Grow Your

Own Optimist!

Olivie Blake

A Witch Way Anthology:

Book 1: The Answer You Are Looking for is Yes

Book 2: Grow Your Own Optimist!

ALSO *by* OLIVIE BLAKE:

Masters of Death

Lovely Tangled Vices

One For My Enemy

La Petite Mort

The Atlas Six

The Atlas Paradox

Alone With You in the Ether

Fairytales of the Macabre (Fairytale Collections, Vol. I)

Midsummer Night Dreams (Fairytale Collections, Vol. II)

The Lovers Grim (Fairytale Collections, Vol. III)

By OLIVIE BLAKE *and*

LITTLE CHMURA:

Alpha

Alpha, Vol. II: Rising

First Edition, 2023

Witch Way Publishing
3436 Magazine Street
#460
New Orleans, LA 70115
www.witchwaypublishing.com

Editor: Tonya Brown
Cover Designer: Olivie Blake

Printed in the United States of America

ISBN Paperback: 978-1-0879-9558-8
ISBN E-Book: 978-1-0879-9626-4

To those we loved in lockdown

Dear Reader,

The stories you will find in this anthology were written during and after the onset of COVID-19, over a period of time when most of us were confined to our homes. Which is not to say the pandemic itself is resolved or even over from my vantage point as I write this now, but to point out that these stories represent a period of my life when I had plenty of time to introspect and absolutely nowhere to go to do it.

I was also pregnant during the height of the pandemic—and the 2020 U.S. presidential election—and wrestling with the question of what it meant to bring a child into a world where life, even at the best of times, often felt confounding; untenable. I couldn't guarantee my future child's bodily autonomy or even safety. I didn't—and still don't—know how to exist ethically as an individual in a world with such systemic and institutional disrepair. I wanted answers I didn't have, and so I found a way to work through them. The only things I really understand about the meaning of life are documented in some way via these stories, and for that reason they are filled with as much honesty as I possess.

All of which is to say that while my previous stories for *Witch Way Magazine* have been romances, these stories are less concerned with the conventions of romantic relationships. They are, however, all love stories. I hope that, if and when you find yourself at the end of this particular collection, you will understand what I mean.

xx, Olivie

TABLE *of* CONTENTS

LOVE IN THE TIME OF DYSTOPIA 11

    PART I: LOCKDOWN 13

    PART II: WITCH HUNT 33

    PART III: REALITY BITES 53

THE DEVIL'S ADVOCATE 77

    PART I: INTRODUCTION TO TORTS 79

    PART II: PROPERTY LAW 99

    PART III: THEORETICAL JURISPRUDENCE.............. 115

ONCE UPON A TIME IN SUBURBIA 129

    PART I: NEW IN TOWN 131

    PART II: PARANORMAL ACTIVITY 155

    PART III: WITCHES DON'T BURN 181

TOXIC 217

    PART I: HE'S JUST NOT THAT INTO YOU 219

    PART II: YOU GOTTA GET WITH MY FRIENDS 243

    PART III: IF IT COMES BACK TO YOU, IT'S YOURS 267

GROW YOUR OWN OPTIMIST! 287

    PART I: LIFE IS STUPID 289

    PART II: JOY IS FLEETING 311

    PART III: PEOPLE ARE DISAPPOINTING 335

GEOFF AND THE MAIDEN 361

LOVE IN THE TIME OF DYSTOPIA (MAY - JULY 2020)

REALITY TELEVISION IS FAR FROM REALITY, so when a group of the country's best amateur chefs are invited to compete in a new cooking show while living in the same house, it's generally understood that things might devolve into baser human urges. Alliances, rivalries, and romances are all expected outcomes for the twenty-four chefs—but when an outbreak of a dangerous virus forces production to shut down for a mandatory quarantine, the show soon becomes the backdrop for a nightmare of supernatural proportions.

Olivie Blake

PART I: LOCKDOWN

Presumably you've seen the interviews by now. Or maybe you've heard about the documentary soon to stream on Netflix? Not that ours was the only interesting story, given the nature of a pandemic. It's easy to say from the aftermath that we should have seen it coming, but in our story, like most people's stories, there's no portent at all. No ill winds, no red skies, nothing like that. One day everything proceeds as normal, and the next, everything you know about the world has changed. We understand how that particular element of panic was not unique to us.

That being said, ours was... a special case.

†

Some of the big networks are incorrectly calling us the contestants of a dating show, which we weren't. It was a cooking show primarily, though with two dozen singles ranging from early-twenties to mid-thirties living together in one house, it was a fairly racy concept. The "human factor" is what the experts call the propensity for an audience to want certain characters (sorry, *competitors*) to go far, or to interact, or to be friends or to simply be humiliated, so what could be better than a show that was half-*Bachelor*, half-*Chopped*, where everyone involved had an equal chance of hooking up as they did of winning the feature in *Bon Appetit*? We all knew when we signed the liability waivers and cleared our physical exams that we were walking into a production, not a competition. Sure, we were each the best chefs that any of us personally knew—some of us with restaurant experience, some with fussy grandmothers, some just self-taught with our own food blogs and YouTube channels—but we knew there was another factor: the *it* factor. Deciding which of us had that was going to be the *Heatin' Up!* audience's job, not ours.

There were some definite frontrunners. Marcus, for example. He was a bartender from New Orleans, with that smooth mixed-Creole skin tone and ample height that made him unmissable in a crowd. It was easy to see why he'd been chosen—his food was hot, and frankly, so was he. He looked like he belonged on the cover of some erotica novel, clutching a woman to his chest with his shirt blown open on a pirate ship.

There was also Audrey, a wide-eyed delicacy who wore Breton stripes and ballet flats and specialized in vegan pastries and desserts. She was like if crème brûlée were a person—no, if crème brûlée *french toast* were a person. Her origins in the Pacific Northwest gave her that extra little edge: she had the most successful food blog out of all of us *and* an Instagram account of half a million followers, having already carved out a niche for herself as someone who cared as much about her carbon footprint as she did about the flavors of her food. The things she could do with fermented soybeans and cashew milk can only be described as, well, Faustian.

Last of the three formidable threats was Elisa, who looked like a cross between royal wedding Meghan Markle and a competitor on *America's Next Top Model*—so basically, if the Duchess of Sussex were half a foot taller and elusively Latina, she might have a little something on Elisa. (And yes, we know that sounds deranged. Imagine how the rest of us felt.) Almost all of us had used our food to get people into bed before, but simply put: Elisa didn't need it. You can see, then, how perfectly unfair it was that she could do more with a handful of peppers and greens than the rest of us could do with a trip to Whole Foods and a full afternoon.

There were more than just those three, obviously. We all thought we were the best and most likely to win or we wouldn't have bothered to come, and the irony of the whole thing turning into a certifiable witch hunt (more on that later) was that there wasn't a single person in the house who *wasn't* secretly convinced they were capable of low-grade witchcraft.

Would any of us have *admitted* that we believed in spirits or demons or whatever it was that Thom initially claimed was filling the house? Of course not. But we *were* magic in the kitchen, weren't we? For us, cooking was deeply personal—it was so embedded in our souls and love languages and cultures that we believed in it more than religion. All of us had that *something*, those unidentifiable reflexes. The palates we relied upon that came from something undeniable inside us; some intrinsic, vestigial quality that couldn't be taught or even explained.

Even those of us who had learned to cook later in life would still admit to having something instinctual to guide us. How much pepper *precisely?* Some of us had blogs and were required to choose a number after one or two dozen tries, but most of us simply felt it in our bones, like whale migration. We knew when something was the proper thickness or whether two ingredients could not be substituted based on something innate—and to us, that was magic.

If, at the time of our respective decisions to audition, we'd been polled about our spiritual beliefs instead of our sexual preferences, all of us would have said without hesitation that magic was real, and that we had already created it in that elusive béchamel, or in the way we could always conjure up a meal from whatever bits of nothing we had in the pantry. It didn't matter whether we could explain it or to what extent we believed it. We believed it nonetheless.

†

It's hard to say whether things might have gone differently if not for the show's cataclysmic timing. The day we all arrived there had been whispers of handwashing, sure, but we had barely slept two nights in the house before it became a full-blown pandemic. We were barred from re-distributing to our places of origin around the country; promised over and over that shooting would commence again the moment we received the all-clear; we were told in daily—no, *hourly*—emails from production staff not to panic, to *stay calm*, even while they were also telling us to conserve our food and consider not touching our faces. We all felt sorriest for Artie, the first among us to be pegged for elimination, because he was forced to deal with our pity after an uncharacteristically bad day in the kitchen. Privately, we recognized that any of us could have been in his position—after all, who among us hadn't misjudged the stiffness of our meringue once or twice? Hard enough to be trapped in a house full of strangers. Harder still to be called out as the weakest link, told to pack a bag and then inexplicably forced to stay.

As for the pandemic itself, Gia's grandmother was the first to test positive, terrifying her and anyone in her vicinity. *All* of our parents were getting older, such being the nature of linear time, and before long, that sense of mortal doom began to infect even those of us who hadn't spoken with them for years. Holly's younger sister and Amal's favorite client (Amal having been an au pair for a family of four) were severely immunocompromised. All of us had friends or relatives that we worried about from within our little quarantine, so understandably, requiring all production to cease didn't help our claustrophobic suspicions that we were being held captive by some unseen force of vengeful paranormal.

In the end, there's little difference between a cinematic apocalypse and a simple matter of preventative social isolation.

Trust us—we would know.

✝

There was fear everywhere, even for those of us who were more stoic by nature, so maybe that's what made everything seem so fleeting, so precious. There was passion and ardor where there might have only been attraction or sex. There was loathing and suspicion, capital crimes of feeling where there might have been merely pettiness or jealousy under different circumstances. We were an experiment in what happens when you take a group of people and force them to mean something to each other, good or bad, and since we were each other's only company, we were also each other's only entertainment.

Except, that is, for Marcus and Elisa—who were that much more interesting to the rest of us for the way they seemed to live in their own little world—and, of course, Audrey.

Though, what happened to Audrey is a story that might take a while to tell.

✝

The story for us began as stories usually begin: with a hero and a villain.

Before joining the show, each of us had been asked to come up with a series of answers to trivial questions about our lives for purposes of marketing—something to help define our various archetypes, and to no doubt craft a narrative for the audience to follow. For example, Raj said his last meal would be his mother's samosas, his grandmother's butter chicken, and a glass of watermelon agua fresca from his favorite vegan place down the street. Nino said his would be the lasagna he'd eaten while visiting family in Italy, which contained a mystery ingredient he had never been able to place. If we could be anyone else in history, Oscar said he would be Columbus just to do everything differently, adding that he resented his own fondness for Thanksgiving (and his elote stuffing, which he described as "perfect" and, despite great effort, none of the rest of us could disagree). To the *Better than sex?* question, Nadya described in sinful detail her morning meditation of melting peanut butter into a bowl of brown sugar oatmeal. Viv's favorite place was a coffeeshop in Edinburgh where she had once had the perfect lavender latte after ducking in from a torrential downpour of summer rain, and where she had returned every afternoon since, rain or shine, for the remainder of her semester abroad. The point is that all of us were the sentimental sort, and most of us connected our feelings and memories with food.

Which is why we couldn't understand why Marcus never seemed to consume anything aside from protein shakes, even going so far as to decline the paella Chantal had made that first night—before the quarantine had even started.

We all saw Chantal's face fall and immediately had the same thought in our collective subconscious: that Marcus was clearly our villain. Here was someone among us who hadn't reflexively thought "hey, let me plug in my phone and call my loved ones," but rather "hey, let me drop everything to prepare a meal on our first night together as a group," and Marcus— exceedingly handsome and therefore hateable already on the basis of either bitter envy or unprecedented attraction (just ask Calvin)—was blatantly dismissing that. We all heard the sound of the blender whirring from the kitchen and gravitated naturally to Elisa, who looked the angriest of us all.

"It's *so* rude," she said in an open flare-up of irritation, and though we nodded and mumbled our agreement, we still felt the compulsive urge to freeze in place when she suddenly shot to her feet. "I'm going to have a chat with him," she declared.

A weak chorus of "wait, no, don't" naturally followed in her wake, but Elisa was the sort of pretty girl whose beauty had a sense of danger to it. She had clearly not been told no very often in her life, and therefore reacted badly (we assumed) whenever it did happen. Besides, if anyone was going to take on Marcus—whom we had all collectively agreed, with the certainty of being five minutes into the first day, was a monster—it should obviously be Elisa. We were pack animals within hours of arrival, unwilling to be either too strong or too weak, so if she wanted to be the righteous one who made herself vulnerable to attack, we were all perfectly keen to let her.

None of us know exactly what happened during their confrontation in the kitchen (we're all still dying to know, given everything) but we were sure of one thing: all twenty or so of us can attest to having heard snippets of an argument. *"Rude, distasteful—" "—none of your business," "Since when—" "Oh, well if that's the case"*—the usual causticity that accompanied two very combative people butting heads. Elisa's voice started out angry, an open call to arms, with Marcus's defensive replies so deep in timbre that even seven-foot-tall Thom looked a little unnerved.

But then, suddenly and without warning, there was silence. We all looked at each other in the absence of voices, unsure what to make of it. To us it was the sort of silence that suggested secrecy. It was a silence filled with something very interesting, which all of us were straining against any conceivable plausibility to hear.

Audrey, whom we didn't know yet was also going to become interesting, audibly cleared her throat and turned to Chantal. "So, are these Chilean prawns?" she asked loudly, establishing herself as someone with a moral opposition to eavesdropping, but before Chantal could answer (yes, they were the Trader Joe's variety and had been stocked in the house's freezer), Elisa and Marcus had both re-entered the room.

Uninvited, Marcus announced to the rest of us "I'm a bit sensitive to shellfish." He sat down next to Xavier, who was pining hopelessly after Elisa from afar (as he would continue to do for weeks), and Calvin, whom we would later find in Lizzie's bed up until *she* found him in Viv's.

"Not an allergy," Marcus qualified, taking a sip from his intensely green smoothie that smelled to the rest of us like mint, cucumber, and strawberry, "but I suppose I might have mentioned it sooner."

"Didn't you submit a shrimp creole with cornbread pancakes as your first date dish?" asked Gia, who in that moment revealed herself to be the resident Virgo queen and chief researcher among us. We would later guiltily learn that she had not only read each of our icebreakers and committed them to memory but also followed all of us on our various social media platforms the moment she learned who we were.

"I did," Marcus confirmed, "but I don't eat it myself. It's just a good recipe."

A glance around the room suggested we all knew this to be not only upsetting, but blasphemous. How did any of us know how to prepare something properly without tasting it several times over the course of its creation? That was the first rule of cooking, amateur or otherwise, and Samad—who had actually gone to a culinary academy for some period of time—looked at Marcus like he'd grown an extra head.

We waited for Elisa to say something, since she'd already established herself as the foil to whatever the hell Marcus was. She didn't, so Audrey, being right next to her, again broke the uncomfortable silence.

"What did you submit as your signature recipe?" she asked Elisa tangentially, all Oregonian politeness, and in response, Elisa's smile twisted wryly upward.

"I didn't," she said. "Just slept with a producer and walked on."

Obviously we laughed it off uncomfortably and then dove back through our icebreakers the moment we were alone to see if it was true (Gia was something of an inspiration to us by that point). To our collective disappointment, it wasn't. Elisa had submitted a spectacular sounding recipe for iced horchata lattes made with oat milk that she'd paired with tres leches cinnamon rolls, adding a lovely anecdote about how breakfast with her younger sisters had always been her favorite meal. She had a sweet tooth, she said, a fondness for coffee dates, and a real knack for pastry dough that rose up fluffy every time.

Disappointing.

More interesting to us, then, was Elisa's answer to the *Better than sex?* question.

Anyone who thinks anything's better than sex isn't having enough of it, she said, so the investigative exercise wasn't entirely unproductive after all.

†

The competition officially began the following morning. Basia had made breakfast so as not to be outdone by Chantal, but as it was so early for most of us—especially those who had flown in from the West Coast—we weren't quite as grateful for breakfast as we had been for dinner. Most of us artlessly shoved the sweetened challah into our mouths (custardy with batter, plus a little burnt sugar around the edges to give it some bite) and stumbled over ourselves onto the charter bus that transported us the handful of miles to the studio kitchen set.

We never saw the judges again after that, so we won't focus on them long. You'll have heard of them, probably—one was a restauranteur with two Michelin stars, another a television personality who had recently published her own cookbook, and the last was a celebrity chef who'd taken something of a downgrade after being one of the showrunners on a Food Network show suffering some MeToo-related backlash. They're not important to the story, really, and outside of the four ingredients we were assigned—snap peas, almond extract, barberries, and gorgonzola—there was nothing remarkable to report.

It was certainly a challenge, as gorgonzola isn't the easiest cheese to make palatable. As we mentioned, Artie's savory mini pies (and specifically their limp meringue, which the restauranteur unflatteringly referred to as "flaccid") got the lowest scores from the judges, rendering him eligible for elimination after what would be our second day. Since we were all grateful it wasn't us on the chopping block (especially Nadya, who hadn't exactly wowed anyone with her ultra-basic gorgonzola mousse), we all went smugly out of our way to reassure him. Simone in particular was sensitive to Artie's disappointment, loudly shielding him from any criticism.

"Jesus, he's a grown man," scoffed Elisa at the time, though really, Artie was a software developer in his early twenties who was best known for having operated a highly successful and profoundly illegal restaurant out of his dorm room at MIT. He'd slurred to Cara after a mere two glasses of wine that he also ran a side hustle preparing private dinners for people staying in

AirBnBs, which was also questionably permissible. (Ultimately we would conclude that he was neither a child nor arguably grown.)

In any case—"He doesn't need to be coddled," Elisa concluded, falling into a chair and crossing one long leg over the other. (She was already an expert in ignoring those of us who followed the motion, a reflex that would only grow less subtle over time.)

"Well, he'll get 'em next time, anyway—won't you, Art?" Nadya said, earning her a weak smile from Artie.

"That or I'll go home" was Artie's glum reply, prompting all of the women except for Elisa (and with the addition of Nino, who at the time was trying to convince Holly that he fit somewhere within the constraints of the "good guy" heterosexual archetype before abandoning both goodness and heterosexuality) to coo over Artie again like a Greek chorus of motherly empathy.

Ultimately—and this, too, we've already mentioned—Artie would neither "get 'em" nor go home. We all woke the following morning to Thom, Jonathan, and Cole watching the news—"*So* straight white male of you," commented a glistening Amal, whom we learned with communal disbelief was an early riser who devoted an hour of every morning to impressively mindful (and dexterous) sun salutations—and reporting to the rest of us that the growing epidemic from two days ago had become a global crisis overnight. Flights and events were canceled, universities and schools were closing, people exhibiting symptoms were advised to quarantine immediately... even *Disneyland* had closed.

And then, in an episode of uncanny timing, the house phone rang.

"Hello?" said Marcus, turning to the phone that none of us wanted to answer. (Perhaps he wasn't a villain, we all expressed in glances exchanged across the room, and *was*, instead, a very soothing presence we had all gravely misunderstood.)

"I see," said Marcus into the receiver before pausing. "Mmhmm. Yes. Okay." Another pause. "And do we have any reason to be concerned?" Pause. "All right. I'll pass that along."

He hung up the phone and turned to Elisa, a choice we all observed with steadily increasing curiosity. Unfortunately for us, the most interesting thing in the room was about to take a hard turn for the worse.

"We're being quarantined in the house for the next two weeks," Marcus informed us, causing most of us to explode in panicked outbursts. After all, we were *amateur* chefs—most of us had day jobs. We'd scrimped and saved and pleaded, using up our hard-fought vacation days for this competition and knowing, as all gig economists know, that even an hour's loss of income could prove irreversible and crippling. A delay in the show's production meant we'd likely be on the phone with our bosses for longer than we'd have liked, assuming we didn't lose our jobs entirely.

"It's not just us. The entire network is shutting down production across the board," Marcus assured us, with a tranquility tacitly suggesting we ought to look to him for leadership. We, of course, were more than happy to comply, and our attention was rapt when he said—as if he had been out in the world instead of here, in this same house with all of us—"Listen, people are really panicking out there, but it's important to be preventative. Better safe than sorry, right?"

Again, he seemed for a moment to be asking Elisa directly. She met his gaze for a lingering second before turning to where Audrey sat next to her.

"Guess we'll all have to think of something to amuse ourselves," Elisa said. Audrey gave her a polite but uneasy smile, intending to skirt the innuendo, but from where he was perched nearby on the edge of the couch, Cole suddenly perked up.

"Why don't we do a potluck?" he suggested, turning to Marcus for approval. Cole was a bit like Artie in terms of puppy-ish enthusiasm, so none of us had reason to suspect he would be anything important. His soufflé from the first round of competition had been good but unthreatening, and he, like his origins, was largely forgettable. (He was from the Chicago suburbs and had a deft hand with comfort foods. His kielbasa mac 'n cheese pierogis were plenty good, but hardly enough to change our answers to the 'last meal" question like Nino's baked ziti.) None of us remember Elisa paying him any attention at all.

"I'm happy to do a main dish," Marcus said. "Short rib? Maybe you can do a vegetarian option," he offered to Elisa.

"Why me?" asked Elisa irritably, rising to her feet from the sofa. "I've got a pulled chicken recipe that'll make your eyes roll back in your head," she informed him, and Marcus gave her a look that said quite plainly, *I bet you do.*

"I can do some black bean tostadas," Cole suggested, sprouting up to follow them. Most of us who held out hope for the competition's reprisal assumed his eagerness had something to do with proving he had range, but we later learned to associate all his actions with that very early memory of following Marcus and Elisa into the kitchen. "Or something like jackfruit chilaquiles?"

"Well, there we go, then," said Marcus absently, still exchanging a glance with Elisa as if nobody else in the room had existed aside from the two of them.

None of us knows what exactly happened during the time that Elisa, Cole, and Marcus made us all so much food that we had to lie down in a tangled heap on the floor until Oscar had the brilliant idea to dig up some mescal, but we all knew that something had shifted—especially between Elisa and Marcus. There was something that bound the two of them together, something they only shared with each other and not with any of us, and for the rest of the time, we all privately longed to be part of it, none of us ever coming close.

†

Knowing only that we had to manage on our own for two weeks, we unanimously agreed to do all the cooking in shifts. This made each meal an exercise in not only curing our extravagant boredom, but also sizing up our competition. If we weren't battling it out properly on the show like we'd planned, then we would do it informally, presenting our best and most creative recipes to stake our claim in the house's unspoken hierarchy via food.

On a more humanitarian note, we were definitely each other's best test audiences; certainly more so than everyone else in our lives who'd lacked our same devotion to its creation. As much as all of us had every intention to win (even Artie, who gradually convinced us his early loss *was*, in fact, a total fluke), we all understood the sharp, exquisite sensation of the perfect first bite. Food was like sex at first for us, indulgent and full of craving, until sex eventually became sex. But that, too, is a story for later.

We usually worked in randomly assigned groups of three or four, given that there were two dozen of us to feed and little else to do in the house. Later on we would establish preferences in the kitchen—Basia would sing Disney songs while making soups with Chantal, Amal would make use of Samad's palette in her specialty lamb meatballs, Nino and Viv would make everything ten times creamier—but at first we were all happy to mix and match on the basis of whoever happened to be closest to the kitchen.

The only people who consistently worked together were Elisa and Marcus, leaving the rest of us torn. We felt the tacit exclusion of the way the two of them murmured privately to each other, moving in such synchronicity that he would be there to hand her something before she even requested it or she would be at his elbow receiving something he'd only just finished with, and we were highly suspicious of it. It wasn't unlike the experience of watching two colleagues at work who were definitely sleeping together, except Gia, Viv, and Nadya, Elisa's roommates, assured us it wasn't true. It was something else, something incarnate, like watching two magnetic poles come together, and we hated it as much as we admired it. Juvenile as our suspicions were, we were all old enough to understand that wanting still felt like spite sometimes.

Nobody ever achieved the harmony of flavors that Elisa and Marcus seemed to hit us with each time their collective turn arose. It made it so that our current competition—making food that *we* liked to eat—was less about impressing the judges than it was about reaching the effortless decadence accomplished by the other two.

The only one of us who ever came close was Audrey, who seemed to prefer to work alone. Cole, who worked with her once after the first dinner with Elisa and Marcus, said she had an almost laser focus and would sometimes not respond to questions or summons, as if she were briefly unable to hear or see anything outside of her own work. She had also, somehow, managed to bring some of her own potted herbs into the house, explaining to Chantal in clipped sentences that when it came to flavor, soil was everything.

Audrey seemed to disapprove of the rest of us in a number of ways, being a primarily plant-based enthusiast and also highly concerned with climate change. We found it moderately irritating, but since she kept to herself and didn't criticize us openly, we refrained from debating her. Only Thom ever thought to argue with her, which is probably why we didn't notice Jonathan coughing. In our defense, it seemed a trivial detail at the time.

"There are ways to consume animal products ethically, without buying from factory farms. And you do realize 'vegan leather' is just plastic, right?" Thom had said, doggedly following Audrey around the kitchen. "You lot only think you're being sustainable, when really you're just contributing to capitalistic systems of industrial waste."

"My lot?" Audrey echoed. According to Calvin and Samad, the other two in the kitchen, she had given him a scathing look that someone her size shouldn't have been able to deliver so effectively. She said nothing else, though Thom pressed the issue at every opportunity even when most of us suspected he probably shouldn't.

Put it this way: we were all instinctively on edge around Audrey, though none of us would have come out and said she was dangerous. A lot of us were introverts and loners by nature, especially those of us who preferred the solitude of baking. Some of us were left-brained, all about chemistry and proportions, fully content to let the Elisas and Marcuses of the world distract us with flash and sleight of hand while we focused in on the details: the piping, the plating, the garnishes that some of us, like Lizzie, would always get right. To us, Audrey's success was explained by the composition of her flavors, which were dense. Rich. Earthy, which was something none of us had ever used to describe anything outside of kale or really dreggy wine. She plainly made use of minimal seasoning, letting the ingredients be the star, and to us that was trendy, farm-to-table stuff, not witchcraft. And most of us argued that we had known people like Audrey before—she was passionate, sure, but not retaliatory. She wasn't ill-intentioned or cruel.

But by the second week, after Jonathan was examined remotely and Marcus informed us that we would all be shut down and quarantined indefinitely, some of us began to disagree.

†

The story gets a bit wilder each time it's told, but there are some details that stay the same each time. It was the thirteenth day of our quarantine, sometime before eight in the morning, and though we argue about who'd been in the living room when the story was relayed to the group at large, we all agree on who'd been in the bathroom with Thom when the events actually happened. Cole was there and so was Artie, and later we found out Xavier had been there as well, though we tacitly understood why he wasn't quick to admit it. (These were basically dorm-style bathrooms, one on each floor, and with all these daily culinary wonders, some of us were learning which of our stomachs were more sensitive to certain things than others.) Given how bad the first scare was, it wasn't hard to believe that Thom eventually became the most adamant about ferreting out which of us was causing all the disturbances. We were all in agreement that none of us would have reacted well to the spiders, either. Much less anything that came next.

It was Artie who'd dropped his toothpaste and run to the shower stall when Thom screamed bloody murder. Cole, who had been shaving at the time, ran downstairs to tell the rest of us what happened with half his face still foamed up, the other half featuring a thin trickle of blood that slid past a sheen of razor-edged cleanliness.

29

According to Artie, who shook for at least half an hour afterward in Chantal's arms, the spiders had all come crawling out of the showerhead. "It was like an army of them," he said, his teeth chattering, and Marcus, by then our designated leader, was already on the phone to the producers, demanding that someone come by to check the pipes. They would later refuse, which we now agree had prompted us to wonder how bad things had become outside our little quarantine. It would only be a matter of days later that Lucien cracked a joke about zombies and end days to which none of us could manage a laugh.

Not all of us had been awake when it happened, but gradually we'd all been dragged from our beds to hear what all the commotion was about. "They were just pouring out," Artie continued to babble, rocking himself back and forth. "They wouldn't stop coming, they wouldn't stop, I couldn't stop it—"

Thom was frozen and silent, violently scratching himself from time to time like he still felt something crawling over his skin. He hadn't said much in the time since Oscar and Raj had basically flagellated him with towels, though that was understandable. This wasn't the sort of thing anyone wanted to go through at all, much less naked, and even though we'd whispered behind Thom's back about how full of himself he seemed to be (which everyone except for Marcus and Elisa agreed he was—though maybe they did too, just not to us) we wouldn't have thought to punish him with anything like this.

"We have to get out of here," Elisa said firmly, who had been listening at Marcus' side until he stepped out for the phone call. (We had all glanced at Gia to confirm whether they'd come into the room together, but she told us later that she had been the one to wake Elisa herself.) "This is total negligence. I mean, did they really not check the house before we all showed up here?"

"Oh please," scoffed Amal, who shuddered at the same moment Thom fervently resumed scratching himself. "They knew what they were doing when they had us sign a waiver."

"What makes you all so sure this is a problem with the house?" demanded Oscar. "You didn't see the way those spiders were moving. It was like they were in a trance or something—totally unnatural."

"Okay, so what are you suggesting, then," Elisa said with a roll of her eyes, "a ghost? A poltergeist or something?"

"It's not totally out of the question," said Cole. "Are we on a ley line?"

"Jesus, Cole, this isn't *Ghostbusters*," said Elisa, as Marcus finally returned to the room and sidled up to her.

"Okay, so, apparently they won't be able to send anyone over yet," he said, holding up a hand as we all—save for Artie and Thom—burst into an explosion of opposition. "Apparently we each need to be tested for the virus before anyone else can come into the house."

"Seriously? What if we need medical attention?" demanded Chantal. We nodded fiercely, conspiratorially shouting *yeah, what she said!*, or at least quietly mouthing it. "Surely if Jonathan has it, we *all* have it by now. Kara's already got a sore throat," she added, and Kara gave her a look of total betrayal, having obviously mentioned it in supreme confidence.

"They assured me they're working diligently on it," said Marcus, which prompted a new flame of outrage. "Guys, guys, calm down—"

"What's going on?" asked Audrey, whom none of us had noticed—and on this we *all* agree—had been absent from the room until that moment. She walked in with her parsley plant in hand, having clearly been tending to it somewhere upstairs, possibly on the roof. We all looked to each other deciding who should explain (again, our pack nature was why Marcus and Elisa had endeared themselves to us so quickly), but before we could, Audrey frowned distractedly at her little terra cotta pot, brushing one finger against it gently.

"Huh, look at that," she said, eyeing something microscopic on her finger. "Spider." She smiled at it briefly, letting it travel across the peaks of her knuckles, then looked up at the rest of us as if she'd just remembered we were there.

"What's wrong?" she asked us again.

And then, like the slow build of a distant air raid siren, Thom began to howl.

PART II: WITCH HUNT

We understand that the clips and blurbs you've read (the clickbait and such) might have confused you as to the events that actually took place during our time of quarantine in the *Heatin' Up!* house. You may be struggling to understand what was real and what wasn't, and in fairness, we are struggling as well. If it had *all* been real or *all* in our imagination, there wouldn't be anything interesting about the story, which as you know has made most of us exceedingly fascinating to the general public. Not that we begrudge Amal her cookbook deal or Oscar his appointment as a celebrity guest judge in the Food Network circuit, but obviously we wouldn't be here if everything that happened could be easily explained.

Here's what we know for sure: it all started when Jonathan got the virus everyone was talking about, which led to us being quarantined en masse. We didn't understand why none of us were technically being tested, though speaking with our relatives and friends (and employers, some of which had only rung to cut us loose) outside the house indicated that the entire process was being wildly mismanaged in general. Was it any surprise that our production team was any different? They seemed to think of us as an egregious hassle, given that we were in their care and yet they, as non-essential workers, weren't supposed to be coming into work to pay us any attention anyway. We were given the impression that the needs of twenty-four unattached amateur chefs—all of whom were generally healthy and at low risk to any comorbidities, as proven by our pre-filming physical exams—

fell dangerously low on the show's concerns. Once Jonathan ran a fever, they certainly weren't going to risk the safety of their own families by coming anywhere near us, and that we could understand.

Not that our sympathy for them made the next six months any easier.

†

So in terms of what was real and what wasn't, let's start there. The virus was in our house, and for that reason, nobody else was entering it. No one was to leave it, either. We understood this in a lucid sort of way, for as long as we could prolong our collective lucidity. But living in a house with two dozen strangers was not especially conducive to sanity—not when we were sharing each other's space, four to a room, crammed in like tinned Vienna sausage. Or so it felt to us.

The trouble with our microcosm of the degradation of human society is, of course, its slowness. Madness doesn't happen overnight. If we had to put it into some sort of order, like the stages of grief, we'd say... Well, actually, we'd say it's quite similar. Denial, anger, bargaining, depression, and somewhere near the end, paranoia with regard to anything supernatural, uncanny, or occult.

Though that last one might be unique to us.

†

We can't neglect to mention that lurking between all of those stages at any given time was the constancy of sex. Again, there were two dozen of us, all single, all of an appropriate age. Artie, the youngest, was newly twenty-four while Chantal, the oldest, was thirty-three, rendering any of us an acceptable combination; some less fathomable than others, sure, but nothing terribly offensive to anyone's morality. We'd already learned by the first drunken night that we fell on nearly every shade of the sexuality spectrum, though some of us learned it in more surprising ways as our experiment in social isolation went on. (Just ask Nino, who began by pursuing Holly only to find himself all but filing his taxes from Samad's bedsheets; or Gia, who'd sworn off men only to get caught *in flagrante delicto* with Xavier; or Calvin, who started with Lizzie, got caught with Viv, then ended up in a trio with both until they dumped him for each other.)

None of us should have been surprised by anything, given our game of musical beds, but of course we all assumed Elisa and Marcus were a foregone conclusion. They were our leaders, and given that both were so intensely attractive, we weren't at all surprised to see them gravitate to each other like a pair of colliding stars. They never cooked with anyone but each other—easy to forget, given everything we've just described, that we were primarily there as amateur chefs and so passion, for us, meant *food*—and while they didn't exclude anyone outright, there was a certain... *other energy* when they were both in the same room. Obviously when the Cole incident happened we all had to hit pause and second-guess ourselves, reconsidering our observations that had led us to believe Elisa and Marcus were a singular, indivisible unit in the first place. We would retrace our steps and think weren't they canoodling on the sofa, or hadn't we seen them kiss once or twice? In retrospect no, it had never been anything like that. In fact they were rarely touching. More often we'd recall Elisa curled up on the sofa watching tv with Viv and Nadya, her roommates, while Marcus would be reading a few feet away, neither of them looking at each other. But there was something about their combined presence that all of us could feel, and though we still can't prove it, we feel confident that Marcus would occasionally look up, and so would Elisa, and they would each secure themselves in the knowledge that the other wasn't far away.

But then, like we said, there was Cole, which we couldn't explain, but there were so many things that we couldn't explain by then that you can probably tell we're finally getting to the juicy bits. A lot of our quarantine was thoroughly unremarkable—don't let us convince you that we were doing anything remotely interesting most of the time; even sex got to be as mundane as making "another goddamn panna cotta," as Simone so eloquently put it—but then again, there were the spiders.

You'll remember the spiders, probably? That was the first so-called episode. It's such a compelling visual (and so memorably horrifying) that a spider is now a feature in Lucien's logo, though at the time it was hard to imagine we'd ever recover enough to be in on the joke. Thom, you'll recall, had been accosted by a trickle of spiders crawling from the showerhead (in the stall we all refused to use afterward, many of us forgoing showers altogether for as long as we could) and Audrey—petite, dainty, vegan little Audrey—came down the stairs with her parsley plant, withdrawing a spider with the tip of her finger and delivering Thom to a nightmarish howl.

As for what followed, some of us remember slightly different things. Raj swears he saw Audrey give Thom a little warning smile (you might recall that she and Thom had recently argued) and Xavier and Cole agreed that they had seen it, too. Cara and Holly, on the other hand, distinctly remember Audrey looking concerned, although they later described it as something of a put-on distress; almost as if she'd rehearsed it. Chantal, Oscar, and Basia all say Audrey rushed forward to help Thom, who was screaming, but Calvin and Amal say they saw her whisper something in his ear; a threat, they assumed, because it only made him scream louder, up until Viv finally had the bright idea to help him up to bed.

Jonathan, the carrier of the virus whom all of us had been avoiding, called weakly from his room about what was going on (we're not heartless, by the way, he was fine—just feverish and achy) but nobody knew what to tell him. What was there to tell? That there had been some kind of voodoo attack by a swarm of cursed spiders? Elisa was the only person to assure us we were overreacting and we believed her, sort of. Mostly. And then Marcus echoed that of course it was just a plumbing mishap, so we believed it slightly more.

Only Artie, who was still half-catatonic from being the one to try to come to Thom's aid, was shaking his head, though none of us can remember who actually started the accusations. Some of us are positive it was Artie; that he had glared fiercely at Audrey in a way that suggested *I know what you did.* Some of us remember it being Holly, who was already very into crystals and tarot, who confirmed that these things were known to happen when bad energies were trapped in an uncleansed space.

What all of us know for sure, though, is that Elisa and Marcus *didn't* believe it... at first.

"Are all of you completely demented? Audrey is not some kind of *witch*," Elisa scoffed. "First of all, misogyny much? Secondly, it's nonsense."

"I think we're just letting our imaginations run away with us," Marcus diplomatically agreed. "Obviously Audrey would never have done something like this."

For the record, some of us would remember Marcus having his arm around Elisa during this conversation while others of us would insist they weren't even standing in the same place in the room. What all of us agree, though, is that Audrey reacted very strangely to this. Not that any of us considered what we might have done if *we* were being paranormally blamed for another person's abject misery, but we were all fairly certain that none of us would have reacted the way she did.

"I don't need you to defend me," Audrey snapped at Marcus, and at the time, most of us were giving her enough credit to recognize she might have been hurt or insulted or angry and simply happened to take it out on the person closest to her. Regardless, she rounded on both Marcus and Elisa, drawing herself up to her full diminutive height and hissing something at them both. (Unsurprisingly, we do not agree as to what that something was; some say it was obscure Latin they recalled from church while others say it was a run-of-the-mill threat, like *back off*.)

Marcus apologized, peacekeeper that he was, but Elisa's response spoke volumes. She said nothing, perhaps having learned by then that we considered every word out of her mouth especially memorable and therefore subject to excess scrutiny, but her eyes had narrowed. Her lips had thinned. The more cinematic among us would say there was a line drawn in the sand between Elisa and Audrey: invisible and yet totally unmissable.

That's when the witch hunt really began.

✝

The spiders were uniquely creepy because no one (save for Audrey, apparently) likes spiders. Certainly it's fair to say that nobody craves the sensation of being covered in spiders when one is expecting hot water and a decent wash. Even the appearance of *cold* water in place of hot would be enough for a day-ruining disturbance, so to find another consistency altogether (i.e. alive, multi-legged, swarming) was thoroughly unforgivable.

It took Thom another two days to fully recover, if one could even say that he did. Certainly none of us would have said so.

Which is why, at first, we thought it was all in Thom's head when he claimed something about weird sounds following him throughout the house. It was very clear to us that seven-foot Thom was now jumping at every sound like an overstimulated Chihuahua, and therefore there was little to no chance of any real threat. There was creaking, he insisted, and voices, things that woke him in the night. His roommates, all sound sleepers, were convinced he was in some sort of post-traumatic hysterics.

Marcus, intent on putting the issue to bed, offered to swap places with Cole in order to sleep in Thom's room. We were certain the whole thing was in Thom's head and that Marcus would inevitably prove it. Unfortunately, we were wrong.

"It's not in Thom's head," Marcus said the next morning. We were eating carrot cake pancakes; many of us remember the cream cheese frosting sticking in our throats at that particular moment. "He's right, there's... something."

Creaking, he said. Voices. Murmurs or something. We were all fascinated as to why Thom was the continued epicenter of these episodes until Gia heard it, too. Viv wasn't sure about what she'd heard, exactly, but Elisa very interestingly said nothing. We took this as a troubling sign: if Elisa wasn't dismissing the whole thing as a farce *and* Marcus had already judged it to be real, then surely there was something to be said for it. Perhaps it wasn't so farcical after all.

According to Gia, the voices were speaking an obscure language. Oscar, who was devoutly Catholic, reported back to us that it was definitely Latin. For most of us, who were agnostic at best until it came time to pray for our custards to magically set despite indisputable evidence they would not, we found the implication of anything remotely close to Catholicism to be especially alarming. (Blame *The Exorcist* for that.)

Presumably you're wondering what Audrey was doing around this time. Candidly, so were we. Now that things have generally passed, we're free to admit that none of us handled this particularly well, and one way or another, all of us found a reason to avoid Audrey like the plague; or, indeed, like a witch. Most of our reasoning was tainted by our initial impression of her: a mix of our envy of her success, her general isolation from the rest of us, and the way she seemed to pass judgment on us by merely looking this way or that. We were all a bit put out by the way she cooked alone, to the point where we began to question why someone of her ilk would even agree to be on the show. Some of us felt it was the obvious—money, notoriety, and, like *Bachelor* contestants, some amount of social media-TMZ microfame—and disliked her for those reasons.

Others of us felt it was... something far more sinister, and *that* group eventually came to outnumber the rest.

†

Before you go thinking we were paranoid, we think it's fair to point out that the people who were victims of the various supernatural attacks were coincidentally (or not) the same people who'd had altercations with Audrey before. For example, we already know Thom was the first to pick a fight with Audrey, but most of us weren't surprised at all when Nadya was next to run shrieking from the stairwell. (Nadya was nice, but nosy, and also slightly insincere. She didn't have the baldness of Thom's aggression toward Audrey, but from the start Nadya had said a number of things in whispers about Audrey's unfriendliness. To our recollection, Nadya was the first one to drop the B word behind Audrey's back, and many suspected her gratuitous praise after Artie's brush with elimination to be a method of poorly concealing her own glee at not being in his place. Not that she was a bad person by means, but, you know. Sorry, Nadya. We are what we are.)

To this day, we're not sure if the scrawling on the corridor walls was actually blood. None of us really wanted to look into it. Lizzie was insistent it was only pig's blood, but when we asked her if "only" was really the right term for the occasion, she agreed that it probably wasn't. In the end, Marcus cleaned it up with Elisa, and Cole joined them, tagging along as he so often did. The rest of us volunteered to comfort Nadya, who for understandable reasons had not appreciated the picture of her, mouthless, that was plastered beside the words *NOBODY SPEAK, NOBODY GET CHOKED*.

You may recognize these words as the somewhat deadpanned lyrics to the chorus of *Nobody Speak*, the 2016 DJ Shadows track featuring the rap duo Run the Jewels. Needless to say, they were unfamiliar words to us, registering only as a haunting threat. Perhaps because spiders and viruses were on the mind (Jonathan seemed to be doing better, though none of us would go anywhere near him), we leapt right to the prospect of asphyxiation. Chantal began to voice her concern that night about sleeping in the same room as Audrey, while Basia and Amal, the other two occupants, assured her she was being paranoid.

They soon changed their minds when all three women woke to the sensation of being—what else?—*choked*.

Their room was above the kitchen, Marcus pointed out, so maybe it was a simple matter of carbon monoxide poisoning or something of that ilk, but when conversation eventually came around to the uneasy question of where Audrey had been while that was happening, nobody knew the answer. Her bed was empty.

"That doesn't mean anything," Marcus reminded us.

Naturally we wanted to agree. Unfortunately, none of us actually could.

†

We were all a little bit afraid of Audrey by then, again because the victims seemed to be those who'd had even the smallest encounters with her right before. Oscar had accidentally grabbed the wrong bag of toiletries and used her all-natural toothpaste. Xavier had knocked over one of her plants. Simone had used the last of the vegan chicken seasoning when she'd been too lazy to look for more bouillon cubes. So was it any surprise, then, that Oscar woke up to find the ceiling of his room plastered with images of himself with his teeth photoshopped out? Or that Xavier woke with his feet resting on massive piles of dirt? Or that Simone, in the most traumatic bathroom episode since Thom and the spiders, found herself locked into the shower stall right before it filled with thick steam and hot water, leaving her shrieking that she would be boiled alive?

The most troubling thing about all of this was that none of our offenses were actually done or spoken in Audrey's presence. We had no idea how she knew about any of the wrongs that had been committed against her, but she was the common thread. Thom now openly behaved as if she were a witch—or, more accurately, he behaved as if everything Audrey touched was somehow poison—and we could all admit to having considered it. How could we not, when the loudest among us were making their suspicions clear? By the time Cole was coughing up soap and telling us pitifully that all he'd done was suggest to Audrey that she should help with the dishes since she was only making a kale-pistachio pesto in the food processor anyway, we realized we all believed it. There had been no defining shift; no moment of revelation. At one point none of us had believed we could possibly be living with a witch, and then gradually, we noticed that we had all tacitly accepted it.

But, then again, we had *also* accepted that Marcus and Elisa were an indivisible pair, right up until the day Elisa kissed Cole.

†

By two months in, most of us had already decided that it was in our best interest to sleep together. We don't exclusively mean this in the sexual sense, although there was plenty of that going on. (Probably too much, if we're being honest, but feel free to make the requisite conclusions about consent and condoms, et cetera.) No, the important thing here was the rise in personal crises, which hit all of us at different times. During the day we were needlessly combative, sick of discovering people in every nook and cranny we demanded for ourselves and our sanities, all of which were waning fast. But at night it was a different story. At night we became like children, clinging to each other in the dark, unsure which of us would find ourselves the next target for magical revenge.

In some respects we'd all settled into a rhythm. We'd wake up, make awkward excuses to whoever we'd woken up with (true for at least half of us on any given day), stumble downstairs and discover what fresh horror might have occurred during the night (it wasn't every day, but often enough that it was worth the asking), and then we'd reach longingly out to the world outside. At night we'd get as drunk as possible or as stoned as we could manage to be without losing our capacity to fend off vengeful spirits, which Basia had started shouting at like a Jewish grandmother. (We think she felt that whatever Audrey might have set loose in the house simply needed a firmer hand.)

But, of course, things eventually changed, and as one might expect given the circumstances, they did not do so for the better.

†

Logistics first: we didn't have quite as much food as before. (We are chefs, so naturally food was our priority, even beyond the stipulations of Maslow's Hierarchy of basic needs.) By the end of the first month, we noticed that our contactless grocery deliveries were starting to make substitutions when we asked for the usual pantry staples. By the second month, there were gaping holes in our grocery requests. Suddenly, every meal became a culinary challenge, and by the start of the third month, an odd form of scarcity had become part of the game. We weren't starving by any means, but it occurred to us that production was now having to cover the costs of hosting us beyond the intended length of filming. Surely they would not care to do so for long.

By the fourth month, none of us were surprised (although we *were* abysmally displeased, the majority of us having been furloughed and forced to rely on our non-existent savings) when the deliveries slowed to an eventual halt. It would be on us to cover the food from then on, and worse, the Wi-Fi had stopped working, and then the electricity went. We were all officially contributing financial crumbs like university housemates, subsisting by candlelight while Marcus made calls and levied demands. We got sick (colds, sinus infections, one or two cases of the flu that *might* have been the virus, though we'd never know for sure) and then got better, though Jonathan's stigma for being the first to fall victim to the illness meant we generally avoided him, associating him inextricably with our own mortality. Even after he stopped coughing, the only person we avoided more intuitively was Audrey, who found ways to remain out of sight from the rest of us for days at a time.

So, if you're keeping track, the markers were there for the toppling of our little makeshift society. We were in total isolation, cut off from the outside world, beginning to fear that our nightmare would never end or that we would simply choke on a Saltine and be left to rot somewhere in our increasingly disgusting house. We became feral, as reliant on each other as we were consumed by our loathing for each other. (Some of us had come to the show for the possibility of love, but none of us had actually expected to spend a *lifetime* in each other's company. We were not surprised when the vast majority of us promptly broke up and begged our exes for second chances upon return to civilization.)

In the midst of all this uncertainty, we relied upon our constants: Marcus and Elisa. Chantal's baking. Raj's singing whenever he had any gin in his system. Nino and Samad's insistence that there was nothing going on between them. (They're married now; the ceremony was lovely. Not a dry eye in the house.)

The entire backbone of our existence were the things we had come to reliably expect. We developed our own rituals and superstitions. We sought out patterns, things we could safely predict, which science (and a host of anxiety disorders) would retroactively suggest were merely correlations. Maybe we'd be spared anything too harrowing if we wore silver jewelry? If we cooked with extra garlic? Not that there were any vampires in the house that we knew of, but we couldn't rule it out. We couldn't get access to holy water, so what was the next best thing? We thought maybe Cara's grandmother's cross was protecting her until eventually the power went out while she was reading alone in her room. (When it came back, all her belongings had been overturned; the page in the book she'd been reading had been censored so that only the words YOU'RE and NEXT were visible between thick black bars.)

"There's something odd about this," Marcus said when Cara told us. As usual, Elisa was near him, the rest of us lumped together on the sofa in something of a leery pack.

"Odd as in uncanny, you mean?" asked Cole, who was usually popping up with commentary whenever Marcus was speaking. The rest of us shuddered at the reminder that there was more going on in this house, or possibly even beyond this realm. (We'd all begun having conversations about the possibility of a veil, and before the internet had gone out, we'd been researching whether other things had happened here. Say the house was built on a Native burial ground. Maybe that would explain things...?)

"No, I mean odd as in weirdly coincidental," said Marcus. He glanced at Elisa. "Don't you think?"

"Are you about to tell me what I think?" she asked him.

He smirked, or smiled. "It just feels very suspicious to me. These so-called supernatural events. The circumstances of all of this. I mean, haven't you ever seen *Ghost Hunters*?"

"No," said Elisa listlessly. "I have other things to do."

"What does *Ghost Hunters* have to do with this?" asked Cole, chiming in again. "It's not like we can call someone in to investigate."

"No, I just meant the show usually has someone who's an expert in construction," Marcus said. "Old houses and stuff. The problems are almost always in the walls or floors." He glanced at Elisa, who again said nothing.

"But there are clearly targets," said Cole, lowering his voice. Per usual Audrey was not in the room, though we still had yet to understand how she was hearing us. (We assumed based on that comment alone that Cole would be next.)

"Yes, and it's interesting who gets targeted," said Marcus. "Isn't it?"

At that point, Elisa gave a loud, long-suffering sigh.

"You're boring me, Marcus," she said, and then, to all of our shock, she leaned over—most of us remember the ripple of her hair swinging, a rich black that shone lustrous in the afternoon sun—and pulled Cole's face to hers.

It's difficult to describe what makes a kiss cinematic, but whatever it was that made so many of us want to rewatch love scenes in films, Elisa offered an excellent showing. She dug her fingers into Cole's jaw and reached around to the back of his neck, dark nails punctuating the blond strands of his hair. She was all sensuality, touch and breath, to the point where many of us forgot to look away in discomfort.

All of us who were present and close enough to see detail will admit: it was all we could do not to stare.

Elisa pulled away and Cole stumbled forward, half-collapsing in her absence. She rose to her feet and strode to the corridor, pausing only to say, "Are you coming?"

All of us gaped at Cole, who looked dazed.

Then, obviously (the "obviously" here being a contribution from all of the men and a good handful of the women), Cole scrambled to his feet, chasing Elisa up the stairs until only Marcus remained as the subject for our intrigue, his brow slightly furrowed in their wake.

Amal was the first to do the calculations, realizing that if Elisa was off the table, that meant Marcus (bronze-skinned, muscled, deep-voiced and phantasmagorically attractive) was now a plausible option. "Hey," she said, sliding closer to him and beating us to the punch while the rest of us considered whether our current partners were worth abandoning on Marcus' behalf.

(In most cases, yes. Almost unanimously.)

"Are you all right?" Amal asked him, having cleverly thought to let one shoulder of her oversized sweater dip below her clavicle.

But Marcus, rather than acknowledge her, simply frowned into space, opening his mouth only to venture the one thing we hadn't suspected he'd ask.

"Where's Audrey?"

†

We admit we were gleeful at the idea that Marcus might soon seek out romantically-driven revenge. Why else would he ask for *Audrey*, whom none of us would admit to suspecting of witchcraft but whom *all* of us, without exception, did? We hadn't thought to use Audrey intentionally, whether for good or otherwise, but surely that was Marcus' intent. Elisa had not been the victim of anything especially terrible until then, but surely with how openly she'd rejected Marcus, retribution was soon to come.

We hunkered down and waited for news of something terrible. Her eyebrows gone in the night. The lovers waking up with dead rodents in their bed. One of the bathroom mirrors hosting accusations drawn in lipstick.

Something.

For several days we were unusually peaceful. We (you may have noticed Marcus and Elisa had always been elevated above the "we" in question) were startled by the loss of our golden couple, but we were also electrified by the idea of open warfare. We'd read all the books in the house by then and made every recipe twice over. Perhaps it's understandable that we were voracious for something new.

The next time Elisa and Marcus were together in front of a group was some days later. (Oscar says it was a full week because he remembered thinking he needed to shave just before Elisa came down the stairs.) Up until then, Elisa and Cole had been doing whatever it was Elisa and Cole were doing, and Marcus had been avoiding us. On that particular day, Audrey was in the living room too, which was part of the intrigue. We collected our friends and anyone else we could find from the other rooms without speaking a word as to why, suddenly certain that something was about to go down.

"Look, we get that things have been weird lately," Marcus said, proving us right. (And we so loved to be proven right.) "We haven't all been together in awhile, have we? And Elisa and I just want to make sure you guys know there's no hard feelings between us."

(We were disappointed, but still intrigued.)

"We thought a toast would be appropriate," Elisa added, producing a bottle of cheap champagne while Marcus stepped aside to reveal he'd already fetched us some glasses. "Marcus, would you pour?"

The rest of us exchanged glances, wary of how absurdly calm Elisa and Marcus both seemed to be; they were our divorced parents telling us how they'd agreed we'd split the holidays. Elisa popped the cork and handed it to Marcus, leaning over to brush her lips against the side of Cole's neck, and we glared at him: *You're not our real dad.* Across the room, Jonathan coughed loudly. Audrey said nothing, though she silently accepted her glass.

Ultimately we don't remember what we talked about while we sipped our champagne for those awkward fifteen minutes or so of realizing that twenty-four was a lot more people than the same five or six we kept bumping into. (We all had our primary lovers, enemies, and friends, most of whom had been determined for us by details as mundane as which bathroom we were forced to share.)

What we *do* remember is a sound: specifically, a thunk.

Elisa looked up from where she was chatting with Viv and walked over to Cole, whose head had fallen forward into the bowl of fake fruits on the coffee table. She motioned to Marcus, who nodded and stepped around to the edge of the room, and the rest of us waited, breaths withheld, as Elisa bent down to put her ear to Cole's back.

We held our breaths. Had it been Audrey?

Elsewhere, there was a crash of glass hitting the floor.

"We're good," said Marcus.

The rest of us whipped around to the sound of his voice, startled to discover Jonathan's head was now lolling forward, leaving him to slump across Artie's lap. Jonathan's champagne glass, which had fallen from his hand, lay in slivers on the hardwood.

The rest of us looked down at our own glasses, some of which had already been consumed. Would we be next?

"It's just them," Elisa assured us, and we exchanged another glance: Why?

At that precise moment, Audrey gave a small throat-clearing cough and rose daintily to her feet.

"So, here's what's really been happening," Audrey began, and though many of us would have said at that point that her voice was unnaturally deep or tending to cackle, we were surprised to discover it was actually more charming and bright than we remembered. It was as if by hearing her speak, a fog had been lifted from us somehow, or maybe we merely thought in terms of incorporeal fogs because we'd been so supernaturally incapacitated over the last four months.

(Or, as it turned out... not?)

"We're definitely on a reality show," Audrey explained. "But it's not the one that we thought."

PART III: REALITY BITES

We're coming around to the end of our story now, which is probably the part of the story you already know. The problem with modern times and our endless access to information-sharing is the massive prevalence of spoilers, and considering how the twist in this case is what really got people's attention, you probably already know it.

But just in case you don't, we want to remind you of how things had been for us: the isolation. The fear. The anxiety that even if this state of existence ever ended, we couldn't be comfortably sure that whatever came next would be better. People are always eager for things to return to normal, but what *is* normal, exactly? Is it something that can even exist after you've seen how unpredictable the *abnormal* can be? The trouble with the uncanny is that it can't be put back the same way you found it. In our case, clinging to our preconceived notions of reality was like the effort of folding a fitted sheet; conceivable in theory, but in practice not so much. We lacked the proficiency to fit neatly into the shapes we used to take.

Presumably you, like many others, consider the twist in our narrative to be redemptive in some way, or perhaps even encouraging. The triumph of the human spirit or somesuch, assuming you consider us the protagonists in this story, which selfishly we hope you do. Having been tormented as we were, we feel our choices were... if not entirely *admirable*, then certainly understandable.

Presumably you also feel the relief of clarity, possessing in retrospect the explanation for our suffering that had driven us to near-madness during our time of isolation. We understand why this offers you such profound satisfaction, because if not for having the answers that you do, you wouldn't believe our story at all. We as a species do not sit well with the unexplained, much less the inexplicable.

Put simply: we are happy to relieve you. It brings us the pleasure that we ourselves still sometimes lack. Not to say that we're unhappy by any means, or that this time meant nothing to us, or that we would willingly choose to unlive it. If experience is what makes us, then of course this experience produced whatever we all now are, which we hope will continue to be of some use to the world. (And financially rewarding, given the boost in our otherwise non-existent careers.)

But before we arrive at our moment of redemption, we have to first revisit the crime: our haunting by what we believed to be a vengeful witch.

So, Audrey. You'll remember that we told you Audrey was important to the story from the beginning, though we may have misled you as to why. She's been relatively quiet in recent days, finding solace, we suspect, in the tranquility of being left alone. (Amal wanted us to add here that people are always terribly suspicious of women who want to be left alone; look at nearly every fairy tale and tell her otherwise. She'll wait.) Ironically, Audrey's publicly beloved now, which is merited, though it's worth observing that public adoration was never what she wanted in the first place. We hear she's turned down the countless offers she's received, ranging from *Bon Appetit* to Ballantine Publications to The Food Network, opting instead to maintain her focus on her little blog community, which has since been flourishing. We heard her Patreon earnings have allowed her to set about publishing her plant-based cookbook independently, and her store on Etsy, which features handmade gardening tools, is one of the site's highest earning shops.

We all follow her account, though she follows none of us back; Chantal finds this perfectly understandable while Nadya finds it annoying, with the rest of us falling somewhere between their two extremes. Recently, though, Oscar noticed (and we did not question his vigilance, most of us being sympathetic to his morbid curiosity) that Audrey had quietly followed a new account. None of us were surprised to see who they were, though we felt another collective wash of shame for the reminder of what the rest of us had failed to see.

Not to get ahead of ourselves, of course.

†

"We're definitely on a reality show, but it's not the one that we thought," said Audrey on the day our outlooks would change—which, it's worth noting, was already well into month five of our containment. (We like to speak of it that way, as if we were captives, which it turned out we definitely were, even if we technically weren't.)

At the time, we had just witnessed Cole and Jonathan being what we presumed to be drugged; we probably should have been more concerned, but we had very little else to entertain us.

For those who require reminding: Elisa, the startlingly attractive alpha female we tried very hard not to describe as spicy the same way we tried not to think of Simone as sassy, had recently begun a tryst with the inoffensive but also somehow unworthy Cole, offsetting the cornerstone of the house's ecosystem. (In our defense, we had been living with a retaliatory witch who was targeting us all paranormally. We were not our best selves.) At the time,

Marcus and Elisa, our painfully estranged—or so we thought—leaders, had disrupted our suspicions of a jealous spat between them to startle us with the knowledge that this had never been a lovers' quarrel after all.

Considering how overturned our stability already was, we were not especially receptive to the idea of another roadblock in our fragile existence. At this point, Audrey was informing us something so heretofore unconsidered that she would have to explain it to us several times.

What we collectively recall is a very neutral, schooled tone of, "There's a reason Cole's been so shady with the information he reveals about himself. It's because he's not what we think he is."

"So wait, he's not from Boston?" asked Xavier.

"He's from Chicago, right?" said Calvin. "I think."

"Is he older than twenty-four?" asked Artie.

"He's like, twenty-nine," said Gia.

"What? No," said Lucien. "Wait, is he?"

"Okay, very helpful, thank you for proving my point," said Audrey, whom you might recall was someone we still believed to be a witch at that point in time, so we all quieted down, though not, perhaps, for purely respectful or even good reasons. "I actually didn't come up with this on my own," she admitted, glancing briefly at Elisa, who was inspecting her nails. "But the point is Cole is actually a... television producer."

The rest of us exchanged glances, then looked back at her.

"So?" said Chantal.

"Right, sorry, okay. So is Jonathan," said Audrey, possibly realizing that we'd need our explanation much quicker. "I actually think it's possible that Jonathan was never sick. I think he faked it," she explained slowly, "so that we would believe we had a reason to be quarantined in this house."

There were a lot of "What"s and "Huh"s going around, so Marcus cleverly stepped in.

"After a bit of skullduggery on our part," he said with a reference to Audrey and Elisa, "we came to the conclusion that Cole and Jonathan have been staging all the supposedly 'paranormal' activity within the house in order to encourage us to turn on each other. It was never actually a cooking show. Apparently," he added, leading us to frown at each other in total bewilderment, "the premise was to combine a bunch of people in one house and then wait for them to turn on each other. The show would eventually be released under the title *Witch Hunt*," he explained, which would have been an instantly damning piece of information if we were quicker on the uptake.

"So wait. It was never *Heatin' Up*?" asked Lizzie slowly.

"No," said Marcus.

"But then the judges," Viv realized faintly.

"Yep," said Marcus.

"Is that even legal?" demanded Nino.

"Kinda, yeah," said Marcus. "We did sign paperwork agreeing to be filmed, so it's probably in the contract."

"Surely it's still some kind of ethics violation," protested Thom, whom you might recall had been nightmarishly showered with spiders.

"Probably," Marcus agreed. "But I'm guessing they didn't think we'd catch on."

At this point, several of us were starting to piece together the fact that we'd been blaming Audrey for all the unnatural things that had happened to us over the past five months. Perhaps you're familiar with the Stanford Prison Experiment? It was a social psychology experiment designed to explore the subject of perceived power between prisoners and prison guards. Upon hearing the results of the experiment, most people typically insist they would never behave that way if put in that position. We, who were just learning that we had all been the unknowing prison guards for one helpless prisoner, were increasingly unable to meet Audrey's eye.

"I think they had someone else in mind at first," Audrey said, perhaps cottoning onto our discomfort. "But I saw Jonathan moving around the house when he was supposed to be bedridden, so..." She shrugged. "I guess he wanted to keep me quiet."

This made us feel incredibly worse, because Jonathan's plan had worked flawlessly, hadn't it? But then someone remembered that, actually, he and Cole must have overlooked something, because obviously someone hadn't been fooled. (We think it was Raj who first looked at Elisa, though Raj claims it was Holly.)

"Mm," acknowledged Elisa, noticing our attention swiveling to her. "Yeah, well, it always seemed pretty unlikely to me. And also, Cole is sketchy is hell," she added, pulling the rug out from beneath us yet again. Not that we'd ever understood what she liked about him, but we had believed it, which said a lot about what people in our position can be made to believe. "Anyway," Elisa continued, "I happened to see that Run the Jewels song on his workout playlist"—you'll remember, possibly, the lettering on the walls of NOBODY SPEAK, NOBODY GET CHOKED, which at the time the rest of us were unaware was actually a fairly well-known song—"and I was like yeah, okay, this is all messed up somewhere—"

"Which is why she prevented me from speculating in front of him," contributed Marcus, acknowledging their public fallout from the week prior. "And anyway, it took a bit, but this is all confirmed now. We're being filmed," he said, pointing to the cameras we assumed had been disarmed, and also lifting a plant that had wires hidden at the base of its potted soil.

"The show never shut down. This *is* the show, and according to the filming schedule we found, we're going to be trapped here for another month."

There was an outburst at that point from almost everyone, and Elisa, never one for patience, waved her hand to silence us.

"They're going to wake up soon," she said, pointing to Jonathan and Cole, and explained to us that the way they'd been arranging all our mishaps—aside from anything to do with the plumbing, which was carried out by Jonathan, whose "illness" had worked to his benefit twofold—was by interfering with the house itself, or by drugging us. "They'll wake the same way you did," Elisa continued, indicating that she must have uncovered Cole's stash. "Shocked and disoriented, but feeling as if no time has passed."

This was eerie to us for obvious reasons, so you might imagine that our instincts ranged from vitriolic to litigious. "We should sue," declared Samad, and we all nodded vigorously, all beginning to discuss the piece of our mind that we would inevitably give Cole and Jonathan the moment they came to, but then Elisa cleared her throat again.

"Actually," she said, "I have a better idea about how we could spend the next month," and by now you're probably beginning to understand why our story was so compelling. VICTIMS OF REALITY TELEVISION HOAX TURN PERPETRATORS OF RIGHTEOUS VENGEANCE is actually a pretty good headline, all things considered. Anna Wintour and *Vogue* found it worth a look, as did Forbes; even SyFy ran our story as a speculative piece about reality television and the future of the surveillance state. We're told there's *also* an HBO adaptation in the works, and that Jordan Peele is executive producing it, though we're not entirely sure how he's going to approach the ending.

Not to get ahead of ourselves. Again.

Anyway, Cole woke up with his arm around Elisa, and Jonathan woke with a fresh glass in his hand. Audrey was now tucked into the corner of the room.

"To friendship," said Marcus, lifting his glass.

"To friendship," we agreed, as if we had not spent the last hour plotting the downfall of the two men who'd done their damndest to recreate our own personal living hell.

Worth noting is that Elisa played her part here flawlessly, smiling at Cole as if nothing had changed. True, for her it hadn't, because she'd gone after him with a motive of suspicion from the start. We had dismissed her as a hypersexual person to begin with, given that she had led us to that conclusion, so maybe we'd allowed that to cloud our judgment of what she really was. There wasn't a single person among us who didn't watch her gaze adoringly at Cole and wonder, fleetingly, if we shouldn't be a little more afraid of her than we were—but it didn't matter, we thought, soothing ourselves; after all, she was on our side.

†

We agreed that Marcus should be the one to test our theory. Once Elisa explained that Cole and Jonathan had been carefully inspecting their secret recordings for any conceivable slights against Audrey, their chosen target, we all decided to manufacture a perfect opportunity for supernatural revenge. We agreed that Marcus and Elisa would cook with Audrey, and Marcus would stage a conflict. Then the rest of us would plant our own hidden phone cameras, turning the game on Cole and Jonathan themselves.

Elisa had already found evidence that Cole was limiting our grocery supply, and she managed to send an email to the grocery provider without him knowing. Now that we knew what to watch for, we saw Cole's face warp a little in disbelief when we got our first full delivery of fresh produce in nearly two months. "So weird!" he exclaimed, which in his mind, it probably was. After all, he and Jonathan had plotted out one thing flawlessly: that keeping a group of two dozen people just on the wrong side of hungry was enough to drive them all insane.

Elisa talked us out of turning the internet back on, though, adding that Cole might begin to notice things were *too* fishy, and reminded us that an end date made all the difference. If this was really happening, she said, then it would be over in a month—and sure, that was a long time, but we'd gone through worse. We agreed on the tentative terms that our staging would be successful, and having determined our stakes, we hunkered down in our individual whisper networks to wait.

After Marcus suggested that Audrey's baba ganoush needed more salt (a truly horrendous thing to say, one chef to another), it was Xavier's phone in the bathroom that recorded the proof we needed: Jonathan slipping something into the bristles of Marcus' toothbrush, of all things, after which point Cole entered the bathroom and the two argued quietly about whether he had used enough to successfully numb Marcus' entire mouth. Cole, whom we later found out was a very well-preserved thirty-two, accused Jonathan of being useless and implied they would not get the finale they desired if they did not get Marcus on board. Jonathan, whom we later discovered was a fraternity brother of Cole's from a very wealthy family who happened to owe a great deal of money to the government, growled in response that Cole's dalliance with Elisa was the actual source of their issues.

"I'm working on Elisa," said Cole, which of course Jonathan did not believe (nor did any of the rest of us). "Don't you get it?" Cole hissed. "This has to be a *blowout.* Every single member of this house has to believe there's

61

a witch or there goes our budget. You can kiss series renewal goodbye if Marcus doesn't convince everyone that someone cursed the shit out of his tongue!"

As you might imagine, our response to this was one of brutal fury. From that moment on, none of us doubted Marcus and Elisa's idea. WiFi be damned. We had a better plan.

†

Having realized we were all victims of a massive gaslighting campaign, we were quick to turn our attention to the architects. How to punish them appropriately? By giving them what they wanted.

At first.

We allowed Cole and Jonathan to continue victimizing us without any intervention; we behaved as normal, only slightly jumpy about what might or might not be drugged, and continued to speculate as a group about the presence of a witch. This time, though, we allowed ourselves to consider other options.

"What if it's not Audrey?" said Viv to Lizzie in the presence of the potted plant camera. "I mean, Cole was there, too."

"You guys, don't be ridiculous. It's not Cole," Elisa said, playing the role of girlfriend so effortlessly that even we weren't completely sure we shouldn't be convinced. "What about him screams *evil*? Or any sort of supernatural, for that matter," she added, glancing at her fingernails.

"It's just interesting," Lizzie said, backing down just enough to be persuasively unsure. "He was there in the bathroom with Thom the first time too, wasn't he?"

The first stage of our plan kept going like that, the thread of suspicions fraying; the loud bemoaning of our belief that we might be trapped there indefinitely despite knowing our days were purposefully numbered. We started gradually cozying up to Jonathan, coaxing him into a false sense of security. We mentioned our suspicions of Cole and watched his overtaxed accomplice struggle not to give the game away, unable to prevent a slip of glee here and there when Cole's popularity took a turn. Not that Cole had ever been anyone's favorite, but by all accounts he was unobjectionable, universally accepted, while Jonathan had been a pariah due to his "contraction" of the virus.

It became clear that even Jonathan had suffered from five-and-spare change months of isolation, to the point where he was willing to throw Cole under the bus for the tiniest scraps of social acceptance.

✝

Seeing how easily Cole and Jonathan's alliance could be splintered, we were overwhelmed with the first sense of accomplishment that any of us had encountered in weeks. After a week of playing along, carefully (breathlessly!) plotting our transition, we started the next phase of our plan. We wanted Cole and Jonathan to *suffer*, of course, as we had; retribution for our months of slow devolution, the degradation of our little society that had crumbled at their hands. But we wouldn't accept just *any* suffering. Discomfort? Pain? No. We wanted something that would last. Something perpetual, that would exceed our residency in quarantine. It was cold-blooded of us, maybe—but so, we would argue, was surveilling us for months without our permission while also restricting our food supply. (Which was not even to mention the psychological trauma and/or spiders therein.)

This we did in stages. First we wanted to spook Jonathan, the less dominant of the two, so we experimented on each other. We used the same tactics, the same tricks, only this time we intentionally provoked Cole first in order to set the stage for our amateur theatrics. Chantal had a particularly harrowing scream, so we started with her, encouraging her to first "drunkenly" slosh the front of Cole's signature crisp t-shirt with a glass of cheap Pinot Noir before then soaking her bedsheets in it, leaving her to "awaken" in a puddle of "blood."

Cole, we could see, was thoroughly shaken, and though he'd been a good actor thus far, he wasn't exactly a once-in-a-generation thespian. That first successful mission electrified us, our survival responses greedily attuned to the fight.

Initially we were not very creative, being unaccustomed to sadism as we largely were. We put packets of food dye (natural, per Audrey's insistence) into the showerhead so that it looked like blood was coating Xavier's shoulders when he and Cole were alone in the bathroom, which we now recognize had a certain similar undertone to Chantal's bed-wetting. (Our tactical revenge teams had gotten their wires crossed, as we now suspect.) Luckily we had the element of surprise on our side, precisely as Cole and Jonathan had once had against us. At some point after this excursion, our footage caught Cole accusing Jonathan of going rogue, which was how we knew our methods were working. Jonathan was pale-faced and panicked, insisting it hadn't been him, and to Cole's insistence that if it wasn't him then *who*, Jonathan clearly didn't want to answer.

"What does it matter if they think it's you?" Jonathan demanded, once it had become clear that the tide of the house's suspicion—procedurally paced thanks to Marcus, who kept us from running away with our growing enthusiasm—was turning. "It still proves the same thing, doesn't it? The show still holds up," Jonathan said, visibly spooked.

Up to this point we had kept pace with Cole and Jonathan's schedule of horrors, collaborating as a group to chart every time the rest of us had been targeted and following a similar pattern of every two to three days. We were still only playing tricks on each other, each of us cheerfully wiping away makeup-ed bruises or discarding our efforts at drafting menacing messages to leave on the walls, but once it seemed obvious that Jonathan was beginning to turn, we started to escalate.

This time, we picked a new target: Jonathan himself.

†

We imagine there is nothing worse than believing yourself to be the orchestrator of torment only to unexpectedly find yourself a victim. Is this not the lesson behind the seminal film *Matilda*, based on the literary masterpiece of the same name? Bullies do not like to be bullied, and perhaps because they are so attuned to their own cruelty, they are exceptionally sensitive when it happens to them. Initially we did almost nothing, drugging Jonathan only to rearrange his room just slightly; just enough that he would wake with a dry mouth and realize things were... inexplicably out of place. His paranoia sank in immediately, and this time, we noticed, he did not run first to Cole. Instead he turned to his roommates, Samad and Nino, who were kind enough to be giddily sympathetic.

We caught an audio recording later between Cole and Jonathan that was difficult to hear, perhaps because Jonathan was panting. We know the exchange that followed was essentially "it isn't me" "okay then prove it" "how am I supposed to prove it, maybe it's you" "it isn't me I swear," which was playing out so beautifully that we could hardly stand it ourselves.

"Elisa will never believe it," Cole had growled to Jonathan, which concerned us at first, because he was correct that Elisa would not have believed it before, and in fact obviously hadn't when the target had been Audrey. (Audrey, during this time, had become our chief engineer of misery, though most of us were still unable to speak casually with her, having now suffered a mass storm of guilt that surpassed even our previous cloud of fear.) We wondered how Elisa planned to execute the turning of her own belief, since her opinion on the matter was obviously essential.

What we failed to notice at the time was how expertly Elisa had cultivated her position as the linchpin of our plan. True, we understood on some basic level that Cole was using her as a symbol of rationality, but we hadn't realized yet that he had put the last of his sanity *in* her. He was not only using her, he was *relying on* her, and so long as Elisa did not feel there was madness afoot, Cole could believe it, too. Which made the finale of our plan very clear.

During the final week before production was supposed to shut down, Audrey told us that all tomfoolery and psychological buffoonery would stop. Stop? we echoed doubtfully. Stop, cease, desist, she replied, unfazed. We wondered why, and she told us it was obvious: that waiting for the drop was the most tormenting thing of all. We had our doubts initially, but soon discovered she must have been right. The tension was so stiff that the air itself was thick with paranoia, all of us sustaining a single withdrawn breath.

†

None of us knew what was coming until it arrived, but by the time it was happening, it was obvious. After all, none of us had ever been able to look away when Marcus and Elisa were in the same room. Knowing something significant loomed had only heightened our observation.

Not that we were technically *in* the room. We weren't even sure what had made them so convinced we'd overhear. Instinct? Possibly. They were more attuned to us than we were to them, even if we were exorbitantly watchful. Possibly they knew that by doing something quietly—something near-silent, as they had that first night when Elisa first confronted Marcus in the kitchen—we would all be that much more likely to listen. Whatever their intentions, they accomplished it easily, in low and almost secret tones.

"I don't like him for you," said Marcus, without preamble.

(They were cooking, of course. It always came back to the kitchen for us, and don't mistake us: this detail of context is significant.)

Elisa's reply was swift and harsh. "I don't think I asked for your opinion, did I?"

"It doesn't have to be him."

"Then who else would it be?"

A pause.

"You know who," Marcus said, and on our side of the wall, Holly's eyes widened while Viv raised a hand to her mouth, entranced.

"Do I?"

There was the sound of something, a rustle of motion, and the sound of chopping stopped. We estimated Marcus had taken the knife from Elisa's hand to pause her mid-mirepoix, and by then even Thom couldn't pretend not to be listening intently.

"There's something wrong with him," Marcus said softly. "I know you know it."

There was a collective intake of breath on our side of the conversation, all of us purposefully not looking at Cole until, one by one, we did. Nadya, Basia, Gia, Amal, Xavier, Oscar... most of us can list off in precise sequential order the way we all slowly let our attention turn to him.

In that moment, waiting to hear what Elisa would say, Cole could feel us turning against him. There was no fear in us anymore, thanks to our strength in numbers. We, the collective, now *blamed* him. He could see it, practically taste it, how there was only one voice left to defend him, and she had very carefully chosen to take her time.

"Just tell me," Marcus said. "Tell me I'm not crazy."

"Oh, you're definitely crazy," Elisa said quickly; too-quickly. "But..."

And here, time briefly stopped.

"You're right," she said, and Calvin inhaled sharply. "Something's... something's wrong," Elisa murmured. "With Cole."

We watched Cole's mouth tighten.

"Do you trust him?" Marcus asked.

"No," said Elisa.

"Do you love him?"

"No."

At this point Cole was visibly deteriorating, his cheeks turning red, and by the time Jonathan looked at him, joining the ranks of the mob, it must have been enough. It must have been too much.

"Do you love *me*?" Marcus asked.

At that moment, all of us bracing for Elisa's answer, Cole feverishly tore through the room, upending the chair he'd been sitting in and bursting into the kitchen with all of us leaping up in his wake. He let out a primal something, a growl or some other animal sound, and Elisa, already half-in Marcus' arms, whirled to face him. (This is the account we have from

Lucien, who was closest to the door, which has also been confirmed by Basia. Raj says they were already kissing, but Raj has a tendency to exaggerate.)

"So will it be me next, then?" Elisa asked Cole, and we have to admit, she was brilliant. There were pricks of tears in her eyes, sharp thorns in her trembling voice, and Cole was wild—as wild as we had been for months before the truth had soothed us. He was maniacal with disbelief, and that was when we realized that we had done it: that now, even Cole suspected himself of being the sliver, the flaw.

Marcus, noticing Cole's departure from lucidity, pulled Elisa closer to him, which seemed to break Cole even more.

"It's not... it's not *witchcraft*," Cole spat, furious, before he finally broke down and confessed. "It's... it's part of a show, it's all fake, none of it's real—"

"Get away from her," Marcus warned, his hand twitching at his side. According to Raj, whom we've already acknowledged as only half-trustworthy, Marcus had been the first to glance at the chef's knife where it had been mislaid on the cutting board beside the carrots.

"I'm telling you," Cole said hysterically, "it's all just a—"

Marcus, still playing the role of protector, moved Elisa behind him to shield her, and she, to what must have been Cole's disbelief, went. That seemed to be the breaking point for him, and with a glint in his eye, he lurched forward; maybe to do nothing more than shove Marcus out of the way, or to reassure Elisa.

Given the knife's position on the counter, though, maybe not.

What actually happened is difficult for any of us to explain. In fact, to this day, we can't. We get asked all the time by our families and Ellen Degeneres alike what happened, or who planned this part of our little revenge concept, but we don't actually know how the knife rose up of its own accord from the cutting board. We also don't know what made the kitchen ingredients rise up in a cyclone and spin, tighter and tighter, until Cole let out another primal scream, and then they froze.

How can anyone explain that?

Cole certainly couldn't. He stared at his hands, lunging for Marcus again, but then the cyclone continued and he stopped. He threw out a palm, wordlessly pleading for Marcus to wait, to let him explain, possibly to insist once again that it wasn't him—and then the knife slowly angled itself around, the blade perilously aimed at Marcus's throat.

"No," said Cole in a whimper, "no," and at that moment, we saw the idea latch into place. We watched a theory become reality, and at the moment we weren't sure whether to be horrified or vindicated, agonized or proud, because in the end, against all odds, Cole's television production had accomplished precisely what it set out to prove.

He had convinced everyone in the house, himself included, that he was a witch.

✝

We're told that what happened to Cole has been officially diagnosed as a psychotic break. We don't know if this is something his lawyers cooked up in order to prevent him from being prosecuted, which Jonathan was, or if Cole *actually* lost his last grip on reality. The media is calling it the devolution of a man's sanity, the unsettling but satisfying conclusion to the sort of vengeance tale that Quentin Tarantino would write, but the rest of us are still too mystified to understand it. We know what we were responsible for and what Cole was responsible for, so at this point we've agreed that maybe we imagined the end of it. Maybe by then our herd mentality had exceeded normality to the point that all of us temporarily hallucinated as one.

After all, Thom had told Amal, who hadn't been able to fit through the doorway, and Artie had told Samad, and Cara had described it to Viv... so maybe we all invented it.

That's the story we're going with, anyway. Though as a group, we all laughingly take credit for it, as if that final detail had been nothing more than an actionable item in the scheme of comeuppance we'd carefully planned.

Jonathan broke shortly after, blubbering then packing then shrieking, and we received word from the network via the house's phone that we would be sent home immediately, the next morning. We were relieved, elated, victorious, and though the virus itself hadn't been entirely eradicated, we were famous enough by then—thanks to Holly, who had "friends in journalism"—to be tested and proven uncontaminated, finally able to make our way home.

We had all agreed among ourselves that Elisa and Marcus were probably acting, just playing their parts in our quest to drive Cole to confession, so we didn't read that much into what we'd heard in the kitchen. Nino and Samad, though, soon assured us otherwise, the two of them separately messaging our group chat the following day from where they'd decided to stay at Nino's parent's lakehouse. (At the time we initially heard from them, we were all still pretending we believed this to be a platonic arrangement.)

There was a moment, they both said, when Elisa and Marcus were alone together at the foot of the stairwell that led to the living room. Nino and Samad, who were having a secret tryst of their own, managed not to interrupt, though they disagree about the details. Mostly they agree that Elisa and Marcus were standing in the panes of moonlight that came through the windows. (Which is atmospherically pleasing, at least.)

"You know it's always been you," Elisa said quietly, and according to Nino, Marcus's entire face changed when he looked at her, like he was watching the sun come up in her eyes.

"Yeah?" he echoed.

"Yeah."

Samad says this is when Marcus turned to Elisa and took her face in his hands, caressing her cheeks and tenderly pressing his lips to her forehead. Nino says that neither of them actually moved, but Marcus was looking at Elisa, and she was looking back at him.

"So anyway, maybe I'll see you again," Elisa said casually, breaking the spell, and Marcus laughed.

"You're impossible."

"Am I?"

"Yes."

"Hm."

There was a comfortable silence then that convinced Nino the previous conversation between them, the one staged for Cole's benefit, hadn't been entirely an act. Marcus had broached something unplanned, something she hadn't heard from him before—*Do you love me?*—and in her silence, she had communicated something back.

"You knew I wanted you from that first night," Marcus said.

"And that makes me impossible?" Elisa asked.

"Yes," he said, "because you knew you wanted me, too."

She either slid him a caustic glance or kissed his fingers, depending who tells the story.

"Yeah, well, I didn't want you like *this*," she said, referencing the house and its confinement. This made sense to both Nino and Samad, who'd spent the last half year trying to avoid the scrutiny of the house's occupants themselves. Apparently, Elisa giving voice to their own suspicions—i.e., that madness was the root of our six months, and therefore the entire time was rendered suspect, suspended by a thread of delirium, somehow false or inauthentic or at very least gossamer, fairy-made—was the revelation they needed to understand their own need for secrecy, their guarded hesitation. It encouraged them to later reveal the nature of their relationship to us (once they'd first relayed what they'd seen that night).

"So how do you want me, then?" Marcus asked Elisa in his low voice, and she looked up at him, shaking her head.

"You're just a cocky little bastard, aren't you?"

"Maybe so. Answer the question."

"I want lots of people, you know."

"I know. But not in the same way."

"And you know this because...?"

"Elisa." A step closer. "Answer the question."

She sighed, gradually resigned. "Honestly?"

"Do your worst."

So, Simone texted eagerly at this point, *how did she want him??????*

Tell us right now or we'll find you both and kill you, said Amal.

Jesus Christ, said Nino, *calm down you maniacs—*

"Wickedly," was apparently what Elisa replied, or so they think, though on this, at least, Nino and Samad both agree: Elisa and Marcus leaned in at once, in synchronicity, bending toward each other like stalks on a breeze, and in the moonlight they shared a kiss that would end in wordless, sightless quiet, charting all the voyages the rest of us would never see.

†

Life was different after our time in the *Heatin' Up!* house, which had actually been the *Witch Hunt* house all along—though, considering that show would never air, we can't really bring ourselves to call it that. We were in constant contact with each other for a few weeks, all of us trying to settle back into a world that had only just begun coming out of its shell. We reminisced about the meals we'd eaten together (all of us had very different palettes from where we started, which certainly helped Artie expand the delivery-based cafe he later established in place of his AirBnB scheme, and also gave Lizzie and Viv an edge in their fusion catering business) and the more memorable gaslighting we'd ourselves committed (such as the time we'd all drunkenly written notes for Simone to find in her underwear after she'd written a passive-aggressive one to implicate Cole. Ours were not so much frightening as highly inept). We sent each other articles and clips, including memes of ourselves and satirical headlines. We were both heralded as the most remarkable people of the year in *Time* Magazine and mocked relentlessly on Twitter, so we leaned on each other, just as we had during our time in quarantine. After all, we, unlike even our friends and family, were the only ones who could possibly understand.

Eventually, though, we stopped answering messages right away, or resorted only to GIFs and reactions or the odd baby picture from Chantal (she'd gotten back with her ex, much to Thom's disappointment), and then gradually we didn't talk at all. It was only recently that we'd begun to speak again, owing mostly to what Oscar found during one of his aforementioned visits to Audrey's cooking blog.

At that point, so much time had passed that we were beginning to misremember things, or to remember things we'd forgotten, and so we told the story again to each other, all trying to collectively make sense of it.

Wouldn't it be hilarious if there had been an actual witch in the house all along? said Oscar.

We all wanted to groan; to deadpan that all this experience had taught us was that witches weren't real, but truthfully we had our reservations. After all, what had actually happened when Cole faced down Elisa and Marcus? Had we imagined it? Had it been a trick that someone had managed without the rest of us knowing? Calvin, an engineer, had always been quietly suspected of being involved, but he assured us he wasn't. He also assured us there was no explanation for it, so at that point, Cara was the one who decided we ought to write it down. It was cathartic, her therapist said, to try to give shape to a story. To help us make sense of reality, and thereby find the line between that and our imaginations again.

So here it is, our story, which has belonged to the public for perhaps a little too long. Obviously some parts are missing; we never asked Cole or Jonathan how they felt about messing with us like this because, for obvious reasons, we don't care. We also apologized to Audrey many times, unsuccessfully; all of us shared screenshots of emails or DMs from her that said, essentially, "Don't worry about it," with no attempt to mend the rift. Fair enough. As for Marcus and Elisa, none of us ever heard from them again. Given the massive outpouring of public scrutiny, they shut down their personal social media accounts, disappearing into thin air.

... *Until*, that is, the day Oscar dug up the account that Audrey had recently followed: @KitchenWitches, a new cooking blog mixing classic Latin American staples with Creole-inspired soul food. Interesting, right? We thought so, all of us collectively energized once again as we zoomed as far as we could into the screenshot Oscar sent us of the account's photograph. Elisa's hair is shorter and Marcus's is longer, but it's definitely them, or so we've confirmed as a group. You'd think this would drive us somehow crazier—kitchen *witches*, is that some sort of joke, or a confession of guilt, or...?—but honestly, the truth is that it's a relief. We'd managed to be right about something the whole time, and it's affirming, really, having gone through everything we have, to know that at least one thing was always true. Whether or not we can ever explain what happened in the house or how much of it was natural, we can finally close the door on the whole thing now, our cravings finally satiated by the truth.

That in the midst of our personal dystopia, there had been love all along.

THE DEVIL'S ADVOCATE (MARCH - MAY 2021)

ANY FIRST YEAR LAW STUDENT WILL TELL YOU that a contract is an invaluable thing; for many a headache, for others a thing of beauty, and for some a matter of eternalism itself. The art of moral clarity forms the primary vocation for Elaine Estrada, who considers her employer's contracts to be nothing more than a straightforward deal—until she meets someone whose impractical search for lost souls puts her no-nonsense approach to the test.

PART I: INTRODUCTION TO TORTS

What is a soul for, *anyway?*

Elaine Estrada reconsiders the query at hand and backspaces a bit.

What is *a soul, anyway?*

Better.

Is it some fundamental life source; the spark which lights the cosmos itself? Is life *the same as a soul? Is sentience? There is some contention as to which species even contain souls, which are sometimes considered housed within a body. Other definitions exceed corporeal limitations.*

She pauses to ponder it, then continues.

There is arguably no purpose to having a soul at all. After all, countless organisms exist with nothing but genetic function and a preternatural, species-driven pattern of instinct without any need for a collective higher purpose. What is it that makes souls so valuable that we are willing to assign them such incomprehensible value? In consideration of

"Ehem," says Mr. Up. "Ms. Estrada? We've discussed this."

Elaine should be startled by the unexpected interruption, but of course she isn't. It's much too frequent.

"I'm not going to submit it anywhere," she informs her uninvited guest. "Unless you haven't noticed, it's a slow day," she adds, referencing the perimeter of her office, which would be empty if not for Mr. Up, who is standing very awkwardly beside the coat rack.

"Ms. Estrada," Mr. Up attempts again, with another throat-clearing sound of unease that is typical of his frequent appearances. (Elaine makes him very nervous, as do most people and things.) "Your employment contract clearly states—"

"Since when do you have any idea what my employment contract states?" Elaine replies, typing madly away in her document without much regard for diction, as she knows she has less than a minute to finish her thought. "Regardless, you work for the prosecution, Mr. Up," she reminds him, "and last I checked, I have no obligation to share my findings with you."

"Now, now," Mr. Up exclaims, aghast. "There's really no reason to be so hostile."

If Mr. Up were an actual man, Elaine would point out that she wasn't being hostile, merely factual, and furthermore, that being told "now, now" was, much like being told to "calm down," unproductive. But it's not Mr. Up's fault he doesn't understand her.

"Mm," she replies, still typing.

A seam of the wall unzips and Elaine's cramped office is now officially at capacity.

"Ms. Estrada," says Mr. Down. His voice is deeper than Mr. Up's and considerably more collected, though it is no less unwelcome. Nor is it any less a surprise.

"Mr. Down," Elaine replies, and his hand moves, or perhaps she imagines it. Either way her manuscript is wiped clean, as if it had never existed to begin with. "Excuse me," she protests, glancing up at him. He's wearing a very odd coat with a wide variety of buttons, all different sizes and shapes of brass: anchors, bows, oversized coins. Either he has never quite gotten the hang of human fashions or he feels obligated to wear it.

For fun, she imagines Mr. Up gave it to him. "I wasn't finished."

"You know the rules," says Mr. Down.

"In fact I do," Elaine retorts, irritated, but again, unsurprised. This is not the first time they've played this little game, nor is it likely to be the last. "There is nothing in my contract that states I can't speculate as to what I've witnessed over the course of my employment."

"It's poor gamesmanship," Mr. Down informs her, glancing sideways at Mr. Up.

"I do believe I'm in agreement with my colleague," agrees Mr. Up, anxiously.

"Well, ultimately the two of you are far more alike than you think," Elaine reminds them. "I'd have added that to my findings if you'd ever let me get beyond the introductory paragraphs. It's very foolish, you know, the way people so fundamentally fail to understand the simple bureaucracy of the whole thing. They hate lawyers nearly as much as they hate you," she points out, glancing specifically at Mr. Down while she gestures to her diploma on the wall from UC Hastings law school. "And yet *your* side gets off scot-free," she says to Mr. Up.

"Regrettable indeed," Mr. Up blusters in apology.

"Hush," Mr. Down tells him, not unkindly. Secretly Elaine suspects them of being quite good friends, perhaps meeting up for a weekly game of poker. "And as for you," Mr. Down says, directing his attention to Elaine this time, "boredom is no excuse for insubordination. If this keeps up I'll have to submit a formal report."

"Oh no," says Elaine, who is responsible for formal reports. (She's technically legal, not HR, but there's some latitude.)

"Yes." Mr. Down confirms gravely. "And there will be another tide of supplicants soon. There nearly always is. You've seen the state of politics, the economy," he offers reassuringly. "Believe me Ms. Estrada, another peak of mortal desperation is nigh."

"Oh goody," says Elaine, then glances at Mr. Up. "Seems like you should take some sort of pre-emptive measure for this kind of thing, if everyone knows it's coming?"

"Strike that from the record," Mr. Down says at once. "Upstairs has its own legal counsel."

"Indeed, so stricken," agrees an agreeable Mr. Up, and there's an imperceptible blink of time where Elaine's words have been undone; her meaning unfelt. "If you could please return to work now, Ms. Estrada."

It's four p.m. on a Friday and Elaine would like some nachos. A previous version of her would say she'd kill for them, especially with a bit of carne asada mixed in (heavenly and sinful all at once, much like the current contents of her office) but she's learned to be a bit more careful with the specifics of her phrasing.

"As you wish," Elaine replies, as Mr. Up filters out through the air conditioning vent and Mr. Down melts into the floors.

†

In a previous version of herself, Elaine Estrada was eminently sensible. Not that she isn't now, but sensibility has its place. She possesses the pragmatism of an eldest daughter who selected her university degrees based not on prestige, but on the projected minimisation of her student loans. She waited until after marriage before losing her virginity, just in case. She was once primarily agnostic, appreciative of the self-sufficiency of domestic house cats, and to this day does not have a sweet tooth. Her morality is coded purely on the functions of the law itself.

Elaine was married at twenty-five to a fellow law student, Justin

Frusciante, which all parties agreed was a very sensible choice; he was respectful and kind and intelligent and had a very bright future as a law clerk to a federal judge whilst she'd set her course in transactional law. Elaine considered their sex life adequate, but was not surprised when her husband confessed he had fallen for someone else. An artist, which was by all accounts an unsensible career path. In any case, Elaine wished him well and chose to move out of San Francisco, which was much too expensive to live practically on a single income, in favor of Tulsa, Oklahoma, where she could have a two-bedroom apartment all to herself along with a stable income. Because she was so eminently practical, though, she did not disable her profile on various job-hunting sites, allowing the door to remain open for greener pastures.

Which is how she came to be invited for an exclusive interview by Mr. Down. The salary was extremely competitive, complete with phenomenal benefits, and her hours as his employer's in-house attorney would be strictly nine-to-five, with all holidays off and two weeks paid vacation. Elaine had never envisioned herself as private counsel, but she had also never envisioned herself divorced and living in Tulsa, and ultimately neither of those things caused her much grief. She also learned the name (or rather, title) of the employer and did not flinch.

"Any questions?" Mr. Down asked at the end of Elaine's interview, after which time he informed her the more trifling details of the job. Primarily she would be handling contracts and any subsequent legal concerns, though they had long since been standardized and were unlikely to be complicated. In short, nothing that would keep her in the office past five.

"What are the opportunities for advancement?" Elaine asked.

"You will be in a department of one, Ms. Estrada," replied Mr. Down.

"How has your role changed since working for your employer?"

"It hasn't. Certainly not in the last six thousand years."

"What does a typical day look like?"

"There is occasional wailing and gnashing of teeth. Otherwise fairly normal."

"Can you tell me about your new products or plans for growth?"

"This is more of a business-as-usual position, Ms. Estrada," replied Mr. Down.

"I see." She paused. "I suppose I always assumed this sort of job was usually held by some kind of slimeball Harvard grad with a senator for an uncle." She had never actually thought about it as a vocation before, technically speaking. More as self-appointed form of torture from fellow law students who enjoyed the sound of their own voice. But it stood to reason that where there were contracts, there was an attorney involved.

Mr. Down nodded. "A common misconception. But we find the job is best handled by someone more sensible. You must understand, Ms. Estrada," he added, "that emotions will not serve you well here. Many supplicants will grieve and beg. None, however, will present a sound legal argument."

"Isn't it my job to determine that?" Elaine asked. "If you give me the job, that is."

"Yes." Mr. Down considered her with his head tilted, then nodded approvingly. "So. Are you available to start immediately?"

"Immediately as in Monday or immediately as in now?"

The room which had been Mr. Down's office reversed itself so that Elaine was the one sitting in the desk. Meanwhile, Mr. Down rose to his feet in a fluid motion of supreme ambiguity. The walls shrank down to a proportion of about 15% its original size.

"Ah, much cozier," Elaine said.

"Indeed," agreed Mr. Down, before dissolving into several tiny pieces that carried away on a breeze.

✝

Elaine's job is not very complicated, which is probably why her employer does not see the necessity of a Harvard degree. She has never met him—her employer, that is, for whom Mr. Down serves as a proxy—though she doesn't consider that unusual. At her old firm she was very unlikely to run into any of the partners, and anyway, the office she works out of now is not in any sort of corporate headquarters where such a thing might be possible. It sits innocuously atop a barbershop and a vacant ice cream parlor, neither of which disrupt her work in any way.

Elaine has a business card. It reads *Elaine Estrada, Devil's Advocate.* People find it exceedingly amusing when she puts it in for free lunch raffles at nearby delis and cafes, though the supplicants who come to her office clutching it in hand feel differently. Mr. Down was correct that they are typically very upset, and there is a fair amount of teeth gnashing. Ultimately, though, the job is very simple.

"I'm afraid the contract is solid," Elaine once told an artist who'd traded his soul for a work of true greatness. Greatness did not sell well, evidently. The artist was struggling to pay his rent and Elaine was sympathetic, but sympathy didn't pay her bills. "You specifically said 'a work of true greatness.' You never specified a monetary valuation."

A novelist felt similarly about their possession of The Next Great American Novel, which no agent seemed to find sufficiently compelling. They couldn't relate to the characters, they said. The novelist seemed very dismal about this and Elaine could certainly see why. "Publishing is a difficult industry," she said. "You'll get there."

"*But my soul*," wailed the novelist.

"It was worth a very great work of literature," Elaine pointed out. But by the increase in volume of the wailing, it did not help.

There were a fair amount of politicians who were slipperier, their contracts reviewed in advance by their own in-house counsel. Tech billionaires, accustomed to terms and conditions, arrive better prepared. Elaine does not hear from them much, since she is not the originator of the deals. That, as she understands it, is a matter for the recruitment department, followed by the collections department, neither of which she has ever been to or seen. Her only job is to defend her employer's legal liability, and it is not a difficult job.

It is, though, a monotonous one.

Which is not to say she doesn't enjoy the complexity of the legal arguments. They aren't stupid, the supplicants who come to her doors; not always. Desperate, yes. Stupid, no. They often know they're being intentionally inflicted with anything from emotional damage to negligence, and the request for a remedy is an understandable one.

The problem is that the devil's original advocate—as in, whoever it was who wrote the standardized contract that Elaine is so often called upon to defend—understood the law to a degree so pervasive that no argument stands successfully. In legalese, the supplicant must prove with a preponderance of evidence (by all accounts a lower standard than "beyond a reasonable doubt") that the suspected tortfeasor (Elaine's employer) is the undisputed originator of a legally recognized cause of harm.

This is a very tricky legal puzzle, which nobody has yet to solve. Not even Elaine, though she tries to. The problem is that nobody understands a soul besides the person (or metaphysical concept/being) who collects them.

On the Monday after Elaine is caught once again attempting to put into legal (or at least technical) terms the value of a human soul, she arrives at her office promptly at nine. Her office is well-stocked with coffee and filters. She fixes herself a cup and sits down with her dayplanner, which says things like *dentist appointment* and *oil change* but nothing of a professional nature. While contractual disagreements in her previous firm had a tendency to last for weeks on end, much of which was spent preparing for arbitration or trial, nothing has ever exceeded the length of time necessary for her to immediately square it away at her desk. She goes on Twitter, scrolling for anything of interest or the occasional joke. Only two social media sites are banned: Myspace and Tumblr. They are operated by Mr. Up's people, which is unfortunately not very blessed with technological proficiency.

At ten in the morning, someone enters. A young girl. No, a twenty-something woman who only looks very young. But she does indeed look very young.

"I've been wronged," the young woman says.

"Sit," Elaine replies.

The young woman sits.

"Your name?"

"Nessa. Er, Vanessa."

"Last name, please?"

"Smith."

"Date of birth?"

"July 1, 1996." So the age estimate was correct, then.

Elaine finds Nessa's file in the system, which is fully automated and actually quite good. The database is extremely organized. "I see here you offered your soul in exchange for two weekend passes to Coachella?"

"I was joking." Nessa's face is unchanged. "It was like... sarcasm, you know?"

"I'm afraid the contract does not recognize sarcasm, Miss Smith."

"Well," Nessa sighs, "I was kind of with this guy my mother thought was a terrible influence. Turns out she was right, but anyway—"

"Did he summon my employer on your behalf?" Perhaps it would be an interesting legal argument if the supplicant in question were some kind of collateral damage. Elaine hasn't come across that yet.

"No, he just... We were really bombed one night, and—"

Ah, Elaine thinks morosely. This is a very common argument. "Your state of mind at the time of contract signing shows you to be lucid and below the legal limit at the actual time of signing."

"I... duress, then?" Nessa attempts. Elaine suspects she's been told to say that, and wonders if Mr. Up's people have anything to do with it.

"Were you threatened, Miss Smith? In fear for your life?"

"Well, it was really friggin' weird—"

"Answer the question, Miss Smith."

"I just—" Nessa exhales through her (gritted, but not quite gnashed) teeth. "Surely you can see this is an unfair bargain. He must have been able to foresee the damage. Doesn't that count as liability?"

Ah yes. She has definitely been coached.

"Miss Smith," Elaine says. "You're right that it's a very stupid situation."

"Thank you," Nessa exhales, flopping back in her chair. "See? I knew you wouldn't be unreasonable."

"Unfortunately," Elaine continues, "excessive stupidity is not a compelling legal argument."

Nessa blinks. "What?"

Elaine, finding this all exhaustingly redundant, proposes, "If you could prove you were genuinely incapacitated at the time of the agreement—"

Nessa gawks at her. "I told you, I was wasted!"

"I do not mean under the influence," Elaine clarifies. "I mean truly incapacitated, as in mid-seizure, or perhaps in the midst of a schizophrenic break—"

Nessa shoots to her feet, jaw clenched. "I'm not crazy."

"Well, that's a pity, given everything," Elaine says, selecting 'resolved' on Vanessa Smith's contract file. She notices, though, that Nessa hasn't left, and is instead pacing the office.

Elaine has a good hour and a half until lunch, so she decides to indulge her curiosity a bit.

"What does it feel like?" Elaine asks her. "Having promised your soul away."

"What?" Nessa stops her pacing and turns to Elaine. "Don't you know?"

Elaine shakes her head. "I have a very straightforward employment contract." She receives a W-2, with bountiful retirement benefits and an annual bonus.

"Oh." Nessa sinks into the chair again, chewing her lip. "Well, I still have it, technically."

Elaine leans forward. "Technically?"

Nessa nods. "The echo of it, I guess. I can feel the places it used to be."

"Like empty space?"

"Yeah, or like, something I forgot at home. Kind of like I left the oven on."

"That doesn't sound so bad," Elaine says. Annoying, sure. But certainly livable. The human body is very adaptable. Humans are capable of stupendous flexibility in general. They can adapt to severe heat and cold. The human spirit—is that the same as a soul?—is famously resilient. She has never actually known why the devil collects them, except that she suspects he uses them to power his house.

"It's horrid," Nessa says. "Or at least I think it is."

"You think?" Elaine echoes.

"Well, I don't know anymore," Nessa says with a shrug. "I taste things, but feel nothing about them. I see a sunrise or a sunset and there's nothing but a hollowness, and maybe half a memory about how I used to feel. I still have my thoughts but none of my... passions."

"Passions?" Elaine says, intrigued.

"Yes, my passions," Nessa confirms ruefully. "I went to Coachella, you know. But it was like I didn't even care anymore that I was there."

"Hm," says Elaine. "Interesting."

"Is it?"

"I think so. After all, it means no more heartbreak," Elaine points out. "No more disappointment or grief. No more fear or worry."

Nessa fixes her with a blank look. "I think you're trying to make me feel better, but it won't work. I just told you I don't feel anything."

Privately Elaine thought that was untrue. In her limited experience Nessa still felt frustration, embarrassment, shame.

Still. "I'm afraid your legal argument is unsound," Elaine says.

"Is there a way to appeal that with like... someone above you?" asks Nessa. Whoever coached her is very good, Elaine thinks again.

"You may file to appeal in thirty days," Elaine says, "though I wouldn't be too hopeful."

"Great. I'm not. I never am anymore." Nessa rises to her feet. "Thirty days, you said? Here?"

Elaine nods. "Thirty days."

"Cool. See you then." Nessa turns, closing the door behind her, and

Elaine clicks out of the office database.

"Mr. Up?" she calls.

"Yes?" he says, materializing apprehensively from somewhere behind her eyelids.

"I don't suppose your side is giving legal advice to our supplicants, are they?"

"Ms. Estrada, whatever do you mean?" asks Mr. Up, who knows perfectly well what she means, given his degree of omniscience. Elaine thinks of him as a little algorithm with too much formal politeness programmed in. "You know the rules. None of our side would ever interfere in that way."

"Not even for the promotion of..." She doesn't fully understand the motivations of the Upstairs staff, whose jobs seem no distinct from hers, but she presumes her basic understanding of theological polarity will be sufficient. "For goodness? Morality?"

"Ms. Estrada, I don't mean to suggest an ethical consideration stands between us and you," Mr. Up says, looking troubled by the possibility the adversarial system might somehow be uprooted. "Surely we would, if that were the case. But as you know, the defense is able to request information from the prosecution."

"Yes," Elaine says, though she's never requested anything from him before. She rarely needs to, as nothing ever goes to court. In fact she can't begin to imagine what that process would look like.

Her confusion must show on her face, because Mr. Up continues, "As you yourself have reminded me several times, the prosecution is not able to request any details from the defense."

"Meaning...? Oh." Elaine blinks. "You really don't know what our contracts look like?"

"Nothing has ever been litigated on the matter," Mr. Up says with a shake of his head. "I'm afraid our legal advocates would not be particularly helpful even if someone did come to us with their concerns."

"I see." How strange. "So the only person who would know the process—?"

"Aside from another advocate such as yourself or your associates? Someone who has been a supplicant before," says Mr. Up, with such a potent display of nerves Elaine half-wants to suggest he have a little lie-down and a warm glass of milk.

"How very interesting," Elaine says, considering this even after Mr. Up floats to the ceiling, up, up, up, and beyond.

†

Despite the commonality of the young woman's surname, it isn't very difficult for Elaine to find Miss Smith, who has an outstanding traffic citation and some paperwork for the adoption of a geriatric beagle named Hoop Dreams. She doesn't attend any odd megachurches or anything like that, so it's not a celebrity pastor. (That was Elaine's first guess; more than one has found themselves in her office, either having grown a conscience somewhere along the way or attempting to squeeze more out of an already lucrative deal by shepherding other souls into the bargain.) Miss Smith doesn't have any unusual social media habits, either. She's not on any extreme alt-right apps or deep into the world of Reddit, where Elaine expected to find at least one Faustian thread. (She finds seventeen on the subject of devil's advocates, many of which are close to accurate, but not quite right.) All of this leads Elaine to conclude that perhaps she was simply imagining things. After all, who would select Nessa Smith as a successful candidate for appeal?

Small rebellions aside, Elaine is too sensible for such thoughts of paranoia.

Over the course of the next few weeks, though, Elaine finds herself encountering a variety of claims that she considers... if not entirely *successful*, then increasingly interesting. She hears two arguments of negligence. One supplicant is actually the *son* of a supplicant who wants to be freed from the collateral damage of his father's deal. Another supplicant attempts to file a countersuit, alleging the soul she'd traded was never hers to give away, and the contract was therefore null and void on the basis of some larger theoretical precedent that would undo *all* deals. It didn't work, obviously, but it was interesting: the argument of a soul as an inherent spark of something that the individual in question did not actually own and was therefore not free to bargain with. Not an asset, then, but a right. Theoretically very compelling.

"Careful," Mr. Down warns. "You sound very nearly impractical."

He's perched at the edge of Elaine's desk like she's dreamed him there.

"I take it not even my thoughts are free from interception?" she asks him.

"I can't imagine you'd be surprised," he replies. "Your legal education served to reprogram your thoughts, forcing them into prescribed formulas under the law. But of course you did not have such a pleasant concierge to assist you in your thinking at the time."

Mr. Down doesn't smile, but then again he never does.

"Why does it matter whether I think about the value of a soul?" Elaine asks him.

"It's in your employment contract that you agreed not to," Mr. Down points out.

She did read her contract before she signed it, so this is an infallible argument.

"Fine," she says. "But you can't stop what I think about outside of the office."

"True," Mr. Down agrees. "But very insensible of you, don't you think? To exceed your contracted hours for the purpose of work."

"It's not work," Elaine says. "Just natural curiosity. It's what we do, you know, as humans? Occasionally we inconvenience ourselves by thinking about why we exist."

Mr. Down typically blinks for her comfort, so as not to unnerve her, but he doesn't for a long time.

"I see," he says.

"But you're right," Elaine assures him. "It's really a waste of my time." After all, if she had to spend time thinking about her reason for existing or the purpose of her soul, she'd have to question why she spent so much of her youth cleaning up after her father or why she married Justin or how she knows her siblings think she's a cold fish because she believes they're irresponsible or how, for some completely stupid reason, she misses her stupid expensive apartment that cost her too much money just so she could live by the soothing cool air of the Bay. The premium she paid to watch the bridge twinkle at night, or to feel normal in a wedding dress. Inconvenient. Stupid.

So when she goes home that night, she thinks she's going to forget about it. Nessa Smith and all of it.

But then she thinks... What if Nessa Smith was just a test case? Something to experiment with, but not to win?

And all that human inconvenience begins anew.

†

When Nessa Smith returns thirty days later to file her appeal, Elaine is ready for her. Or at least she thinks she is.

"Are you in contact with an attorney? Did someone force you to file this appeal?"

"What? No," says Nessa, signing her name to the document and frowning at Elaine. "Why?"

"Have you been paid? Threatened?"

"No, and definitely not—what's this about?"

"Nothing," Elaine says, disheartened. She hits submit on the appeal. "If this appeal moves forward—which I doubt it will," she adds, "just as a professional consideration—"

"Noted," says Nessa.

"I'll contact you."

"Anything I should do in the meantime?"

"I suppose not," Elaine says glumly, and she's about to let Nessa go when she determines she ought to give it one last shot. "Who instructed you to appeal?" she asks, which is admittedly a much less leading question than her initial phrasing. Typically it's worth being more careful with her wording.

"Nobody *instructed* me," Nessa says. But then, before she disappears through the door, she says, "Though, my therapist did say it would be a good idea if I gave it a try."

"What?" Elaine sits upright again.

"Well, you know how shrinks are. Never quite know whether it comes out of your head or theirs." Nessa rolls her eyes.

"Shrink? What shrink? Who?"

"Uhhh, I only went once. Figured my time was better spent here, you know, working on this appeal, so—"

"What's the therapist's name?" presses Elaine.

"Delilah something. Sampson," Nessa says, recalling with a blink. "Yeah, that's it."

What an obvious false name. "A woman?"

"Yeah, why?"

Somehow Elaine had just assumed it would be a man, the same way she might have assumed the devil's advocate to be a man if not for occupying the post herself.

"No reason. I'll be in touch," Elaine says, knowing she won't be. The Nessa Smith file has already been returned from the appellate level, whoever they were: APPEAL DENIED.

"Cool," says Nessa, shutting the door.

Mr. Down walks promptly through it.

"Let me guess," Elaine sighs. "You're going to stop me from following up on this?"

Mr. Down doesn't smile or blink. Instead, he simply AirDrops something to her computer.

DELILAH SAMPSON, PSY.D.
ALTERNATIVE TREATMENT & SPIRIT WORK

The title is followed by an address. She's here in Tulsa.

"Ah," Elaine says. "And here I thought it'd be some sort of wild goose chase."

Mr. Down gives her a look like such a thing could very well weary him into nonexistence.

"Why the effort at convenience?" she adds suspiciously. "Given my insensible human inconvenience."

He shrugs, a gesture that looks as strange on him as the rest of his maudlin garments. Today it is a black velvet capelet fastened with a tiny brass violin.

"You know the rules," Mr. Down reminds her as a parting statement, vanishing into the pixels on her screen.

PART II: PROPERTY LAW

The outside of the building is no less unimpressive than Elaine's own well-camouflaged office. Swap the aging barbershop with a tiny FedEx office center and the vacant ice cream parlor with a Vietnamese restaurant and there would be functionally no difference. After procuring a slightly soggy bánh mì for purposes of stalling, Elaine finally brings herself to buzz the intercom beside the narrow stairwell leading to the offices on the second floor.

"-ello?" comes the crackling voice on the other end. It is indistinct and ageless.

"Hi, I'm looking for Dr. Sampson," says Elaine, leaning into the speaker. "I don't have an appointment, but—"

"-refer not to be -led doct-r," comes the voice. For a second Elaine mishears, thinks the voice says Dr. Sampson is not available, but then belatedly makes the connection.

"Ms. Sampson, then? Delilah?"

There's a buzz that Elaine takes to be permission for entry. She nearly misses it, tugs on the door once, badly, and then a second time successfully. Then she is inside the stairwell, which leads to a door or perhaps multiple doors, one of which will take her to approximately the end of what she has thus far imagined.

Since receiving information about Delilah Sampson, Psy.D., Elaine has been pragmatically considering the purpose of her visit, to very little avail. The short answer, she suspects, is curiosity. Very few people understand what she does for a living or by whom she is employed. In fact, most people think she is joking. This has never bothered Elaine, who again took the job as devil's advocate merely as a means to a capitalist end (i.e., rent, health insurance, federal income tax, and contribution to The Economy, itself an obscure deity of sorts). But after years of monotony within the auspices of Mr. Down, the prospect of a counterpart is somewhat savory; the possibility of an adversary juicily more so. After all, if it is indeed Delilah Sampson who has been sending supplicants her way, that must mean something of cosmic significance. Balance and all that.

"Don't get carried away," was Mr. Down's helpful warning. "The contracts are legally sound."

"I'm aware," said Elaine, who couldn't help adding, "So why encourage my inquiry?"

"My employer is familiar with human nature," said Mr. Down.

"So this is a command from... him, then?"

"Do you think of me as a 'him'?" asked Mr. Down.

"Yes," admitted Elaine, uncertain now whether she should reconsider.

"Then yes," confirmed Mr. Down. "And for what it's worth, I don't disagree."

Elaine is reminded how much she does not particularly hate Mr. Down, who today is wearing a sweater vest patterned with tiny images of cracked eggs. In truth, it's very difficult to conjure any opinions about him whatsoever. It strikes her that perhaps the Downstairs offices *do* understand humans very well, probably much better than their counterparts upstairs.

In terms of Elaine's personal motivations there is a certain marked indifference; a lack of emotional response that means she does not particularly care about the outcome of her meeting with Delilah Sampson. She does not wish ill on her employer. Though, from a purely moral standpoint, she can't rule out the possibility of harm.

The frosted glass door which reads DELILAH SAMPSON, PSY.D. is on her left. Elaine knocks briskly, twice, to find that the door is ajar, and to then discover that it opens to a narrow waiting room which contains only one chair, a large bamboo plant, and a floor-based trickling fountain. The outer door opens inward while the inner door opens outward, so that briefly Elaine is trapped in the waiting room threshold while someone darts out from the office. There is a brief dance—"sorry, you go ahead," "no, you go, sorry"—and then the outgoing person, ostensibly *not* Delilah Sampson, exits the premises. Elaine observes there is a switch beside the inner office door that reads "waiting," and so she flips it and she waits.

She sits down, wondering how long it will be. When sufficient time has passed to suspect she may be waiting a few minutes, she pulls out her phone only to then be interrupted.

"You wanted an appointment?" asks a breathless woman who looks to be at least partially East Asian. She is wearing a tank top and cargo pants. Very aughts, Elaine thinks.

Elaine considers admitting that no, she doesn't want an appointment, she merely wants answers, but instead she decides to spare the time. "Yes," she says. She wonders if Delilah Sampson, Psy.D., has any idea that she is currently being visited by the devil's advocate, and if either way she should tell her. There was never any outright ban on candor. "Do you know who I am?" Elaine decides to ask instead.

"Yes," says the woman, who despite being winded does not look bothered. "Please," she says, pushing the inner door fully open so that Elaine has little room left to sit, and therefore little choice but to enter. "Do come in."

†

This is Delilah Sampson's office: four white walls, a fluffy shag rug in a neutral gray pattern, a soothing painting of the ocean, and several large pictures in frames that rest along the floor. One depicts the boxer Mike Tyson, the other Anne Frank, the others unidentifiable. There is also a side table containing a coffee maker and an electric kettle, so despite all evidence suggesting she ought to do otherwise, Elaine accepts a cup of tea.

Typically there is something about Elaine's mannerisms that does not invite people to waste her time. In business dealings she is very brusque, almost to the point of rudeness. (This was listed verbatim in one of Mr. Down's quarterly reviews as a testament to her skill. She would later receive a hefty winter bonus.) By contrast, Delilah squirrels away nearly five entire minutes chattering about the inception of oolong, and then she takes a seat and falls abruptly silent.

Elaine, who does not know what a typical appointment looks like for someone possessing the credentials Psy.D., lowers herself onto the sofa and stares at the painting behind Delilah's head. Then she glances at the Tyson picture on the floor. "Did you just move in?"

"No," says Delilah, adding, "Tell me about your parents."

"There's not much to say," says Elaine. "How did you know about me?"

"Saw your picture on your LinkedIn." Delilah sips her tea. "How is your relationship with your inner child?"

"I can't say we've ever met. How did you know to look for me?"

"We could do an introduction if you'd like. Maybe later." Another sip. "And professionally speaking it seemed relevant."

"Is your real name Delilah Sampson?" asks Elaine.

"Yes. My father had a sense of humor I can only call unnecessary." Delilah curls her legs underneath her and withdraws a large, clawlike clip from one of the pockets of her utility trousers, using it to sweep half her shoulder-length hair atop her head.

"Had?" asks Elaine.

Delilah smiles at her over her cup.

"Ask me," she says.

"Ask you what?"

"What you came here to ask me."

"If I don't know what that is, I doubt you do," says Elaine.

"Nonsense. You want to know if I've ever made a deal with the devil."

"I don't need to know that. I could have looked it up in the database."

She hasn't, though.

"You haven't, though," says Delilah.

"Well, did you?" Make a deal, she means.

"Did *you*?"

Elaine sighs aloud.

"Look," she says eventually. "I don't actually want whatever this is."

"Psychotherapy," offers Delilah.

"Right, sure, that. I just want to know why you sent Vanessa Smith to me."

"Vanessa Smith... oh, yes, Nessa. What a doll, honestly." Delilah smiles faintly into nothing. "Enrapturingly narcissistic, too. Fascinating ego. Really makes you reconsider whether Freud had a point."

"Should you discuss your clients like that?" asks Elaine, unnerved.

"Absolutely not," Delilah says. "But she never submitted her paperwork and anyway, her case had no merit. Besides, it doesn't matter anymore."

Elaine isn't sure what that means, being generally unfamiliar with the terms of patient confidentiality, but also doesn't want to ask. "The others," she says. "You've been sending them to me as well, I take it?"

Delilah shrugs. "I specialize in what I like to call an activated self-dialogue."

"By telling them to see me? Seems more like a dialogue, full stop."

"I know," Delilah says with a laugh. "Funny how that one routinely slips by them."

Elaine shifts in her seat, unsettled.

"You thought I'd be nicer," Delilah observes.

"Well, it seemed..." Elaine hesitates. "It seemed there was a chance you were a bit more... philanthropic." What she means to say is that she was expecting someone nicer.

"You got that from me advising my clients to appeal their impossible legal contracts with the underworld only to be denied?" asks Delilah, apparently for purposes of clarification. "By that logic I'm no more philanthropic than the average personal injury lawyer."

"Lawyers are not inherently untrustworthy," argues Elaine, defensively.

"Who said anything about trust?" counters Delilah.

She sips her tea again and falls silent. Elaine is beginning to suspect it is a tactic.

"You're actively sending people to me," she says, deciding to simply move forward. "Why?"

"I have a vested interest in lost souls," says Delilah.

"A personal one?"

For a moment it looks as if Delilah doesn't intend to answer.

She does, though. "Is *your* vocation personal?" she counters.

"No," says Elaine.

Delilah shrugs, then kicks off one shoe. "Sometimes we simply attend to our contracts." She gestures upward. "You know how it goes."

Elaine blinks. Delilah's work, well-intentioned as it is, must exist within the purview of the divine, which would certainly make her the adversary Elaine was expecting. "But then you're not—" Elaine stops, remembering Mr. Up saying that only someone who worked in the downstairs offices could know what their contracts contain. "But I thought the Upstairs wasn't allowed to—"

"Oh, no, you misunderstand me," Delilah says with a careless shake of her head. "I don't work for either of the offices."

"Then what do you do?" asks Elaine.

Delilah's smile darkens.

"It's not what I do," she says. "It's what I did."

✝

Delilah Sampson was a sunny child, eternally optimistic. The third youngest of four, she was known for her fanciful imagination, her idealistic dreams, and her absurd, almost pitiable gullibility, which would have been depressing if not for being as laughable as it was. She was safest inside her own head, which bloomed and bore fruit with an infernal brilliance. Whatever she touched she was either dismally unskilled at or prodigiously adept, no in-between.

In short, nothing about her was practical. She was a feral thing, shoeless and unreliable and eternally, annoyingly late. Her parents, one an accountant and the other a doctor, were staunch atheists soothed only by science and reason, which in their dispassionate way were constraints within which Delilah's mind did not excel. She sought out the fevers of literature, the mania of art, the formlessness of history, redundant with its lessons never learned. When boundless entropy of mind failed to pacify her nature, she studied minds themselves, and madness, until she found an anchor in the last place she thought to look.

It was not until her college years that Delilah first entered a church, though when she did so it was only by accident, because she was dating a boy who wanted to wait chastely for marriage and Delilah, recklessly in love for the hundred and seventy-fifth time, had told a series of cheerful lies about probably being baptized. Once they entered the church, Delilah became aware of an eerie serenity, a brutal sense of peace. There was a voracious demand for order, the art filled with violence and the architecture seeming more to scale with the heavens than with the earth. Tongues of fire were holy but also damnation was flame, water was floods but also ritual, it was all so arbitrarily enchanting in exactly the way Delilah loved. The main character of the book was a father and also a son and also a spirit, simultaneously bringer of doom and savior of men, like BPD but better. To achieve the eternal blessing, she need only commune with the omniscient ghost. And it was all so sinisterly final that it rewired her somehow. Bolstered her. Or at very least, distracted her with something new.

It was a nervous man who came to her later in a dream. He explained very apprehensively that it was not really a contract, not *as such*, because only the other side did contracts and recruitment Downstairs was a totally different thing, much more finite, and—this he said with extreme discomfort—damning. Upstairs it was more a matter of points! This was much more upbeat, even promising. Good deeds, good results, explained the nervous man who shook her hand and called himself Mr. Up, adding as if he'd nearly forgotten that the final tally was taken somewhere near the end. Of what? When would that be? Oh, don't worry about it, it wasn't very complicated actually, although she ought to consider keeping an eye on her carbon footprint. The rules were written down in the book in case she forgot. And then he left and Delilah had the queerest feeling that she later began to identify as doubt.

Starting with the most obvious problems: Delilah found the book very confusing. She disliked that there was no transparency to her point total. How did she know if she was succeeding in her mission? She sought out a career to help people only to find that most people could not, for whatever reason, be helped. That seemed unfair. Did she fail if they failed? Delilah fell in love for the two hundred and thirtieth time and married a cheerful elementary school teacher named Craig who woke her every morning with a song and convinced her to buy a house somewhere below open sky, and also talked her into yoga. They volunteered together, worshipped together, had increasingly average sex together, and adopted three dogs of varying health and behavior and nursed them together. Morally speaking, it was a dream.

But then, alarmingly, her husband revealed he had fallen in love with the teenager (apparently she was in her twenties but Delilah simply couldn't see how) who worked the front desk at the dog rescue, and he took the dogs but left Delilah with the mortgage. Her practice was doing moderately well by then; hardly lucrative but far better than, say, the assets of a public school teacher who had recently been laid off, so, needless to say she was crushed financially as well as emotionally. She rented out an extra room in her house only to discover the tenant refused to leave. By the time the house was in ruins, Delilah was out of defenses as to how a professional psychologist had been taken in by a grifter who would ultimately cost her more in legal fees than the house was even worth. She waited for Mr. Up to make an appearance, to assure her that her point tally, at least, was untouched, but he was nowhere to be found. On the evening her debit card was declined while buying milk and tampons, Delilah finally closed her eyes and thought with desperation: I will do anything.

I will do anything to make this end.

In place of Mr. Up was a spindly man wearing a suit of tartan. His buttons were tiny enamel covers of the works of Charles Dickens.

"I hear you may have some interest in a contract," he said. Delilah did not think to ask if there was some preexisting conflict of interest. She merely signed and figured that if anything was invalid, well, so be it. Someone really ought to have checked in.

Within a single evening, Delilah's unwanted tenant was gone. Vanished. Later she would struggle to remember how she worded it, precisely. What she had said. What she had done. There was something about the circumstances of the agreement that left her feeling foggy, unbalanced, almost as if her left hand had betrayed her right. For weeks she was sick with guilt, positively racked with it, and then her ex-husband called to tell her that he would no longer need spousal support, and actually he had won the lottery and returned to her the majority of the money she'd given him (though not all of it). Delilah considered falling in love for the two hundred and thirty-second time with a fellow psychologist who by all accounts was stable and loyal and even a very kind man, widowed young with no children. But as they say: two hundred and thirty-once bitten, two hundred and thirty-twice shy.

It was then that Delilah began to wonder if some essential part of her was absent. She wondered about it, her soul, more than she ever had thought of it before, and wondered if maybe it was impossible to value until after it was already proffered up and gone. She wondered still if it even mattered, and if so how much, and if not how long.

She never stopped fulfilling her contract with Mr. Up, technically. The lost souls who found her—increasingly over time, as if they were drawn to some innate piece of her—still held more interest to Delilah than any of the others with their unending sea of neurotypical problems. (What, after all, was a brain compared to a soul?) She began to collect the supplicants she found, even marketing directly to them. She ran an ad on Instagram that read *Made a deal with the devil?* and added a link to her page.

This, presumably, was how Nessa Smith had found Delilah for a free session. "I just, like, really wanted to go to Coachella," said Nessa blandly.

"Understandable," Delilah said. She had met with several supplicants by then and needed a sort of lab rat. Someone to try out the rumors she'd heard, see how it went. Before Nessa, an attorney who'd made a deal to stop a receding hairline had said there was an appeals process, which was confirmed by a deeply litigious CEO who now had insomnia to go with his healthy stock portfolio. But what Delilah needed was a spy.

Hey girl! she typed a few weeks after her session with Nessa. *How did it go?!?*

If this is about that organic wine subscription I already have an account, said Nessa, and then, a few minutes later, *And fyi they gave me a company car if you're interested in signing up?!*

Delilah quickly explained that no, she wasn't some kind of hashtag-bossbitch looking to be part of a pyramid scheme, she was just touching base after their session. Nessa seemed to remember belatedly and said it hadn't worked, bummer, though the lady in charge was like, kind of a fox tbh. A bitchy fox, but still. Delilah said that was great, but was there anything specifically about the appeal...? Nessa said what appeal. And Delilah was like, okay. This isn't working, never mind.

What she wanted was to understand the process. No, not just the process: the whole system, who was in charge, how it worked. She sent all of her subsequent clients to the devil's advocate, whose name was Elaine Estrada and who by all accounts wasn't magical or demonic or anything and who was apparently also divorced, but to Delilah's frustration, they never got any further. Delilah read and read about Estrada until her eyes crossed and she exited the rabbit hole somewhere around the article on Estrada's essay contest from the seventh grade. She and Delilah were similar in age; Estrada's ex-husband even looked a little bit like Craig, though they seemed to still be amicable whereas Delilah hoped very much that Craig would never show his face in her life again. Estrada was still following her ex on Instagram, which seemed like kind of a big deal. Unless of course he was muted. But anyway, this wasn't the point. If Delilah couldn't get beyond Elaine Estrada, then she'd have to find out some other way.

Whether she was a singular clerical error or a larger legal loophole, Delilah had already made up her mind to find out.

✝

Two hours ago, before what would be Delilah Sampson's final client and before she would meet Elaine Estrada, the spindly man had returned to her office. "I know what you're planning to do," he said after emerging from the base of her waiting room's fountain. "You should also know there are a great many alternatives. The occult, for example. Also, Lilith could do with more volunteers."

"I am no longer interested in the offerings of the mortal world," Delilah said, pouring ethylene glycol into her usual afternoon oolong.

The man, whom she thought of as Mr. Down, watched her without expression. "You know," he said, eyeing her cup, "the Upstairs tends to disapprove of this."

"Are you going to stop me?"

"No."

She glanced up at his unnaturally still face. "Why not?"

He shrugged. "Human nature."

"If you understand human nature so well, then why even allow this sort of error?"

"Complications arise all the time. Not everyone chooses to litigate."

Delilah scoffed, "Shouldn't you have known that I would?"

"Upstairs concerns themselves with plans. We prefer the specific damnation of agency."

"So do you know what will happen?"

Mr. Down shook his head. "Only that we have very effective counsel."

"Effective enough that you'll win?" Even now, Delilah hasn't decided whether or not she wants them to. True, it would mean her soul is claimed, the end, and perpetuity would no doubt be gruesome. But in the war between Upstairs and Downstairs, she isn't sure who she trusts more. Which is maybe why Downstairs expects to win.

"Win, lose, these are meaningless concepts. The difference between lighting a fire and counting grains of sand." He observed her for another few seconds. "You will alarm Miss Estrada," he noted. "She is not familiar with the irrational."

"No? Not even a little?" Delilah joked bitterly, referencing herself. Herself and all her irrationalities and judgments.

"I said she is unfamiliar," said Mr. Down. "Not immune."

From the open window came a glimpse of the jittery Mr. Up, like the flash of a reflective surface.

"Oh dear," Mr. Up exclaimed nervously.

"Never mind," said Mr. Down. "We'll see you in court."

And with that Mr. Down disintegrated into the grains of Delilah's raw cane sugar while Mr. Up vanished into a wisp of steam, the light finally turning on from the waiting room for Delilah's immediate attention.

✝

Needless to say, Elaine does not know any of this. For Elaine, the session is notable only for being bewildering.

"I used to be great fun, you know," Delilah says. "Generally more pleasant."

"You're not unpleasant," lies Elaine.

"Oh, I am," Delilah corrects her. "But the point is, I wasn't before. I was very nearly wonderful before, or so I was given to believe. A very sensitive child. Were you very sensitive as a child? You must know what I mean." She babbles while she sips her tea, fingers curled protectively around it. "Children are so imaginative. It's such a crime that it gets robbed from us. And who do we sue for that? Not the devil. Doubt he has anything to do with it. Wonder if there's a court for disillusionment. Or a church of existential decay." She looks up at Elaine. "Are you spiritual at all?"

Elaine shakes her head.

"Good for you. Life is death, anyway." Delilah barks a laugh. "Birth is a trap."

"Are you quite well?" asks Elaine. Not because of anything Delilah's saying, but because Delilah's forehead is sweaty. Her words are beginning to slur and her head is drooping.

"Hypothetically speaking," Delilah says (slurs), "what do you think a human soul is worth?"

"Oh, I wouldn't," Elaine cautions politely. "My employer really doesn't care for me to speculate." She wants to leave, but it's becoming increasingly clear that doing so will be difficult.

"Do you think it only has value if someone is willing to bargain for it?" asks Delilah, before uncrossing her legs and lying down on the floor's shag carpet.

"Um," says Elaine. "I mean, I suppose that according to Adam Smith—"

"I just want to see what will happen," Delilah says deliriously, rolling onto her stomach. "All those appeals. What a waste. I should have known I would have to do it myself. I suppose I was just being cowardly."

"Well, on the subject of that—"

"What would you do with it?" Delilah asks, looking disarmingly at Elaine from where she's lying prostrate on the ground.

"With my soul?" This is something Elaine was wondered about exactly seventeen times, which is neither upsettingly often nor remarkably rare.

"No." Delilah shakes her head. "With mine."

She's very sweaty now, obviously lethargic. Elaine abandons her cup of tea and bends down to press a hand to Delilah's clammy forehead.

"You've done something," Elaine says.

"I've done nothing. That's the point," says Delilah. "It's the lack of transparency that gets you."

"What?"

"Let them fight over it." Her eyes close. "I'm tired. I don't feel well."

"You don't look well. Miss—I mean. Delilah?"

Delilah murmurs something incoherent, and Elaine presses her ear lower, eventually squirming in her practical skirt suit to lie facing the woman on the floor.

"Tell me again," Elaine says, not softly or quietly but with interest, like a person who suspects she is about to have a very stressful week litigating a contractual dispute that she doesn't fully understand, but who doesn't know it yet.

Delilah is clearly unwell now, and Elaine has to strain to hear her answer.

"Tell them I want to file an appeal," she says.

Before Elaine can say anything in response, Mr. Up manifests like a creak in her spine and then Mr. Down is there, misplaced like a snag in the carpet.

"Shall we?" says Mr. Up to Mr. Down, gesturing into a room that appears in place of Delilah's ocean painting on the wall. One moment it's abstract seascapes, the next it's mahogany pews.

"It appears we must," replies Mr. Down, while Elaine, at least, has the clarity of mind to dial an ambulance before being summoned upstanding in court.

PART III: THEORETICAL JURISPRUDENCE

The courtroom and its contents are almost laughably unexceptional. The things one expects to be made of wood are made of wood and the things one expects to be marble are marble. Though, by the way Mr. Up is currently sitting (legs pulled apprehensively up to his chest, at least a solid half-foot above the bench on the side of the plaintiff) Elaine begins to wonder if most of this is only here for her optical comfort. Whatever everyone else is seeing, she doubts it is the box of stale donuts atop the piles of case files in the judge's chambers. Which, again, she would expect to see. So in that sense it is soothing.

She glances askance at Mr. Down, who looks very grave indeed, as always. His suit today is made of the same material as Delilah Samson's shag carpet, though it is outfitted with little gemstones like the belly buttons of Elaine's childhood Treasure Trolls. (This is less soothing than the donuts.) If he feels her eyes on him, he says nothing.

"Where is the, um. Disputed person?" Elaine asks in a murmur.

"Drifting between stages of renal failure," he replies.

So Delilah isn't dead yet. Just preemptively disputed by two parties with equally contracted claims to her soul. "I meant more... temporally." As in, where is Delilah Samson *right now*, when five minutes ago (to Elaine's circadian rhythms, anyway) she was collapsed on the floor of her own office at the hands of her own poisoning, blearily proclaiming to Elaine that professional standards of ethics no longer mattered and also asking whether Elaine had any relevant thoughts as to the purpose of her soul.

"Suspended," replies Mr. Down, "betwixt the realms of life and death."

"Right, sorry, metaphysically," Elaine attempts again.

"Oh." He shrugs and gestures behind them. "In lock-up."

"Ah." Something in Elaine grows queasy as Mr. Down angles his shoulders in the direction of the area behind the courtroom, facing the room beside the judge's chambers and the stale donuts.

For the record, Elaine has never cared much for litigation, and certainly she has never litigated a case like this one, which despite its transactional nature has undertones of criminal procedure. She wonders briefly if she even has the credentials.

"It doesn't matter," Mr. Down tells her, then pauses. "Apologies," he adds in apparent reference to his uncanny response, "would you prefer I wait for auditory cues?"

"It would be better," Elaine says. "For my sanity."

He seems to understand this is a delicate matter. Fragile, mortal sanity. "Apologies," he says again, though it's unclear what he's making the apology for. Perhaps he's just generally very sorry for her.

"You can finish your thought," Elaine assures him. "It did seem like it was going somewhere helpful."

He shrugs. "I was merely going to point out that your experience in this area is very close to irrelevancy. The stakes are very low."

"Only a single soul?" Elaine jokes.

"Yes, exactly," Mr. Down confirms solemnly. "In fact, I am surprised it will go to trial at all. Typically this is a matter for arbitration."

"Because of the low stakes?" Elaine uses the same tone of levity, but is becoming progressively less sure she is joking.

"Yes." He glances at her. "You do understand the legal argument, do you not?"

"I think so." The judge, who is not a person but a voice (initially just a splice of intersecting colors until Elaine made some discontented noises out of fragile mortal comprehension concerns) has already made quite clear to Elaine what she did not initially understand upon meeting the contracted soul in question. Now, Elaine understands that Delilah Samson is not an adversary but an anomaly, a person whose soul has been contracted twice: once to Elaine's employer and once to whoever it is residing Upstairs, which is ostensibly her employer's opposite.

"Is the judge God?" asks Elaine, frowning. She hadn't considered before whether this might somehow be a conflict of interest. Theologically speaking, is there an equal and opposite to whoever bangs the gavel of this court?

"Is the judge The Creator, you mean? No, no," says Mr. Down. "The judge is Nature."

"Oh." Elaine is learning quite a bit today, though she isn't entirely grateful for the circumstances. Ideally she could have learned this via some guidebook or hypothetical exercise that wouldn't require so much work. Some sort of online training, perhaps. How long do divine contracts even take to litigate?

"You'll be paid overtime," says Mr. Down.

"Auditory cues," she reminds him.

"Right," he says. "Apologies."

†

117

The plaintiff, represented via the auspices of Mr. Up, file a motion to dismiss. The laws of nature say no, this is too icky a debacle and needs to be dealt with ipso facto, on the record. The plaintiff says ugh fine and delivers its case, which is in essence a YouTube playlist of the major events of Delilah Samson's life. Much of what Elaine would like to observe—indeed, much of what Elaine considers relevant to the case, which is ostensibly about the *value* of Delilah Samson's soul—"Incorrect," says Mr. Down, to which Elaine again replies "Auditory cues"—is skipped through at a rate of 8.50 million times the normal playback speed, so she fills in the blanks for herself with things she assumes to be universal. Delilah learns to walk. Delilah becomes obsessed with someone else's doctrine and rearranges herself around them. (Elaine guesses it was the Spice Girls followed by a series of increasingly heartfelt pop-punk bands.) Delilah gets her heart broken. Delilah learns to mistrust rooms with too many men in them. Delilah develops breasts and her father no longer knows what to say to her except to infantilize her or idly reminisce. Delilah finds a sentence in a book/song/film that closes a broken loop inside her heart. Delilah experiences pain. Delilah experiences pleasure. Delilah experiences grief. Delilah bleeds for the first time through a pair of lemon yellow capri pants. Delilah becomes special to someone. Delilah becomes unspecial to someone. Delilah wears white, Delilah wears black, Delilah participates in social rituals that have preceded her existence, Delilah stubs her toe. Delilah's life plays out on the screen and Elaine fills in the blanks, perhaps too liberally, until gradually, Delilah's experience becomes her own.

But the plaintiff slows to normal speed the following scenes: Delilah with her eyes trained on the heavens, basked in the light of the holy apse. The offer, followed by acceptance. Delilah outside of a badly-lit grocery mart: sick, wretched, ugly, signing her name apathetically on the page. Offer and acceptance take two.

The plaintiff files a motion for summary judgment and the laws of nature say no, there should be precedent here, the judgment in this case cannot be rushed, bada-bing bada-boom. So they break for lunch, although it is nearing four in the morning by Elaine's watch.

It is during this time that Elaine realizes she does not know how to present her side of the case. Which isn't to say she doesn't know how to approach a contractual agreement; in that sense she has achieved her ten thousand hours and is, by all accounts, an expert as an advocate. But there is something about Delilah that gives her pause. Perhaps it is the absence of Delilah herself in the proceedings that will define her immortal fate.

Elaine decides, for purposes of relevant research, to pay a visit to whichever part of Delilah is currently being disputed by the court. She approaches the dimly lit lock-up space and pauses on the safe side of the bars, observing that Delilah looks precisely as she did a matter of hours ago, only no longer prostrate or sweating. Again, this may very well be for Elaine's comfort, since there's no telling where Delilah Samson's body is now. Is she alive, still? But that seems a morbid question to ask, so Elaine begins with something else.

"It occurred to me that none of this handy new knowledge is very useful unless I share it with someone who is equally unaware," Elaine begins. What she means to say is that it's very exciting to be speculating about souls when her employment contract specifically says she's not supposed to. In this case, though, it's her *actual job*, and there's no one else to tell about it. Should she write a book? A play? A film? But even an audience of thousands, millions, even billions would still be somewhat insufficient.

Who can be satisfied sharing their news with a stranger? The only person who will truly grasp the stakes is already sitting right here.

One of Delilah's eyes opens. "Do you think we'd have different souls in different bodies?" she asks, which is not necessarily the response Elaine wanted. Then again, she isn't sure what she wants. She supposes that while Delilah might grasp the stakes of the case the right way, she might also be somewhat biased about them. In which case the continued theoretical argument is as good a direction as any.

"Yes," Elaine says. "Yes, I think so."

"I thought I'd feel more aware of my body or something, but I don't." Delilah looks around and shrugs. "Do you think I'm already dead?"

"No," Elaine says. She has no idea, but the alternative seems stressful.

Delilah fidgets. "Do you think I'm crazy? Knowing what I've done and... all that?"

"I'm not an expert in crazy," Elaine offers diplomatically.

"Sure, but even an amateur can weigh in."

That's probably true. "No, I don't think you're crazy." Reality check: Elaine does think Delilah is crazy, sort of, but also, she needs to know too, now. She's glad it's not *her* soul wavering on the precipice of life and death, but she's unquestionably invested in the outcome. It's safely relevant to Elaine's experience, though whatever Delilah turns out to be worth can always be safely embraced or denied compared to Elaine's. And regardless, it feels crucial to witness the valuation process.

"I just need to know The Point," says Delilah. "The Purpose. The Meaning."

"I know," Elaine says, who can hear the implied proper nouns.

"I need to," Delilah insists.

"I know," Elaine says.

Delilah goes silent for a while. "Do you think it's a predator-prey thing?" she asks eventually. "Like, is this all just about consumption?"

She means *for them*. Not the Downstairs division specifically, but Upstairs, too. By contrast, Delilah and Elaine are sitting here on either side of some metaphysical bars discussing what it's like to be mutual occupants of the lobby.

"No," Elaine says. "I think it's a zero-sum game."

Delilah winces. "That's bad news."

"Yes. Kind of. Yes." It means neither can win while the other survives. It means that in the end, something fundamental is taken from one side and given to the other. There is no such thing as sharing souls or splitting glory if Elaine's right. And she often is.

"So you think I'll lose?" asks Delilah.

"What is winning in this scenario?" Really, Elaine would like to know.

"I guess you're right." Which makes Delilah's answer unsatisfactory. "I guess knowing is winning. Having The Answer. Grasping The Point."

"So you win either way?"

"Unless I don't like the answer," Delilah says with a shrug. "Then I lose either way."

There's a mystical chime from the courtroom's interior that reminds Elaine of a childhood bracelet she used to have. It smelled chemical-sweet, like fake strawberries, but seems to serve as a means to draw the occupants back to their seats. Elaine waits to see if Delilah has anything helpful to add, but she doesn't, so Elaine walks away.

One step, two steps. Then she pauses.

"I'm sorry there's no one on your side out there," she says, because she has a role, after all. She has an employer who pays overtime and who, therefore, expects a certain result. Like anyone, Elaine is bound by the terms of her contract. She is not Delilah Samson's advocate. She is not some Better Angel. For better or worse, the title on her business card means she fights for the problematic side.

But Delilah does not seem to take it personally. She doesn't plead for sympathy. She doesn't ask Elaine to Do The Right Thing. In Delilah's head she's thinking: whatever, it's not like she's Captain America.

So, "Yeah," Delilah says. "Same."

†

When Elaine is called upon to make her arguments, she doesn't have any notes. Not because she doesn't want them—she is immensely practical and doesn't trust waiters who don't write things down (the risk of error seems unnecessarily and perhaps even unjustifiably high?)—but because she still hasn't the faintest idea what she's going to say. Which is probably why what comes out of her mouth is a regurgitated lecture from an introductory legal class, almost precisely as delivered to her by her sensible state school several years prior.

"In property law, the value of the property itself has merit," Elaine rambles. "In contracts there is no significant value attributed to the object or service being contracted. The dispute is not the thing, but whether the thing was validly contracted at the time."

"*The dispute is not the thing,*" the courtroom echoes back to her solemnly, like a small group of kindergartners during circle time.

"Of course, what must yet be considered are the damages awarded to the injured party. But who is injured by a clerical error?" The unintended clerical pun is not lost on Elaine, but she sidesteps it. "It depends on the value of the soul in question. Is the soul worth more because it is good or because it is bad, or is it just a soul and therefore every soul is not discrete but rather some interchangeable metric? Is Delilah Samson, by virtue of being an individual and in possession of an individual existence, an inimitable soul—is she inherently valuable, or is she as replicable as a grain of sand? And if indeed th-"

"Ms. Estrada?" says Mr. Up nervously. "The judge has indicated silence in the courtroom."

She had not been paying attention to the shower of rapturously changing lights.

"Oh." Elaine blinks. "So does that mean—?"

"A judgment is to be made," says Mr. Down, who until now has been seated quietly behind her.

"But I haven't finished my argument," she protests with a frown. "I haven't even finished my sentence."

"The judge already knows it," Mr. Down assures her quietly. Intimately, as if perhaps she is embarrassing herself. "If anything, the fact that you delivered it at all was a mere formality. Your position on the subject is known."

"How is it known? I don't even know it." She hasn't brought any notes. She has no knowledge of whether she cares about the outcome or merely craves it like a drug.

"Still, it is known," says Mr. Down.

Vaguely, Elaine thinks that despite her belief that she would be no help to Delilah's case, this is somehow even worse than advocating for the opposite side. Now there will be no knowing. Everyone else in the room Already Knows. So what, then, was The Point of all this?

She is beginning to taste Delilah's particular madness and feels, for the first time, that she genuinely hopes Delilah Samson isn't dead.

"Aren't there plans?" Elaine asks Mr. Down with a faint but noticeable aroma of desperation.

"Upstairs concerns themselves with plans. We prefer—"

"You prefer the specific damnation of agency, yes I know," she acknowledges impatiently, "but shouldn't there be something? Predestination? A point? None of this should be a matter for judgment," Elaine says, tasting devastation, chasing it with bitterness and doubt. "Either it is known or it isn't."

"Of course it is known," says Mr. Down. "It is not yet understood."

"What?"

"I said, of course it is known, it is not yet—"

"Yes, I heard you. I just wondered how it could be known and not understood," Elaine argues, "or what is the point of knowing without understanding, and actually, if something can be known but not understood, then does it have any merit at all? And if a tree falls in the forest—"

"Ms. Estrada," says Mr. Down, "your nose is bleeding."

He hands her a handkerchief that is either a perfect replica of Magna Carta or the real thing, and either way, does it matter?

"Oh," says Elaine, who blots politely at her fragile mortality and sits down.

✝

After Delilah Samson has been in critical renal failure for fifteen hours and fifty-six minutes, the court delivers its judgment.

"The soul," says the incorporeal judge, "will revert to the ownership of Delilah Samson herself until such time as her demise. Previous contracts will be voided. The decision is remanded for reconsideration and subsequent valuation upon time of mortal death."

The bang of the gavel startles both Elaine and the fidgety Mr. Up into jumping. She frowns, bewildered, and turns around to find the courtroom abruptly empty except for Mr. Down. Also, now it is a vacant hardware store.

"You did well," Mr. Down tells her. It is funereal, as always, but she knows it is meant to register as praise. "Well done."

She considers whether to slap him, negotiate a holiday bonus, or ask if he'd like to have lunch.

"I don't understand," she confesses instead. "I don't understand how I did well, or what happened. I don't understand it at all."

"No," he agrees, as if he has expected this.

"I'd like to understand," she clarifies.

"Oh." He blinks several times very quickly. "In the simplest terms, a mortal soul is functionally meaningless," he tells her. "Humanity is very advanced in terms of anthropological systems, but fundamentally it is no different from a herd of cats. Or a murder of crows."

"So... Upstairs and Downstairs just... shook hands? Called it even?" asks Elaine, struggling with an unknown emotional reaction to this terminal prognosis. "There's no loss to either side?"

"Not yet, no. The Upstairs count of eligible souls is higher than you think," says Mr. Down with a shrug. "It's true what that animated film says about dogs."

"And Downstairs has no problem with losing a contracted soul?"

"It will have to go somewhere eventually," says Mr. Down simply. "And you are not privy to this information, but I can assure you that Ms. Samson's Upstairs count is heavily in the red."

"Why?" Elaine doesn't know her well, but in her opinion Delilah Samson is a reasonably fine human being. Neutral, which Elaine supposes she naturally assumes trends upward. No murders, no child abductions, no ritual cannibal acts. If Delilah Samson were a book on Goodreads, Elaine would round up.

"She summoned me," Mr. Down reminds her, which Elaine supposes does tend to be damning. "But things can change."

"How much longer will she live?" Does Delilah Samson have days? Years? Decades? Minutes?

"That answer is known," says Mr. Down.

"And?" prompts Elaine.

"I said it is known. Not that it is for you to know."

Elaine frowns. "But—"

"Enjoy the unknown, Ms. Estrada," Mr. Down tells her, which has the spirit of kindness even if it is not altogether kind. "It is the only truly lovely thing about your situation," he assures her, "which is otherwise very dismal indeed."

Pragmatically speaking, Elaine can see the logic in this. But she waits until Mr. Down has disintegrated into particles of dust.

"It is known," she tells herself. Then the rest of the room melts away and is gone.

†

Unknown: having called the ambulance that saves her, Elaine has restored Delilah Samson's life.

Unknown: how long Delilah Samson's borrowed time will last.

Unknown: what Elaine will do next.

Though gradually, of course, some of the above becomes clearer.

There's a low, steady beep from the mortal technology that has brought Delilah Samson's soul back to the world of the living. She is unconscious still, breathing through a tube, the IV threading her arms, and Elaine has already been interviewed twice about the circumstances of what came to pass that afternoon, as no time has passed since she initially came in for psychotherapy. Well, for answers.

The absence of Elaine's employer's contract with Delilah Samson is revealing itself in chaos already. Despite Elaine's best efforts, Delilah will almost certainly face consequences, and when she opens her eyes, Elaine will not be able to give her an answer to the question Delilah's own desperation has asked.

Here is what is known, Elaine imagines telling her. There is no answer. We are not quantifiable. We are not estimable. We are known to everyone, everything, but ourselves. They have given you back your soul and now it is yours to squander or cherish. It may not be valuable to the auspices of the building, either Upstairs or Down, but either it is valuable to you, Delilah Samson, or it is valueless, and that distinction is the only thing that matters.

That in the end, whether you see this life as a gift or a curse, you'll be right.

Ultimately, though, it takes several more hours for Delilah to wake, and so Elaine no longer has possession of the words. They have coursed through her and now feel silly, overwrought, condescending. So when Delilah opens her eyes, Elaine says, "You asked about my parents?" and Delilah nods.

"Very emotional people," Elaine says. "Volatile, even. Spontaneous to the point of recklessness. Frequent bankruptcies. We moved several times."

"Hence the pragmatism," Delilah observes.

"Hence the pragmatism," Elaine confirms, splicing herself impractically into fractions and marveling when nothing breaks. "Any regrets?" she asks.

"Not falling in love for the two hundred and thirty-third time," says Delilah.

How wild it is to be human, Elaine thinks. How recklessly divine.

"Never too late," she says.

In the end, Elaine calls the office and takes one of her contracted personal days. She and Delilah continue their session as if it was never interrupted, chatting away over the hospital bed until visiting hours are up.

ONCE UPON A TIME IN SUBURBIA (SEPTEMBER - NOVEMBER 2021)

THIRTY YEARS AGO, A TEENAGE GIRL MET A VIOLENT, APPARENTLY SUPERNATURAL DEATH IN SUBURBAN ILLINOIS. On the anniversary of her death, a documentary-style investigation follows the murder case, pursuing the possibility of false accusations, a network of secret covens, and unearthing the truth behind the uncanny circumstances of a notorious occult crime.

Olivie Blake

PART I: NEW IN TOWN

In 1991, the quiet, unremarkable suburb of New Blossom, Illinois was rocked by the mysterious death of a beloved teenage girl. Immediately, the small town was plunged into a desperate age of paranoia. The strange circumstances surrounding seventeen-year-old Serena May's murder and the lingering possibility of supernatural involvement fanned the flames of the community's growing terror, leading to the defining question of the era: how well one can ever know one's neighbors.

Days into the investigation, New Blossom would soon discover damning evidence of foul play, combined with the revelation of a complex network of secret covens living among them. The arrest of Marisol Farrow, a practicing witch, seemed to confirm the community's worst suspicions— but now, decades later, some are beginning to question whether Farrow, herself merely a young woman in her twenties, might have been wrongfully accused.

Was it, indeed, a witch hunt for the age of so-called satanic panic? Or was it the inevitable manifestation of social tension which threatened to break the community from within? And where does the story truly begin? With the crime itself? With the darkness that had infected the town in secret? Or was it something as innocent as the arrival of two young boys that set the fatal events in motion?

On the thirtieth anniversary of young Serena May's death, we investigate the uncanny circumstances of what would come to be one of the most notorious occult crimes of the decade.

†

IN THE LATE EIGHTIES, NEW BLOSSOM, ILLINOIS was the very portrait of American normalcy. A pristine, manufactured bedroom community developed in the 1960s in response to growing demand for middle class housing, the town was a serene escape from the bustle of the inner city—a self-sufficient, neighborhood-oriented oasis of modern amenities perched on the edge of picturesque sprawling farmland.

JOHN CORRINGER
Mayor of New Blossom, 1982-1988

Chicago was a mess then, if you'll pardon my saying. Not trendy like it is now, what with the fancy donuts and all that. Back then it was violence, crime, drugs, you name it. All sorts of unsavory folk.

Ah—I know that look on your face. *[Chuckles grimly.]* But I assure you, I don't see color. I really do not. Everyone's always trying to make it about race these days, or feminism, or whatever they're 'canceling' people for now. Seriously though, you could be black, white, purple, green, I don't care— in the end, facts are facts. Right? People are going to chase that American dream. Fact. They want that white picket fence. Fact. A clean house, good schools. Pretty wife. Respectful, God-fearing household. Kids playing in the yard, all that.

That was what New Blossom provided better than any other town: the dream.

By the late eighties, the town was home to about 20,000 people—mostly young white collar families whose breadwinning patriarchs commuted to the city for work, leaving their children in the hands of a wholesome, growing school district and a thriving community of up-and-coming franchise retail developments.

EMILY NEWSOM

Teacher, New Blossom High School

1986-2004

I was a new teacher back in those days and boy, I remember thinking New Blossom was as good as Eden. I'd done a year of training roundabouts in Indiana—before I saw the advertisements calling for new teachers in the New Blossom district—and it was a nightmare, truly. Old, crappy textbooks. Projectors that seemed more likely to start on fire than actually project anything. Kids with filthy mouths and filthier imaginations. *[Sighs.]*

But in New Blossom, everything was shiny and new—that was pretty much the town's unofficial motto. It might sound, you know, *Stepfordian—[Laughs.]* But it really wasn't. It was just a town full of good, normal people. Yeah, normal. What do I mean by that? Normal as in normal. The demon-worshipping bit came in later. *[Laughs again.]* Or I guess it was there all along, depending on who you believe.

JOHN CORRINGER

The schools were great, of course, but the real draw was the mall. There had been some small shops before then—a little market, a family restaurant, something of a commercial main street—but it was the mall that secured New Blossom as the pride of outer suburbia. It had all the newest stores and restaurants, everything the wives wanted, all in a pretty little package. By far the pride of my administration.

Why? *[Scoffs.]* Well, there was the tax income for one thing. What do you think keeps the grass in New Blossom so green?

LAUREL MAY
Sister of the victim

Ha. *[Shakes head.]* Isn't the answer to that question always 'shit'?

There were also small, scattered farms and micro-communities around the outskirts of New Blossom, which had been unincorporated territory before its formation as a city. One such example was a third-generation family-owned farm called Three Daughters, which provided a locally awarded small batch of specialty wines and cheeses.

JOHN CORRINGER

It wasn't great wine. Not bad, but nothing incredible. A little too sweet for my tastes—I'm a scotch man myself—but it worked out great for our local business office. Some of the people in town were becoming concerned that everything was too commercial, like we were getting away from that quaint small town feel. So we slapped a few local wines on a Bennigan's menu and suddenly everyone was at peace again.

EMILY NEWSOM

Even before everything happened, everyone was convinced the Three Daughters farm was run by witches. Not in a bad way, or a scary way. Just... urban legend is all. Suburban legend, I guess. We also heard rumors that they were, you know. Batting for the other team, if you catch my drift. And there was a longstanding rumor among the younger female staff at the high school, of which I was one at the time—hard to believe, I know, me being young—that you could... *get things* from them. Looking back it was probably just birth control or condoms or something, but it seemed real secretive at the time. Cult-y, almost.

Were they actually witches? Oh, I don't know. Means something different now, doesn't it? There's a whole witch section in the Barnes and Noble for chrissake, so I'm thinking it doesn't mean what we thought it meant back then. People didn't have the same attitudes on that sort of thing—or any attitudes at all, aside from it being, I guess, *un-Christian*. Unneighborly somehow. It was before *Charmed*, before *Sabrina*, before *Buffy*—before it was, you know, *acceptable*. Before we stopped thinking of witches as the Baba Yaga and started seeing them as pretty blonde girls like Melissa Joan Hart.

CAROLINE ROSHAN

Current Manager, Three Daughters

Farm

Look, I know what people say about my mother. *[Roshan's mother, Rainne Roshan, was the farm's manager at the time. She passed away in 2016.]* People would say all sorts of things about her and my aunts *[Rose Roshan, who passed away in 2004, and Rheem Roshan]*, but I truly believe they were just ahead of their time. They saw the gender inequities and the exclusion and wanted to create somewhere safe for people to go. They also happened to make pretty good wine, so yeah.

EMILY NEWSOM

Passable. *Passable* wine. It was certainly potable, which was all that really mattered as far as anyone was concerned at the time.

CAROLINE ROSHAN

Was the farm profitable? Not really, no. Not at the time. Well, not unless you counted the way the town was hassling them to sell our land, which started with a good enough offer and ended with my mother threatening some developer with a sawed-off shotgun. People weren't really paying attention back then to whether or not land was being snatched out from under someone, to tell you the truth. *[Scoff.]* It wasn't quite 'eminent domain,' but it was still a miracle my mother was able to stay where she was. I know the town offered her an arm and a leg for it—whether to own her fields or just get her out of the way, I really don't know. It's not bad land, obviously. *[Roshan gestures to a display of Three Daughters products, rebranded under her ownership, which include the aforementioned wines and cheeses along with signature handcrafted fruit preserves. There are also a few medicinal products, such as lactation teas and digestion aids.]* We get by just fine. And people are all about buying local now.

[When asked if Roshan believes her mother was offering similar products at the time:] I don't know, honestly. I was really young when Marisol was arrested, and all I know is that Mom thought she was innocent. She never said anything else.

While the Three Daughters Farm was owned exclusively by the Roshan sisters—Rainne, Rose, and Rheem—they also took in boarders from time to time, including young Marisol Farrow, then a recent graduate of a small regional teaching program and a first year teacher at New Blossom High School. Marisol quickly became known as the face of the farm.

EMILY NEWSOM

I have never in my life seen the Roshan sisters. Well, minus the daughter who runs it now, sweet girl. Had her in class years later, real quiet thing. But at the time it was Marisol making deliveries, almost like a whole other full-time job. I remember I told her one time, 'Mari, you gotta slow down.' Teaching isn't easy, you know what I mean? Contrary to popular belief, it doesn't end at three when the students go home. But Marisol insisted she owed the sisters.

She was so loyal to them. Made some people wonder what they must've done for her, if you know what I mean.

CAROLINE ROSHAN

Marisol had a bit of a bad reputation, I do know that much. I figured it out right away—kids can be cruel, and I was complicit from birth just for living on this farm, you know? For being my mother's daughter. They called me a witch, a demon... some just called me a slut like Marisol. Their parents probably figured Mom had helped her out of a tight spot—or, like, you know. That she was *in the family way* or whatever they used to say. *[Rolls eyes.]* I know Mom always said people had the wrong idea about her, that she was just a young girl who needed a place to stay. And that she'd gotten real close to Aunt Rheem, who was near her age.

RHEEM ROSHAN

Former Part-Owner, Three Daughters

Farm

Oh, I was a good decade older than Marisol. Everyone makes her sound like some old spinster now, maybe to make themselves feel better about what they did to her, but she was young then, real young. Poor girl was barely eighteen when she came to us. Sopping wet, too, like some abandoned kitten. We never asked where she came from 'cause it didn't seem like a nice conversation, you know what I mean? And sure, Caro might tell you that Marisol had a 'reputation,' but I'll tell you what she *really* had: the wrong look. She wasn't one of them perfect churchy blondes. Everyone thought she was some jezebel, but I'll tell you something, that had nothing to do with Marisol and everything to do with the damn bigots in town. It was those damn boys who made her life hell.

EMILY NEWSOM

Ah. The brothers. It... snowballed. Yeah, snowballed.

CAROLINE ROSHAN

I never actually met the younger one—I mean, I must have, but not that I remember, being so young—but I saw the older one once, years later. I think, even then, I understood it. How they were able to do as much damage as they did. Even with everything Mom said, I understood it. *[Faint smile.]* And if I could be taken in by a pretty face knowing what I already knew, I can only imagine what happened to the rest of this damn town.

✝

IN THE WINTER OF 1988, THE NEW BLOSSOM MALL played host to a national teen music showcase. While the winners of the showcase would go on to tour the country to minor acclaim, for the town of New Blossom, it would always be about the Barrett brothers.

ABBY DAUBMAN
New Blossom Chamber of Commerce
1985-1998

The 1988 showcase? Oh, I don't know, I don't even know where to begin. Hosting it in the New Blossom Mall was quite a get, you understand. There were all sorts of teens in the mall that day, performing and watching and what-have-you. We figured having their parents around would be good for business, but of course it was mostly the teens themselves. Quite a headache. But yes, I remember the Barrett brothers distinctly. They sang... Oh, what was that song? I remember it from my church days. Ah, I can't think of it now. Age. Too much got tangled up in my memories of them. They sang like angels, though. I do remember that. To my ear, anyway. I was in my thirties and unimpressed by boys who needed haircuts. But I assume it was something different to the teen girls.

JOHN CORRINGER

I was there that day for, you know, ceremonial purposes. Ribbon cutting and whatnot, and a bit of hand-shaking and baby-kissing. I introduced the bands and then I was out. I have no memory of the brothers.

EMILY NEWSOM

[Laughing:] Oh god, maybe it was something about having ovaries, I don't know. Like a dog whistle that only teenage girls could hear.

LAUREL MAY

My sister and I were there that day. She was...
Well, I was just seventeen, so she was fifteen. I
remember seeing her eyes light up—it was Jeremy
for her, the younger one. He had floppy hair, a shy
smile, like a baby duckling. *[Shakes head.]* But for
me it was always Joshua.

EMILY NEWSOM

Joshua Barrett was the older one, the heartthrob.
He was the type that was 'in' in those days. The
younger one was more broody and sad, like a
puppy dog. But Joshua was bright, infectious, and
his hair had that sun-bleached tint. He looked so
California—I remember the girls around me saying
that. He looked like a day at the beach. I have no
memory of how the brothers came to stick around,
but I know that within a week, the girls at the high
school were throwing some kind of fundraiser for
them. A bake sale, if I recall correctly. Cupcakes
with hearts that had the boys' initials on them.
[Grimaces.] Like I said. Heartthrob.

LAUREL MAY

By some stroke of luck my friend Tiffany Lundgren—my best friend at the time, or I suppose what the kids now call my 'frenemy'—she got to talk to him. She dragged me along because she was nervous and I always made her look better by comparison. She was competing too, singing in the showcase, though she had absolutely no talent. Nice boobs, though, even then. *[Smiles thinly.]* I remember thinking Josh was such a sweetheart— he didn't even look at her blouse, which she'd unbuttoned just before sidling up to him. He just smiled and told us how nice it was to be in our nice town, in our fancy mall.

[When asked if her sister, Serena, was with her:] Oh, yes. Oh, Serena was everywhere with me in those days. I hated it. *[Sighs.]* Our mother was a rabid church volunteer, and never at home unless it was time to fix supper for my father, so it was always on me to take Serena with me whenever I went somewhere. I was so humiliated at the time because she was always tagging along—trying to be one of us *cool girls*, you know? And I already wasn't very cool, so imagine what having your kid sister around does for the ol' image. *[Smile fades.]* But then she met the brothers and she had a new

idol. She was the one, actually, who invited them to stay.

The May sisters were the daughters of Michael May, a mid-level investment analyst, and Evelyn May, a homemaker who was heavily involved in New Blossom's Lutheran parish. Upon introduction after the showcase, Evelyn May considered it her duty as a member of the congregation to provide a home for the boys.

LAUREL MAY

To be clear, they didn't just move right in or anything. Serena had invited them over for dinner—shameless little sister stuff—and it came up that they didn't have any place to go after the showcase was finished. Joshua had gotten all quiet when it came up—my daddy had asked where they were from and if their parents had come to watch them. He and my mother figured out there must have been something awful going on at home, and honestly, one look at Jeremy would have confirmed it. He was so skittish, half-starved.

TIFFANY LUNDGREN
Friend of the May sisters

I snuck over that first night because Laurel called me. She told me the Barrett brothers were staying in her guest house—you know, showing off, like she often did—and I dared her to... Oh, I don't know. Kid stuff. Write a letter *declaring her love* or something. We snuck down the hall and slipped it under the door, but our timing was awful. Joshua opened the door just before we made our escape, and I remember there was this... strange look on his face. It was all red, beet red, like he'd been yelling or something. But he closed the door behind him real quick and suddenly he was charming again, just like he'd been that day at the showcase. For so long I thought I'd imagined it.

LAUREL MAY

She said that? *[Sarcastically:]* Must be revisionist history. Tiffany was always trying to come over and worm her way into the brothers' room. *[When asked if it was always their room:]* It became their room, yeah, quite quickly. They moved in and never moved out, not that any of us wanted them to. But anyway, Tiffany, she was always trying to be alone with Joshua, and eventually I realized she was never actually visiting *me*. We fought about it later—after, I don't know, a month? And then we never spoke to each other again. Especially not after I went to prom with Joshua.

The Barrett brothers quickly began attending church services along with the May family. Jeremy Barrett, the younger brother, soon enrolled in the high school, with his forms citing Michael and Evelyn May as his legal guardians.

EMILY NEWSOM

We noticed them around town for quite a while before it became clear that the Mays were taking them in. I rarely saw them apart at first—not until after the older one made himself a staple in the community, always showing up at church, singing and whatnot and performing. I think initially I assumed the brothers were twins—fraternal, I guess, since they were about as different as night and day—but then the younger one was enrolled in my algebra class that fall when he should have been in pre-calculus at least.

LAUREL MAY

Joshua was already of age, so he took a job with my father working in Chicago as some kind of financial assistant. I never really asked questions— I was just so excited to have a boyfriend who went to work, you know? Like a real husband. I wanted exactly what my mother had at the time, though of course I had no idea about my father. *[It was revealed during the 1992 trial of Marisol Farrow that Michael May paid the lease monthly on an apartment in Chicago belonging to his mistress and three-year-old son.]*

Was Joshua really my boyfriend? Probably not. *[Sighs.]* No, looking back I can see that the answer was no. But I really thought so at the time. I thought he was just perfect. He used to walk me to school, put his arm around me, offer me his coat. I thought that was what love was.

[When asked about Jeremy:] What was he doing? I don't know. Spending time with Serena, I guess. I appreciated that she was finally off my back. I was much more popular, you understand, with Joshua on my arm, even if he wasn't in my bed or anything. I didn't have any ideas like that anyway. I was a good girl! *[Laughs.]* A good Christian, and so was he—always encouraging me to keep myself sacred. Oh, I just adored him.

You know, it's funny, I remember one of the other cheerleaders saying that my daddy must have bought him for me just like everything else, and I just laughed. I thought wow, she had no idea, you know? Not even a single clue. That if Joshua was bought for me, well, I didn't care. I'd have paid for him myself if I thought it meant I could keep him.

TOBIN RUTHERFORD

Neighbor of the May family

Laurel May... She wasn't much to look at. I'm sorry! *[Shakes his head.]* I'm sorrier than anything to say it, because she really earned my respect toward the end. Everything she did after the trial. But Serena, *she* was the beauty of the family. I went over almost every day with some excuse just to see her. I'm thinking Laurel couldn't see it—you know how sisters are, big sisters especially, annoyed by everything the younger ones do or don't do. But that summer—the summer when Laurel was so smitten with Joshua Barrett, which the whole town could see—that was the summer that Serena May turned sixteen.

[Nostalgically:] Boy, that blonde hair, those curls. Those blue, blue eyes. Those *legs*. *[Whistles.]* There wasn't a boy in a five-mile radius who wasn't in love with her. Jeremy Barrett included.

EMILY NEWSOM

I did feel sort of bad for him, the younger one. I thought he was kind of a sweet dope, you know? He had the right look, but no charisma like

Joshua, who could charm the pants off every mother in the PTA. Which he might have actually done, come to think of it. We never did find out why Evelyn May was so devoted to him—I never fully bought her whole Christian schtick. She seemed more the desperate housewife type.

Anyway, the younger brother, Jeremy, he didn't seem to me like he enjoyed owing everything to the May family, and Serena May, she confirmed that soon enough. She asked if I knew of anywhere he could get a job, and—Well, Marisol was there at the time. Pouring herself a cup of coffee, looking tired as ever, and then she said in that little voice of hers, "Well, I know a place."

And I guess the rest is history, isn't it?

Jeremy Barrett began working for the Three Daughters farm in 1989. Serena May was sixteen, and Jeremy, according to his school records, was seventeen. Marisol Farrow had just turned twenty-three.

CAROLINE ROSHAN

What did Jeremy Barrett do for my mother? Probably the same thing I have my employees do for me now. Help with the planting and bottling and fermenting. It's not terribly interesting. Or maybe she just felt sorry for him and paid him to do small chores around the house. It sounds like something my mother would do. She always liked taking in strays like Marisol.

MARISOL FARROW

Convicted of the murder of Serena May

[Marisol exhales deeply, almost meditationally before speaking. Her voice is scratchy, as if she hasn't used it in months.]

First, let me say I appreciate you being here. I know that... I know that not many people have any interest in hearing what I have to say. *[After being told that actually, many people are interested in her story:]* Oh, they're interested in my story. I understand that. But they don't care for what I have to say.

[When reminded that we're just here to discuss the events as she remembers them:] Right. Yes, I understand. You seem like nice people, I just... There's so much I haven't... I haven't told anyone. So much that I don't know where to start.

[When advised to start at the beginning:] The beginning? Well. *[She laughs.]* Then I guess I have

to start by saying what Jeremy Barrett found one afternoon in the basement of the Roshan farmhouse.

RHEEM ROSHAN

Who told you about that meeting? I guess it doesn't matter now. Not like Caro's kept up anything from our day. The farm isn't anything like it used to be. That's to be expected, I suppose. I hightailed it out of there as soon as I could myself—the whole thing was tainted for me after Marisol. I sold my shares and never looked back.

Sorry, you asked about something? Right. The day that boy stumbled into one of our meetings. Yes, I remember it, vaguely. Very vaguely. Said it was an accident as I recall, though now I'm not so sure. What does that mean? I don't know. No, I really don't.

[When asked if she remembers anything specific:] I said it all to that lawyer, back when my memory was still sharp, and nobody cared. Never even called me as a witness.

You really want to hear what happened? Fine. Means even less now than it did then, but fine. I remember that he didn't look frightened. Didn't look scared. Didn't even look surprised.

Yeah, I know what he said. He said all sorts of things at the trial—all kinds of awful things. Nobody wanted to hear what I had to say back then and I expect they won't now, either. But I saw his eyes, and I know what I saw.

MARISOL FARROW

How did he look?

[She turns to glance out the window, resting her chin on the heel of her hand.]

He looked like he had finally found where he belonged.

PART II: PARANORMAL ACTIVITY

UNBEKNOWNST TO THE DEVELOPERS of New Blossom, Illinois, the acres of sprawling farmland were not nearly as uninhabited as state institutions made them seem—a recurrent underestimation. Once occupied by the Ojibwe, Odawa, and Powatomi nations of indigenous tribes, the vast majority of Native Americans were relocated in 1830 by President Andrew Jackson's Indian Removal Act, disrupting the land's true stewardship. While some scattered residents still remained in the area beyond the nineteenth century, the land that would become New Blossom had been vacant for several decades in the interest of "preserving the showcase" of the 1893 Chicago World's Fair. It wasn't until the 1950s that any developers attempted to make use of the land—by which time, some argued, the damage had been done.

PAULA SMITH

Historical Director, Midwest Cultural

Heritage Center

Are you asking me if the land under New Blossom was cursed or something? No, of course not. Common misconception by the way, that we're all somehow responsible for the demonic brand of mysticism *you* invented. How very fucking

Puritanical, thanks for that. No, there's been nothing but *civilized* outreach in recent times—on our behalf, anyway. Can't speak for everyone else. What I can say is that certainly in the 1990s we'd all have better things to do than curse a little white girl to scare up some bigots.

Do I know anything about the what? The coven? What, like witches? Honey, that's not my area. Sure, okay, witches. Why not. Live and let live, you feel me? Which isn't to say I don't believe that *someone* might have gotten mightily pissed off. There's plenty of people being shoved out of every inch of state-owned land if you just know where to look, and if they upset some witches, well— *[Laughs.]* Isn't that just sweet?

While the land had few documented occupants, the Roshan family's Three Daughters Farm was one such registered deed, along with a handful of other small farms in the area. Most of these popped up shortly after the Dust Bowl drove residents out of the Southern Plains, but unlike other refugee-type settlements, these were situated well away from more traveled roads.

MIKE CHEN

Community Outreach, Illinois
Department of Transportation

We don't have electronic records for anything prior to the seventies—my department didn't really exist then the way it does now, with outreach being the primary goal—but my guess is that someone would have had to reach out to anyone living along a planned highway. Not to force them out, obviously, we're not bullies. Just... for safety reviews, that sort of thing. There's no record of any conversations, though that doesn't necessarily mean anything.

[When asked if the Roshans were ever asked to participate in the development of planned transit arteries, including the town of New Blossom:] Oh, I'm positive they were. The location of their farm is a little bit of an anomaly—the other small settlements like it are scattered around, but Three Daughters is located on an old Native American trackway. As I understand it, it's an area of critical importance, ritually speaking. It would have been ideal for a more major road, but then obviously there was some resistance.

PAULA SMITH

Trackway? No. I know what this is, though. More of that mystic shit. The... what are they called. Lines or whatever. You know? Stonehenge.

Fairies. Once again, that's not us. You do realize I went to UChicago, right? Our director went to DePaul. *[Waving a hand Jedi-style:]* These are not the spooky cult weirdos you're looking for.

CAROLINE ROSHAN
Current Manager, Three Daughters
Farm

There's nothing weird about ley lines. It's not entirely unscientific as a concept. I mean, how else do you explain it, right? All those sacred places being parallel like that? I'm not saying there's any kind of supernatural significance to it—it's not like we're talking crop circles—but these are *defined* pathways, right? All over the world. I assume there's some archaeological significance. Some reason all those people chose to build where they did. Wait, are you just asking about ley lines generally, or...?

Ah, okay, I should have known you were going there with that. Yes, my mom did believe there was something meaningful about the location of our farm, but not... not fairy related. *[Laughs.]* God, that sounds unbelievably stupid to say. I always assumed that her interest in preserving the location was... hereditary, I guess. New Blossom wasn't the only suburb being built at the time, so the writing was on the wall. But she and my aunts were kind of the leaders in the area, and they were definitely the type to stand their ground.

Most nearby farms and hamlets were bought up to make room for the development of New Blossom around the middle of the twentieth century, but a small constellation of residents were bolstered by the Roshan family's decision not to sell. Little was known about these residents aside from their vaguely isolationist practices, including the decision not to send their children to the New Blossom school district.

EMILY NEWSOM

Teacher, New Blossom High School

1986-2004

It wasn't like they were Menanites, you know? Or no, Amish I guess. Those are the ones with no technology, right? Anyway, they still came into town for things every now and then. And the kids, they showed up for certain things, certain classes, and when they did they were normal. Relatively. I never got the feeling there was any real opposition to the New Blossom residents themselves, or any tension with our students. It was more of a rejection of the whole system, I guess.

[When asked if the May sisters would have had an opinion on the so-called "unincorporated population":] Serena May was such a sweetheart, honestly, I doubt she would have made the distinction. And Laurel May was the opposite—too wrapped up in her own life to notice anything that didn't fit.

LAUREL MAY
Sister of the victim

Oh gosh, no... no, I couldn't name one aside from Ms. Farrow. Marisol, I mean. And she wasn't really even one of them, I guess, since she floated into our daily lives. Plus she was an adult, or so she seemed to us at the time. Hard to think so now— who at twenty-two is an *adult*, you know?—but she was our teacher, so.

Anyway no, I don't recall anyone in particular, though Josh *[Joshua Barrett, the elder of the Barrett brothers]* definitely did. I remember we were walking through town—I was wearing this *darling* new sundress and I was so proud to be arm-in-arm with him—and he spotted Marisol walking down the opposite side of the street with someone else. Maybe one of the Roshans? They popped into town every now and again. And I remember he suddenly got very agitated and I was so confused. It was like... *my dress*, you know? 'Look at me. Look at this dress. Look at how nice we look together.' *[Laughs.]* Kids, right? And I thought I was so grown up. But anyway, it really didn't occur to me until later that he seemed very skittish about the whole thing. Really thrown off. I knew he was sort of secretive about his history and everything, but I didn't make that connection until he was called to testify at the trial.

TESTIMONY OF JOSHUA BARRETT

State v. Marisol Farrow, 1992

I just felt there was something fishy about her. I knew it right away, because I'd seen it before. I don't talk about this much, given the unpleasantness, but me and my brother, we didn't exactly have it easy growing up. Our parents... they were good, small town people. Small minded, maybe, or just naive. They didn't know how easy it was to be taken in by those types until it was too late.

[Attorney for the State of Illinois: "Which types of people, exactly?"]

You know. *[Pause.]* Satanists.

RHEEM ROSHAN

Former Part-Owner, Three Daughters

Farm

I remember the silence in the courtroom when he said that—everyone was too busy looking at each other to see the look on his face. Smug bastard was so clearly lying his ass off with every word out of his mouth, but what did they see? A well-pressed suit, paid for by Mr. May and his corporate city job. The May family and their weekly church attendance. His little girlfriend with her eyes all red, crying over her golden, cherubic sister... Not that I don't feel sad for them, of course. Of course I feel sad, I feel sorry for what happened to them. But what he did? What this town turned the whole thing into? *[Shakes head.]*

It wasn't like New Blossom was completely made up of bigots, either, which is the worst part. Plenty of people were capable of keeping their damn heads on straight. Someone should have spoken up. Someone ought to have said something—said that their kids were cared for by Marisol, that there was no way the person selling basil at the farmer's market had suddenly got a taste for *ritual sacrifice*, for Pete's sake. That boy was a classic manipulator, playing on the fears of people who should have known better. The Mays were grieving—okay, fine. But everyone else? No excuse. No excuse but cowardice. And fear. And it set the tone for everything that followed.

EMILY NEWSOM

The thing is, when we first heard Joshua Barrett's story about him and his brother escaping some satanist cult, it was like... oh man, that's just like in the news! What a horrible thing to happen to this child, this *victim*. It didn't occur to us to think, huh, how hard would it be to tell the same story, you know?

I think later someone pointed out that the details were so believable because we had believed them before. It was circular, like a feedback loop. We believed it was happening somewhere, so we believed him when he said it had happened to him.

MARISOL FARROW
Convicted of the murder of Serena May

Did I know the truth about their backgrounds then? No. Jeremy had told me certain things about himself, some things that made me wonder... like his age. The fact that he was older than he said he was, because Joshua had told him strangers would take more kindly to boys than men. It made sense when he explained it, and I thought that was his big secret—that and everything we shared, obviously. But it wasn't until later, when it was already too late to change my story, that he finally broke down and told me the truth. He felt guilty, I guess, that I was protecting him.

What truth did Jeremy tell me? Well, that Joshua had his reasons for covering their tracks. And, of course, the kicker: that they weren't brothers. Not at all.

✝

IN THE SEVENTIES AND EIGHTIES there was a new insidiousness attributed to the concept of strangers—a sudden, generation-defining wariness of what could be lurking in the unknown. With the rise of serial killers like the Alphabet Killer and the Zodiac Killer, people were becoming increasingly afraid of the constancy of danger outside the home. Coupled with the influence of insular conservative politics and the rise of the Evangelical movement, New Blossom wasn't alone in being vulnerable to the collective surge in paranoia. But behind the scenes, a similar struggle existed among those in New Blossom who had very good reason to hide.

AGATHA SMITH*

Name has been changed by request.

Look, I'll get right to the point: Yes, there was a coven in New Blossom at the time. Today it's merged with one of the larger Northern Illinois chapters for obvious reasons, but yes, it existed then. It's not what you think, obviously. Witchcraft has layers to it, like everything. Everything *nuanced,* anyway, which doesn't account for much these days if you go by the Twitter hive-mind, but still.

Was Marisol Farrow a witch, yes. Was she a murderous devil worshipper, no. It's really that simple.

[When asked if there were any in the coven who did subscribe to the "devil worshipping" school of witchcraft, so to speak:] No. Well, not exactly. Even within the witch community there was always disagreement at the time about how far to go with certain abilities. We don't really use the terms "good" witch or "bad" witch—it's really not so

binary—but that being said, was Marisol a good witch? Yes. A thousand percent, yes.

RHEEM ROSHAN

She helped us with planting. She had a green thumb. It's a real fine line between magic and witchcraft, right? Sometimes it just comes down to that ineffable quality, that ability to nurture something that other people couldn't. She wasn't as useful in the kitchen—my sister Rainne was the master of that particular domain—but the garden? All her. She was a gardener as a person. That was her Achilles heel, in the end. She was a gardener who thought that boy was a goddamn rose.

What did I think? All I knew was that it was a bad idea to have that Barrett boy coming around. I'd had a bad feeling about him since the day I saw him walk in on the coven meeting—I could see it on his face, he'd been in one before, and given his circumstances it clearly hadn't ended well. And the way covens work... I'll spare you the mundanities, but you don't usually leave one so much as get removed. And at the time, getting removed meant either you were trouble or something else was going on. Some poison in the root.

Marisol, though, she trusted him. I didn't. And even if he'd been the kindest, gentlest person in the world, I still wouldn't have trusted him. I knew people were keeping a close eye on him, for one thing. He was a little infatuated with Marisol, even before the day of that meeting, but he was too... too *New Blossom*. Too part of the May family narrative. The Mays—you've gotten to know the Mays from their testimony, right? They ran with some real 'fire and brimstone' types. Not a lot of room for gray areas there. Worse, the Barrett boy owed them something and he knew it—hell, even I knew it. I also knew he was keeping a bigger secret than he let on, and it was only a matter of time before someone noticed he wasn't exactly maintaining that wholesome New Blossom facade.

LAUREL MAY

I did notice that Jeremy wasn't around as much, yes. This was a year or so after they'd been living with us, though I only noticed because Joshua noticed. He seemed angry more often at the time, usually at me. I thought that was normal—that I was being a nag, or boring him. I was so scared to lose him. In fact I was so scared to lose him that I kept pushing my sister—I thought if *she* held onto Jeremy, then *I'd* get to keep Joshua. She was sad,

I know that much. She suspected that he loved someone else, but who could believe that? She was perfect. She was beautiful. So beautiful I was almost angry with her—because it wasn't *fair*, you know? That adolescent sense of fairness: it wasn't *fair*. You should have heard the way our parents went on about her—Serena this, Serena that. I was convinced that if I'd had her looks I'd have no trouble keeping Joshua—but that's the worst part, because I ignored what she was actually trying to tell me. I thought her mere existence made a mockery of mine, so I told her to stop moping and go lock down her man.

[When asked what she meant by "locking him down":] I told her to follow him, yes. To find out what was really going on, and she did.

AGATHA SMITH

I really can't speak much to the details of what happened around the time of that poor girl's death. I didn't know Jeremy Barrett well, though I don't think any of us can say that we did. He was very quiet, almost painfully shy. It was like he was already atoning for something. Not that that stopped him coming around, participating in spells. Nothing sinister, mind you. We're a community like any other, no different from the churchgoing people he lived with. We had spells for prosperity, for fertility, for health. What is prayer, anyway? People might not care for that comparison, but it's the truth.

Anyway, we loved Marisol. For her we were willing to tolerate him, though it was clear even to us that if *we* noticed he was spending that much time with her, other people were bound to ask questions. After all, she was a teacher. Her public life, the optics, with all the time they spent together... *[Shakes head.]* We thought we were being polite by staying out of it. Now I wish one of us had been rude.

MARISOL FARROW

At first I thought I was mentoring him, I think. Honestly, I don't know what I thought. I really didn't seek him out—he was the one who found me, most of the time. He'd walk into a room I was in and then look so startled, jumpy as a cat. He'd offer to help me in this quiet voice, and I remember thinking it was so much deeper than I expected.

Then there was the day of the coven meeting, and I knew there was something more going on. He told me soon after that he wasn't really seventeen—he was actually twenty-one, a year younger than me. Joshua was nearly twenty-five. I asked why the pretense, and—well, I already told you. Josh had decided it would be safer, and Jeremy went along with it. At first I asked, you know, why such concern about safety? He'd come to New Blossom as part of a teen showcase. He was pretending to be in *high school*, which wasn't a place any reasonable person wants to go back to. It seemed extreme to me. But I could see the admission made him uncomfortable, and at the time I didn't feel it was my place to push him. I told him we'd obviously have no trouble—he'd walked into a *coven meeting*, right? So I wasn't going to tell his secret if he didn't tell mine.

After that he started spending time with me on purpose—coming to the meetings, helping in the garden. It was several months after that when we kissed for the first time. I remember he smelled like thyme, like rosemary. He tasted like citrus. I don't know what came over me. I was usually much more cautious, but I think I was lonely, in some... intrinsic way. Looking for my other half. For a moment, I really thought I'd found it.

Problems started not long after that, of course. In retrospect we really weren't all that careful. There was a day when Joshua showed up in the Roshans' kitchen—he startled me so much I broke a glass. That was the day Jeremy told me that he and Joshua weren't actually brothers. Again, the lie was for safety. I should have pressed him as to whose safety he meant—and who, exactly, the pair of them were so afraid of—but I didn't. Again, I decided not to pry. After all, I was keeping my own secrets. It felt wrong to ask for his.

EMILY NEWSOM

It was certainly obvious to us that Marisol was seeing somebody. That was a harsh blow for her case, I think, that we all knew something had changed. Almost every parent and teacher who'd been interviewed testified that there had been a change in her demeanor. She seemed happier. *[Sighs.]* How sad is it that happiness is enough to convict a person? But at the time, Marisol's sudden lightness did feel acutely out of place.

RHEEM ROSHAN

Young people in love can't help themselves. Which is why Marisol made a mistake.

MARISOL FARROW

It was a day when I hadn't been very careful—it had been a hard day, some problems with parents who didn't think I had any business teaching their children. That came up a lot. Too often. *[Pause.]* Anyway, Jeremy had taken one look at my face when I pulled up to the farm and he'd taken my hand—probably the most open we'd ever been with each other. Out of the corner of my eye I thought I saw blonde curls, but I wasn't sure.

The next day, Laurel May—who had graduated by then, I think, but it doesn't surprise me that she was able to walk right into the school—stormed into my classroom and slapped me across the face. What did she say? I struggle to remember, honestly. It was so shocking, so fast. For a long time I remembered her threatening me, because that's what the testimony was from Emily Newsom, whose classroom was next door—but I don't think she actually did. I think she just told me to be careful where I stepped because she knew what I really was.

EMILY NEWSOM

I thought it was an accusation of an affair, which seemed plenty bad to me. It was only at Marisol's trial when I realized they were using the conversation I'd overheard as evidence of something much more damning.

MARISOL FARROW

Do I blame Laurel May for that? Or Emily? No. Really, I don't.

LAUREL MAY

I blame myself every day of my life. Though not so much for that as for what happened later that night. Serena and I got into a screaming match that night—well, I was the one screaming, she was stone-cold. Said I didn't understand. I remember the real blow was what she told me about Joshua—'It's obvious,' she said, 'it's so obvious he hates you, he just needs you as a cover.' I stormed out after that, expecting Joshua to come after me and talk me down, but instead he went to talk to her. I remember he sounded very calm. I was waiting outside for my chance to be dramatic, but I heard a strangely gentle tone of voice from him. Then he came out and went looking for Jeremy, which made me angry, so I went to bed. I thought about apologizing, but I didn't.

The next morning, Serena was nowhere to be found.

†

MOST PEOPLE CONSUMING MEDIA IN THE NINETIES will have some memory of Serena May's infamous disappearance and subsequent discovery several days later, her body unearthed near one of the creeks at the edge of New Blossom's western border. Her parents had led a church-sponsored search in the hours after her disappearance, which even then consisted of most of the town. Within days, every detail of Serena May's life had been picked apart and sensationalized in local media, eventually being picked up by the Chicago news outlets. By the time her body was found, the story had made national news.

JOHN CORRINGER
Mayor of New Blossom, 1982-1988

There was more media in town than any of us had ever handled before. My successor, Randy *[Randall Kirkowski, who passed away in 2019]* called me in to help despite my being retired. I always had more of a presence for the camera—Randy was a backstage kind of guy. He wanted to make everything go away, but even then I knew there were weirdos who loved that kind of stuff. Murderheads and what-have-you.

[When asked when he knew it was murder:] Oh, instantly. It just seemed so obvious. The parents were adamant she wouldn't have run away. Her teachers adored her, she had plenty of friends—she was a happy girl, a beautiful girl. A girl like that could have had plenty of boyfriends, so what else could it have been?

JAMES MORRISON

New Blossom Chief of Police, 1990-2011

Look, we tried our best to contain the media at first, but eventually it just seemed best to cast a wide net. The parents were hysterical and we weren't exactly well-funded for that kind of thing. We were relying on the public to help us find her, and they did. It was a civilian who found her. Used the word 'unnatural' quite a bit. Apparently was convinced she was alive, even talked to her for several minutes before realizing... Well, sorry to paint too unpleasant a picture. But you'll know by now, right? Everyone does. Her autopsy came up empty. Cause of death: heart stopped. In a perfectly healthy teenage girl. Her heart just... stopped.

DR. RON FELLMAN

Forensic Pathologist

It was extremely unusual—the most unusual case I've ever been called to consult on, by far. There is so little information to impart even now, though believe me I've been asked. It was very unnatural. Disturbing. I hadn't been to church in years and still, that day I called my mother. Asked her to remind me how the hell to do a rosary. *[Laughs.]*

[When asked what was so disturbing:] Well, there was a symbol on her, some drawing of something, only it was out of place because it was tattooed on her. Not with ink, which we know because we ran a tox screen. It had been tattooed with blood.

LAUREL MAY

I remember very little about those days, to be honest. I was shattered, absolutely shattered. At the time I assumed it was my mother who first suggested it was something satanic, because I think even then I assumed it was one of her little religious oddities. But looking back I think it was Joshua. I think it was Joshua who planted that in my mother's head, and until the day she died she never let it go. Not that, or Serena. It drove her completely mad, this idea that her poor baby had been murdered by a witch—a witch who had corrupted Jeremy, who'd tried to steal him for herself. Even after Jeremy and Joshua were gone, my mother still believed this was the work of a jealous rage, and that if Marisol had simply not existed, everything would have been fine.

AGATHA SMITH

It was a rune, yes, the tattoo. Not a very meaningful one, but it looked the part. A good lawyer would have pointed out that it was far more likely a frame-up job than any actual witchcraft, but Marisol didn't have a good lawyer. She had an overworked PD locked in a custody battle for three children whose mother was also dying of cancer. Sometimes that's just how it goes, isn't it? *[Shakes head.]* If Marisol was really a witch, you'd think she'd just conjure up a spell to post bail, but no. The Roshan sisters did what they could, but I think even Marisol was too shaken to believe any of it was actually happening. From the moment they arrested her, I think she really believed it would just go away,

MARISOL FARROW

Did I think any of it was real? No. I was in shock, utterly in shock. I was bereft with sadness for the Mays, and then doubly stricken to find they were the ones accusing me. The day the police showed up in my classroom... I should have known it was over. That town was never going to unsee that. I should have known right then that I was done.

[Farrow pauses for a long time before continuing:] The thing is, I knew I'd done something untoward with Jeremy, so I just tried to keep him out of it. I thought, even then, that *he* was the one who needed protecting. He was so quiet, so wounded. I thought, surely no one will believe it was me. I just need to keep them away from *him*. And by the time I realized the tide was turning against me, it was too late. Even my lawyer didn't believe me. He wouldn't put me on the stand because he said they'd ask me, are you a witch? And I'd say yes, and the trial would be over. It was already over. And by the time I understood that, the information from Jeremy—the truth about his background, everything about who he was—the

ammunition he might have given me was too late. There wasn't a single person in that courtroom who'd believe a single word out of my mouth.

I don't think Jeremy meant for things to go the way they did. Certainly I didn't think so at the time. I was so convinced of his goodness—so blindly sure that he would have spoken in my defense if he'd known how bad things really were. I wasn't surprised when Joshua testified against me, but when Jeremy didn't testify at all... I've never really known what to think. Which is why I'm doing this, to be honest with you. Not because of Laurel May's petition, though I'm very grateful to her for continuing to speak on my behalf.

Why now? I don't know. Something innate, I guess. I'm innocent, yes, but I've always known that. I never spent much time trying to change an outcome that seemed inevitable from the day Jeremy set foot on the Roshan farm. But I suppose thirty years of contemplation does something to a person, because for whatever reason, there's only one part I can't stand not knowing.

I have to know why Jeremy didn't say anything. I have to know what I sacrificed myself for, and whether my suspicions were correct.

So mainly, I have to know whether Jeremy Barrett
is still alive.

PART III: WITCHES DON'T BURN

SERENA MAY WAS DAYS SHY of her eighteenth birthday when her body was found in one of the fields outside of New Blossom, Illinois. In the hours prior to her death, Serena was last seen by most of the town sitting at church with her mother and father, and her sister, Laurel May. Accompanying the family had been the Barrett brothers, Joshua and Jeremy, who were then rumored to be romantically involved with Laurel and Serena respectively.

TOBIN RUTHERFORD
Neighbor of the May family

Serena May... Well. You've seen pictures, I take it? Though pictures wouldn't do her justice. She had this... this *air* about her, this lightness. I had a crush on her, as did every other teenage boy within ten square miles. She was the teen dream. Probably would have been prom queen if she'd made it one more week. God, I can't tell you how many of us hated Jeremy Barrett. He was her date, I assume. I guess we'll never know, right? I don't remember if anyone else had asked her, though, because it seemed like he was the only person who'd caught her eye.

181

What was he like? Quiet. Kind of a loner. Never really seemed like he wanted to be there, although who did? The ennui of the average high schooler in the early nineties was not what it is today, I'll tell you that much. *[Laughs.]* My kids... they're into all sorts of clubs and teams, honors this, AP that. Back then it wasn't the same. But anyway, he was good-looking enough, I guess. As much as one man can say that about another man. But he wasn't on any sports teams, wasn't a rebel of any sort, wasn't a smooth talker by any means—not like the older one was. He was just... troubled, I guess.

Yeah, looking back, I think that was it. He was a troubled kid. And Serena, she always liked trying to fix broken things. She really seemed pure, you know? Angelic. The girl was a saint, so I guess it makes sense. *[Wistfully:]* Only the good die young.

RHEEM ROSHAN
Former Part-Owner, Three Daughters
Farm

That was the trouble, wasn't it? The perfect angel meets her untimely doom and the whole town mourns because only a monster could have done it. And in a world that insular and simple, so few people understand what true monsters are. They mistake different for demons, and that's what happened in New Blossom all those years ago.

LAUREL MAY
Sister of the Victim

Serena really wasn't... *perfect.* I mean, don't get me wrong, I loved her dearly, and she definitely had fewer flaws than me, but the narrative around her death... It did her a disservice. I will say, though, that they were right about her archetype. She didn't care at all about superficial things, like prom. She was much too insightful for that, almost cerebral, and it drove me insane, honestly. She just did not even care because *of course* she didn't— she'd be prom queen even if she went in her pajamas, which she very nearly did. I'd spent weeks looking for the perfect dress for my own prom, but Serena, she just wanted to borrow something from me. Told me she hadn't even thought about it. I actually remember almost vibrating with sin that morning in church because I was just so *annoyed*, you know? She was so *good.* So infuriatingly good. I guess I pushed her into it, the fight we had. I used to hate that my last memory of her was of such rare and—well, honestly, *unprecedented* cruelty from her, but I like it now, I think. If not for that, I might have given you some bullshit speech about how she was a good person, a loving daughter, a caring friend... everything they say about people who don't really take up space in the world, you know? But now, in the end I can be like yeah, my sister was sweet and she was kind—mercifully kind, considering what a monster she had for a sister—but she was also a bitch when she wanted to be. She knew how to sting. She was just careful about it, and in the end it says a lot about her. That she knew what secrets to see, and how to strike.

For years I've wondered if that's what happened in the end. If she finally struck, but she wasn't careful enough about how she did it, or who she threatened. And then... well, yeah. *[Sadly:]* And then I remember it's probably my fault.

The morning of May 13, 1991 brought with it the news of Serena May's disappearance. Her parents, Evelyn and Michael, were quick to file a missing persons report upon discovering Serena's bed empty that morning.

JAMES MORRISON
New Blossom Chief of Police, 1990-2011

She wasn't the kind of girl who could be missing for long without the police being called. Do you know what I mean? That was the age of latchkey kids, sure, but not the Mays. Never the Mays. The mother was accustomed to waking both the daughters in the morning, sitting down for breakfast as a family. Like a weird, Stepfordian nightmare. Anyway, I hoped it was some teenage rebellion. That she'd had a fight with her sister the night before and left the house in a pubescent revolt, so of course it would be nothing. I told them not to worry, to wait a few hours. That maybe she'd show up at school that day.

EMILY NEWSOM
Teacher, New Blossom High School 1986-2004

I remember that day very clearly because Evelyn May was absolutely losing her mind. She called me several times before school even started. Called me *at home*, even. I told her I wasn't even Serena's homeroom teacher that year but she wouldn't listen. I'm not sure why she came to me, to be honest. I'd taught Laurel and Serena both, but it wasn't like I knew them well.

MARISOL FARROW
Convicted of the Murder of Serena May

I was Serena May's homeroom teacher that year, yes. And her mother did call me, though only at Emily Newsom's insistence. I think Emily was concerned, too, but mostly she couldn't figure out why Evelyn May was holding her *personally* responsible. But I didn't think it was that, really. Evelyn May and Emily O'Neill—she was Miss O'Neill then—they're quite similar in upbringing. Same sorority, even, I think. Aesthetically there was a kinship there. And anyway, I don't think Evelyn May got the answers from me that she was looking for. The... *concern*, I suppose. She held that against me later, saying that only a cold-blooded murderer would be so heartless. But the truth is that as odd as it was for Serena to not be in school that morning, I was focused on Jeremy. He was... distraught, I guess, is the word I would use. Distant, different. And I let it distract me, because I assumed it was Joshua's doing, even then.

TESTIMONY OF JOSHUA
BARRETT
State v. Marisol Farrow, 1992

The day before her disappearance, I was with Serena, trying to calm her down after her little spat with Laurel. They didn't fight often. Or, I should say, *Serena* didn't fight with Laurel much, though Laurel is a bit more tempestuous by nature. I did find it a bit odd, especially because it seemed like Serena was genuinely shaken by something. I wish now that I had intervened when Serena said she wanted to step out for some air.

[Attorney for the State of Illinois: "What happened when she said that?"]

I let her go. I felt she was entitled to her privacy.

["Did she seem anxious or concerned?"]

Yes.

["Yes she seemed anxious, or yes she seemed concerned?"]

Both. It seemed to me like she was going to have a chat with someone, someone she didn't want me to know about. She was being quite secretive. But again, she was Laurel's kid sister, and I had work in the morning... As much as I cared about her, I didn't think it was that strange that she was leaving the house that night.

["What time was it when she left?"]

Sometime after nine. Not terribly late.

["The forensic pathologist estimates that Serena May was killed no later than eleven that evening. Wouldn't that make you the last person to have spoken to her?"]

Aside from the murderer? *[His gaze flicks pointedly to Marisol Farrow in the defendant's box.]* Yes. I imagine so.

["What did you discuss with Serena May that evening?"]

Like I said, I was calming her down after her argument with Laurel. She mentioned her teacher, Miss Farrow, which I thought was a bit odd until I remembered she'd been hanging around Jeremy. He'd mentioned to me the things Farrow had asked him to do, always making excuses to have him around. It occurred to me that she might have been manipulating him.

[*"Manipulating him?"*]

Preying on him. She had a very dark energy around her. Every time he came home from being on the Roshan farm he always seemed drawn and secretive. I suspected something.

[*"What did you suspect?"*]

Jeremy had been unusually volatile. Jumpy. Like he thought someone was watching him. He seemed spooked. And like I said, I have experience with these types of people.

[*"Types of people meaning...?"*]

Witches. Dark ones. And obviously I was right.

MARISOL FARROW

[*Sighing:*] It was clear from his testimony that Joshua Barrett hated me. Everything out of his mouth was a lie, one intended to poison the whole courtroom against me, and I just wish I had realized sooner why that might have been. That, and I wish Serena May—who was clearly just an innocent bystander, *maybe* one who knew too much—had never been involved.

But I suppose we'll never know why one human being uses another. We want it to make sense, but we know it never will.

†

IN THE DAYS LEADING UP TO the discovery of Serena May's body, the town of New Blossom was shaken by her disappearance. The prom was canceled and replaced with a candlelight vigil. Everyone tuned into the morning news to hear the crumbs of details: Jeremy Barrett's time at the Roshan farm, the alleged affair between Jeremy Barrett and Marisol Farrow, the likelihood that Serena May knew and had threatened to tell. As tension heightened, most of the town united in their attempt to locate her, gradually alienating the Roshans and Marisol. Eventually, the story was picked up by national news, with the narrative of Marisol Farrow's inappropriate conduct and likely interest in dark witchcraft gaining steam.

JAMES MORRISON

It was a real flashy case, definitely. It had all the right markers for the time. Young girl goes missing. Virginal, blonde, church-going. Affluent parents. Like a teen JonBenét. Not the type to run off with a boyfriend or anything like that. Nobody would *want* her dead, you know what I mean? It was a little past the era of serial killers but maybe that was worse, because by then everyone already knew to be afraid of 'em, the Ted Bundy types. They were piecing all this together and looking for tragedy. First we had the victimology, then that freaky tattoo on her chest? The state of the body when it was found made it all the more compelling.

DR. RON FELLMAN
Forensic Pathologist

Ah yes, the tattooed rune. It took us a while to find someone who was an expert. It looked Celtic to me, so I found someone who specialized in, you know, that sort of thing. Mythology. There was a professor at UChicago who found it— Well, not Celtic at all, as it turned out, but there was a whole department doing symbology research. They told us it was some symbol for establishing influence over others.

And look, can I just say? I felt sorry for that poor girl. The one they called a witch. Well, she *was* a witch, I guess. But they asked me what the rune meant under oath, so I had to tell them. A dark day for my career, I can tell you that much, but there wasn't much else to say. However Serena May died, it wasn't natural. It wasn't physical or chemical. It was supernatural, and I believe that much with the core of my being. So yeah. I knew it wasn't going to go her way.

AGATHA SMITH
Name has been changed by request.

The coven was outed right away, yes. We didn't feel it was in our best interest to hide, and it... wasn't pretty. Aside from Marisol, I believe nobody suffered more than the Roshans.

CAROLINE ROSHAN
Current Manager, Three Daughters Farm

The theory became that my mother was a witch. *Head* witch, actually. *[Chuckles.]* Which I suppose she was, but I think they pictured it like some kind of terrible, Roald Dahl-ian convention of demons, when really it was just... a green thumb here, some lucky guesses there. I'm sure plenty of people wanted her to suffer over it regardless—she was, at very least, holding meetings for marginalized people outside the town, that much they knew for certain and didn't care for—but in the end, there was no motive. She and my aunts gained nothing from the death of that girl—if anything, it ruined their business. It took a long time for things to recover. In fact I've spent the last ten years of my life trying to take the vestiges of my mother's business and make it viable again—which I guess is why I wanted to be part of this. To say that a lot of people were punished who shouldn't have been, especially with what came after.

AGATHA SMITH

For what it's worth, I will be the first to admit that the rune they found on that poor girl does mean something along the lines of... of influence, or power. Using their metric of 'good' and 'bad' witchcraft, I agree that it is dark, quite dark. Certainly darker than anything Marisol would know about—but of course, who cares about the particularities of any individual's witchcraft when there are witches to be burned? Their story—that Marisol wanted to punish the town for... I don't know. Keeping that boy from her? Was that it?— you can see how flawed it was that I can't even connect the dots logically. I find it hard to believe anyone could, except she was such an easy target.

RHEEM ROSHAN

Marisol was alienated from the town from the beginning. Most of that wasn't her choice, but definitely some of it was a result of her being a real loner type. She kept her distance. She spent time with us, with that boy, instead of going to church with people the town might have deemed *acceptable*. When the detectives started sniffing around the farm I tried to advise her, tried to point out what was happening, that she had to stop skulking around with that Barrett boy because her antisocial tendencies were only making it worse.

I think, though, she wouldn't have heard a word of it, even if she'd seen it the way I had. I'm not the psychic one, you understand. That was Rose. So when I said it, you could see Marisol wasn't listening. She was looking so hard for the magic of it all that she didn't see the writing on the wall was spelled out in plain English.

Within days of the body being discovered, Marisol Farrow would become the prime suspect for the murder of Serena May, owing to her occult involvement and what became painted as a love triangle, with Marisol Farrow being the aggressor. With the case so public and the sentiment against Farrow so deeply entrenched in the narrative of protecting the children, the New Blossom Police Department were pressured to compress the timing of their investigation, leading to her arrest within weeks.

JAMES MORRISON

What was our story? Honestly, it didn't seem like we had much choice in the matter. The investigation kept leading back to the same person. In that sense, the story told itself.

†

THE CRUX OF THE CASE AGAINST MARISOL FARROW was a simple one. Prejudice in the abstract. The investigation conducted over the death of Serena May was in fact so rudimentary and biased that the truth behind the Barrett brothers was not revealed until after the trial had already concluded. By then, Marisol Farrow had already been convicted for the murder of Serena May, and it was not until months later that the truth of the Barrett brothers came to light.

EMILY NEWSOM

The whole town was shaken up once again, I remember. Things had barely gone back to normal since the trial and then there we were again, the subject of more national news. It was really very confusing to even hear about the Barrett brothers, who'd essentially disappeared into the night—first one, then the other. They already felt like such a footnote in the town's tragedy at the time, but it was only a few months, I think, before some P.I. showed up looking for them.

RHEEM ROSHAN

The private investigator was Rose's idea. I was so done by then, I wanted to leave the farm and never come back. I did just that, shortly after. But I did help Rose and Rainne hire the P.I., because they wanted answers. They thought it might help Marisol, but I already had the answers I needed: people are fundamentally terrible beings. Plenty of so-called *good neighbors* were happy to let her rot in there if that's what it took to punish someone, anyone, for what happened to Serena May. But Rose and Rainne, they knew they didn't have a whole lot of time left. They wanted to leave the earth greener than they found it, I suppose. A whole lot less scorched, anyway. And they were my sisters, so I helped them.

FRED LEWIN
Private Investigator

Truthfully I'm not surprised the information I discovered about the so-called Barrett brothers didn't come to light during the trial. You learn very quickly in my business that most cops are looking for easy answers, pieces that neatly fit. They're not looking to find out that the older one—his name was actually Joshua, yeah—was nearing thirty. He'd already pulled the same trick on a number of other towns, usually as a solo act. The other one, his name was Rob. No actual relation. Early twenties, not seventeen or eighteen or whatever he claimed he was. Just a young-looking face is all. He showed up a few jobs in. The tricky thing, oddly, is they might have gotten away with it—well, arguably they *did* get away with it, if you don't count the bar fight that killed Joshua—but anyway, if they'd just kept up their little traveling circus they might never have gotten caught. Instead they decided to settle down with the May family, and it was clear that one of them wasn't very happy about that.

One thing for sure? That story Joshua told, the thing about being abused by satanic witches or whatnot; his torrid backstory, his and Rob's—that wasn't true. Well, it was partially true. He threw the scent off himself that way, calling himself a victim and taking advantage of people who wanted to help. But in fact he was a practicing witch, same as the girl he put behind bars. Worse than her, given everything.

By the end of 1991, New Blossom had discovered the truth about Joshua Barrett: that it was he, in fact, who was a practicing witch, whose own coven had cast him out for exploring the so-called dark arts. Born Joshua Reagan in San Antonio, Texas, the golden boy of the New Blossom teen showcase was actually a chameleonic adult who had a history of capitalizing on the kindness of strangers.

FRED LEWIN

In terms of my investigation—which was sadly much too late—his downfall was his memorability. He could change, blending just enough to fit in, but he couldn't quite disappear. People remembered him as being charming, persuasive. People *remembered* him, which for a con man is already quite a flaw.

LAUREL MAY

I think learning the truth about Joshua was the last straw for my mother's sanity. She became inconsolable, first, and then quiet after that, and she died a long, slow, quiet death a few years later. For me, it was never really over. The trial ended and it seemed like things would go back to normal, but I just couldn't shake the feeling that something was wrong. I brought it up with Joshua several times before he left and— *[Chokes up.]* Sorry. I'm sorry. I just can't help thinking that so much of this is my fault, you know? I let Serena leave the house after that fight. I never told anyone the truth about Joshua, about the way he was so controlling and cold. I kept quiet about what he was really like behind closed doors because I was so desperate to look a certain way to the rest of the town. And honestly, looking back, it's possible I couldn't even *see* the truth about Joshua at the time—I wanted so badly for him to be the person I made him out to be. But in the end he was a lot of things I never mentioned to anyone. Brittle and angry. Quick-tempered. He never laid a hand on me, true, but I honestly think that's because he didn't care enough about me to want me to hurt. He wanted *Marisol Farrow* to hurt—and I guess he wanted Serena to hurt, too. All for a little bit of greed.

I can't believe I fell for it. Well, actually I can. I was a little fool, spoiled and selfish and—now that I see it for what it was—terribly, desperately lonely. Joshua was right to prey on me, with my parents who failed to protect me and my sister from the kind of people who could say the right things, the *Christian* things. Ironic, isn't it? They wanted someone to blame and there he was, living in our house all along.

Shortly after the trial's conclusion, the young man known as Jeremy Barrett quietly disappeared, never returning to New Blossom High School and forgoing graduation. Joshua, perhaps sensing a reckoning soon to come, also disappeared.

FRED LEWIN

It turned out Joshua Reagan—that was his real name, Reagan, not Barrett—was killed in a bar fight in Chicago. Hardly weeks later. He kept a diary, which was the strangest thing of all. He wrote mostly in code, mind you, but it wasn't difficult to unravel. He was angry with Rob, the guy called Jeremy. I got the impression that the two of them had gone through hell together somehow, but there was no telling the specifics.

[When asked why not:] Oh, because Robert Bona, alias Jeremy Barrett, disappeared off the face of the earth once he left New Blossom, Illinois. Joshua knew something of what happened, that's for sure. He knew Jeremy's loyalty was wavering—

knew from that final conversation that Serena understood more about their relationship than she revealed to her sister or to anyone else. It was clear he'd done something that haunted him right up to the end, and I think we all know by now what that was.

Listen, I know you've got lots of questions and you're looking for proof, but I got none. All I have is my gut, you understand? I've been in this business a long time. I understand why the courts didn't feel that anything I produced for the Roshans was enough evidence to overturn that witch's conviction. The likely culprit was already dead. If you ask me, it was obvious Joshua did it. Major anger issues, control issues. Why kill Serena May? Because she knew something, she knew the truth, maybe she taunted him over it. Because the real simple fact of the matter was that he was losing his partner-in-crime, and that's an old story. He took it out on all of them, if you ask me. Killed Serena. Put Marisol behind bars. Went after his partner and killed him.

Jealousy. It's like love but meaner. And believe me, it always ends in tears.

LAUREL MAY

The moment I realized it was Joshua, I started the campaign to overturn Marisol's conviction. I couldn't do much while my parents were alive—they were certain it was her, that they'd put a witch behind bars, and I think they needed that to have any peace about losing Serena—but once they passed away, I got a better lawyer. Using my inheritance, we filed appeal after appeal. I felt it was my responsibility, my doing. The way he disappeared, everything we found out about him after... It was so obvious. It was so *obvious*, and I couldn't live with myself. Eventually I went to law school and took on Marisol's case myself, though as you know we've made very little progress until now. Our next chance to appeal is coming up and we're very hopeful. Very hopeful.

Still, without a better story— *[Sighs.]* Damn Joshua. You'd think after everything he'd have at least done me the favor of writing it more explicitly in his diary: *oh yeah it was me by the way, Marisol Farrow is innocent.* But now Serena is gone and Joshua is gone, and there's no one left to tell the truth.

And you know, I did try to find Jeremy. Or whatever his name is. Was. He's gone, though, so I guess I— Oh, you do know his name? Right, of course, Bona, that's it. Just didn't seem to fit him, but—

Wait. Bona. That's—

What did you say your name was, again?

†

I SUPPOSE NOW IS AS GOOD A TIME as any to pull aside the veil and explain that while this is not my first true crime retrospective covering the paranormal crimes of the nineties, this one in particular is a bit personal for me. You see, my father, Edward Bona, is a witch. As am I. And my uncle, Robert Bona, was a witch as well, and a member of our local coven until his excommunication at the age of twenty, after which time he disappeared.

My father made me promise not to investigate this case while he was alive, but as he passed away last November, it soon became necessary for me to find the answers my father never got. What exactly happened to my uncle Rob, who was my father's favorite brother? My father always described him as an odd comic, a talented mimic. Someone gravely misunderstood, in my father's view. "He was never trying to do anything bad, Cassidy," my father told me on his deathbed. "He was just interested, that's all. I know he was. He wanted to know things, to really understand them, to see what witchcraft could look like beyond the constraints of our little group. Not to use it for ill, obviously. Never. But they cast him out for being curious, and now he's gone."

Knowing intimate details of Jeremy Barrett's real identity made him much easier to find, a feat that neither Laurel May nor even Fred Lewin, the Roshan's P.I., were able to manage. In the end I dug him up in a tiny beach town in Southern California, where he wasn't Jeremy Barrett anymore, nor was he Robert Bona.

ELI WESTMAN
Pastor, Hope Flight Parish

Hi. This is... strange, isn't it? *[Laughs.]* Usually when I do these things I'm not talking about... what was it you said? Witches?

The man formerly known as Jeremy Barrett is now Pastor Eli Westman, a self-professed non-denominational pastor with an impressive following of tireless believers. Pastor Westman is now the shepherd for what he calls his "flock," which consists of over four hundred thousand people—among them several celebrities. He has been head of the Hope Flight parish for the last twenty-nine years after rehabilitation following a severe car accident.

ELI WESTMAN

I'm afraid I don't remember anything before the early aughts. I've been advised to move slowly with this type of thing, given the trauma. I was hospitalized for quite a bit of time.

According to his medical records, which begin in 1992, this is unquestionably true. Eli Westman was, for a time, John Doe, who spent several months in Cedars-Sinai hospital in Los Angeles in the 1990s. Since then, Westman has been in contact with noted psychotherapist Dr. Phillip Gitan, who specializes in long-term memory loss.

DR. PHILLIP GITAN, PSY.D.
Psychiatrist

I would caution against speaking with Eli about anything too personal. The mind is labyrinthine that way, with little fractures for old aches and pains. It might be good for Eli, it might not—I can't say for certain. He's made terrific progress in the time since his hospitalization, but even so. It sounds as if he was in an emotionally abusive relationship with this Joshua Reagan person you mentioned, which would confirm my preliminary diagnoses. Perhaps they bonded over similar beliefs, and then their paths diverged and took a turn for the tragic. It happens. Ultimately, I believe Eli to be a highly sensitive person whose brain is protecting itself by blocking out the trauma of his past.

Dr. Gitan seems adamant that however convenient Pastor Westman's memory loss may seem to be, it is genuine. As for Eli Westman himself, he seems good-natured about the whole thing. His bemusement over who he might have been is detached, even distant.

ELI WESTMAN

We do look a bit alike, don't we, you and I? No offense to you, of course. *[Laughs.]* But of course I'm thrilled to hear from you, regardless of the circumstances. What a blessing to have my family returned to me.

When I mention the Serena May case to Westman, he reacts with minimal emotion—the familiarity of someone who has heard of something but has no personal connection, much like myself and the golden age of MTV.

ELI WESTMAN

Of course I'm familiar with the case. I'm afraid I can't speak to any of the events.

And he can't, of course. Jeremy Barrett was never called to the stand during the trial. Even those of his parish who were actively following the May case have no recollection of seeing their current pastor, though it's hard to deny that Jeremy Barrett and Eli Westman are the same man.

EMILY NEWSOM

Here's a yearbook from 1991 where you can see his senior portrait, and... yes, there he is, right here! *[She points to a picture of Jeremy Barrett in the background of the May trial.]* Yes, I definitely think this is him. How strange.

[When asked if she believes the theory that it was Joshua Barrett who killed Serena May, not Marisol Farrow:] Yes, I do believe that. Joshua Barrett was... magnetic. Very much the type. Sad, though. So sad for Marisol. And so strange! Why kill Serena May, you know what I mean? It's such a ludicrous story, him being some devil-worshipping witch, that he could have simply denied it. And trying to kill his own partner with a car? Why kill one person with a curse and then hit another one with a car...? Seems odd to me, but I suppose we aren't meant to comprehend that sort of evil, are we? *[Shrugs.]* At least now we can let it rest.

LAUREL MAY

It does make sense in retrospect that Joshua had quite an influence over him. He was that way with everyone.

[When asked if her theory is that Joshua masterminded the murder of her sister and subsequent near-fatal accident with Pastor Eli Westman:] Yes, that's my theory. And I may not be able to prove every piece of that theory, but I've been working for years to make sure Marisol eventually goes free. And Joshua had a reason, didn't he, for not wanting the truth revealed? And if Serena knew it— Well, yes, I suppose that means Serena might have known the truth about Jeremy as well. And Marisol would have known too, so— *[She pauses, troubled.]* But still. I don't think it would have been Jeremy. It was Joshua. *[She nods.]* Yes, it must have been Joshua. Looking back, it all makes sense.

†

IT WASN'T EASY TO BREAK THE NEWS to Marisol about Jeremy, whom we'll now call Pastor Westman for the sake of clarity. It's obvious that she's been haunted for some time about his disappearance from her life. When I initially asked if she had any interest in seeing him, Marisol paused for several seconds to organize her thoughts.

MARISOL FARROW

It seems pointless, doesn't it? Talking to him now. He won't remember anything we shared. Even if I felt angry or, I don't know, *wronged*, I'd get no absolution from whoever he's become. But— *[Pause.]* I guess part of me has gotten by this long on the belief that we were star-crossed in some way. That this happened to me only because I was so absurdly lucky to have met him, to have had the brief time with him that I did.

I think sometimes in my darker moments it occurs to me that the universe may not actually be kind. That some people are marked for harder paths. And you know, if that's true, then even a moment of what I had with J— sorry, with... Pastor Westman. *[Pauses.]* Even a moment of that was beautiful. So beautiful that it gets me through this, keeps me going. So yes, I do want to see him. Even just to see his face, to know who he became. I think that would bring a lot of joy to me, whatever happens on this next appeal.

Marisol sounds resigned about the future. Laurel May is hopeful, but she's right that trying to achieve an overturned conviction on a claim of poor police work that played on prejudice and paranoia is, in the end, just another version of a story.

So this morning, before Marisol enters the courtroom yet again, I have arranged for Pastor Eli Westman to visit her. There may not be any justice for Serena May, nor any satisfaction for my late father's lost brother, but at least, in this, there can be something. Thirty years of Marisol Farrow's private mystery can end.

†

AUDIO TRANSCRIPT:

MARISOL FARROW

I... Sorry. *[Clears throat.]* I thought for such a long time about what to say, but now that I'm seeing you in front of me...

ELI WESTMAN

I understand. This must be very strange for you.

MARISOL FARROW

It is. *[Laughs.]* Strange is an understatement.

ELI WESTMAN

I do want to apologize, Ms. Farrow. For not remembering whatever happened between us. I wish I could say there was... some spark, or an inkling, or—

MARISOL FARROW

[Emotionally:] You were magic, do you understand that? We. *We* were magic. I'll never not believe that.

ELI WESTMAN

Ms. Farrow, my faith is—

MARISOL FARROW

I know you think you know who you are. *What* you are. I know that must be your reality now, and I understand. I've seen a few of your services and... Well, I— You've clearly been incredibly successful—

ELI WESTMAN

I've been very blessed.

MARISOL FARROW

Yes. Right. Blessed. *[Pause.]* But still, part of me feels so sure that if you could just—

ELI WESTMAN

I hope you find peace, Ms. Farrow. Whatever happens from here. I do hope you find a way to move forward.

MARISOL FARROW

[Long pause.] You know, it's funny. You told me nearly everything. How you and Joshua were never brothers, how he made the whole story up. You seemed so frightened of him. But I've read the journal pages.

ELI WESTMAN

I'm sorry, Ms. Farrow, I really don't—

MARISOL FARROW

He seems so... sad, in the end. So alone. And I don't know much about whatever happened between the two of you, but I do know loneliness. I also know guilt, having been here for thirty years. I know remorse. I know the *lack* of remorse. But this isn't a man with no feelings. It isn't the voice of someone who's just gotten away with a crime, either. And it's strange, isn't it? That he would be killed? In a bar fight, of all things. He wasn't really like that. You even told me he wasn't like that.

ELI WESTMAN

Really, I can't—

MARISOL FARROW

It made me think maybe it... it wasn't him.

ELI WESTMAN

Ms. Farrow, it isn't for us to know His plans—

MARISOL FARROW

Isn't it, though? Don't some things make *more* sense? Serena May, she had been following Jeremy around. Following *you.* I saw her myself. She might have known something, might have understood more than I did, and—

ELI WESTMAN

I hope you find peace, Ms. Farrow, I really do—

MARISOL FARROW

[Quietly:] I think it was you, Jeremy.

ELI WESTMAN

What?

MARISOL FARROW

[Louder:] I think it was you. It was, wasn't it? You can tell me. It won't make any difference except to me.

ELI WESTMAN

Are you... I'm sorry, is she... well? Is she feeling well, I mean? I worry, maybe this is too stressful. She's been through so much. Is there some sort of medication she should be taking, or—?

MARISOL FARROW

[Laughing.] Oh my god. Oh my *god.* It really was you all along, Jeremy!

ELI WESTMAN

I really have to go. Is this— is there someone here who can take her, or...?

MARISOL FARROW

It was you! This whole time, it was you! *[Crying]* You did this, Jeremy. It was you... It was you, IT WAS YOU, IT WAS YOU—

ELI WESTMAN

Can someone please see to her? Poor thing. She's clearly not well. *[He leans forward and attempts to administer a blessing. Marisol looks as if she's been struck.]* Marisol, please, be well. Okay? I don't think this has done either of us any good. I'm so sorry I wasn't able to help, and I'd like to make sure she's comfortable, that she's taken care of—

MARISOL FARROW

[Sobbing] IT WAS YOU, IT WAS YOU— DON'T TOUCH ME, LET GO OF ME—

In the moment they take Marisol away, I catch sight of something on Eli's arm. It's a tiny symbol, and I ask him about it. He seems distracted; gives me a fleeting smile. It's for luck, he says. I agree it must be very lucky. He is very lucky, really, to have survived such a fatal accident. To have no memory of a crime that has haunted another woman's life. To have lost his partner. To have gained his flock.

His smile in return is not easy. It is the smile of someone who has crawled a long way over broken bones.

Later that day, he delivers a sermon to over a hundred thousand parishioners, most of whom have paid for the right to be present while he speaks. I attend. I listen. But what sticks with me is what he told me just before we parted ways. It is the same thing my father once said to me. It led me here, to what I do. To who I am.

"Cassidy," the man who was once my Uncle Rob told me. "The luckiest person in any room is always the one who is telling the story."

And then he walked through the door and was gone.

TOXIC (NOVEMBER 2020 - JANUARY 2021)

AN UNDERPAID AND OVERWORKED CLASSICS ACADEMICIAN/BARTENDER lives a typical cosmopolitan lifestyle of exorbitant rent, nihilistic brunches, and perennially charging her vibrator, until a chance match on a feminist dating app drives her to Will, a stereotypical start-up bro whose washboard abs initially make up for his obvious disinterest in commitment. However, after an unmemorable one-night stand, Will reveals himself to have hidden layers—or perhaps just one hidden layer.

Is Will the typical Jekyll and Hyde archetype of the modern dating scene, or is it possible he's the host for something entirely . . . else?

PART I: HE'S JUST NOT THAT INTO YOU

It is not a very good time to be a bartender. There are days when I feel relatively convinced it's never a good time to be a bartender, psychologically and metaphysically and perhaps also allegorically speaking, but usually this is not a pressing financial concern. After all, I started bartending at the Ophelia Club—a preeminent society venue for the matriarchs of the Fashionable Upper Crust—as a method of paying my exorbitant grad school tuition. Initially I planned only to work there until the feeble doctoral stipend kicked in, but then I found myself in the lucky position of being arbitrarily promoted to a rather cushy timeslot. There was a time when tips alone at the Gardenia Brunch would more than pay for my monthly rent (in my slovenly flat shared with three other worker bees—Meredith, a nanny whose charges are currently holidaying somewhere in France; Rae, a musician currently relying heavily on her OnlyFans page; and Lea, whose much older boyfriend is leaving his wife "any day now") so I obviously kept at it, since *you* try being a Classics major in a world oversaturated with impoverished academics. There are basically only two feasible roads, education or research, and despite my working knowledge of French and German in addition to the requisite Latin and Greek, I don't have a lot of... shall we say, marketable skills. Though I can make a mean Bellini.

Anyway, back to the point, which is that while the world has mostly returned to normal, the vast majority of my most generous tippers remain scattered elsewhere; largely the Hamptons or the Catskills, but some more permanently absconded to their cabins in Sun Valley or ranches in Montana (family properties, you know how it is). My bank account, usually cushy enough to afford my little hobby of eating and drinking in order to keep myself alive, has dwindled to near-ramen rates. With classes still taking place online, they've canceled the seminar I was supposed to teach (an unusually radical one I'd been ecstatic to be assigned in the first place, about the role of the sexually emancipated woman in Greek tragedies) and cost me that extra bit of... Well, never quite Saturday avocado toasts, but definitely Thursday afternoon lattes.

To make matters worse, Andrew stayed in Savannah to care for his ailing mother instead of returning for the winter term. (For the record: she's fine. She just has a son that's a softhearted, nearsighted Classics academic.) "We really shouldn't be seeing each other anyway," Andrew informed me over FaceTime the last time I tried engaging a bit of a digital get-down, which even then was well past the danger zone as far as person-to-person contamination. "It's not the end of the world. Don't you have a vibrator?"

"Yes, Andrew, I have a vibrator," I sigh. Andrew has never been entirely of this species. "Astonishingly, that's not quite sufficient. Don't you miss me?"

"I really should be going, I have a Zoom lesson in ten minutes," was Andrew's oddly direct reply. Normally he's never so forthcoming.

This—in addition to the constant presence of Meredith's boyfriend Damien, an attractive but fundamentally vile human being who sets my loins afire—has led me to what I can only call "The Apps" in something of a forlorn, misanthropic tone, because of course I would not be here if not for a supreme urgency I'd rather not confess in detail.

Horniness, I have to say, is rather unjustly reserved for men—there's something about the shamelessness of the word, "horny," which does not seem to have a female equivalent. Where else can we express the exigency of our craving? But of course these are not things one can say on The Apps, because social convention demands the mutual drama of concealing our intent. (What is female arousal, if it even exists, if it does not lead to marriage and eventual babies...?) Which is not to say my account isn't filled to the brim with unsolicited phalluses, but while a person can certainly *want* sex without connection, one does not have to settle for it with the sort of man who proudly—nay, shamelessly—unleashes his dick as some sort of exceptional prize. So yes, there must be some pretense involved.

My simple pleasures? The Apps inquire. *Reading a book*, I say, a fairly straightforward answer, which means inevitably that seven men will challenge me as to what book ("Have you read *The Stranger?* It's by Camus, he's a French philosopher, not sure if you've heard of him") while an additional three will say something pornographic and a fourth will ever-so-slyly tell me that he *could* say something pornographic, but won't (wink, wink). Which leaves the genuinely curious, at least half of which will quiz me as to my "actual" knowledge of literature (a very good indication that they, like their Victorian forebears, are threatened by my emasculating literacy) while the remaining, save for one or two, will simply lose interest.

Today, there was only one who did not.

To Will's credit: he is very handsome. Per his surprisingly accurate portfolio of curated images, he has Henry Cavill blue eyes (and Henry Cavill thighs) beneath sun-kissed blond hair and ample, nearly-not-lying 6'2 or so height, plus a strong, masculine chin. To his detriment: he is moderately well-traveled, which means there have been a plethora of dull anecdotes to sift through. Ultimately, it was his availability (and Vile Damien's continued shirtlessness) that won out, which is what brought me to his apartment. Well, more accurately it brought me to the little pop-up cocktail restaurant patio they've set up in the alley, which was relatively charming in a Potential

Boyfriend™ way until Will *happened* to mention that he only lived up the block.

What can't be underestimated or misrepresented was how little his presumptuousness and/or lack of effort put me off. After all, we are talking about the rare presence of a living, breathing, hormone-secreting and—doubly fortunate—*interested* human man. It's been months up to this point, truthfully, and my brain cannot possibly make room for four written languages in addition to impulse control.

Will does not have a roommate, I do not have a viable alternative. The math is staggeringly uncomplex.

†

I once read the statistics on how many men orgasm during a one-night stand versus women. Presumably most people would guess there was a severe orgasm gap, somewhere around the wealth gap of pre-Revolution France, and they'd be right. Surprise! While close to 100% of men will finish on a singular sexual encounter, only 10% of women do. All of which is to say, sociologically speaking there's good reason for women to seek out relationships as opposed to casual sex—and despite my best efforts, I am unfortunately not going to count among the anomalies tonight.

"That was great," says Will, who has already flopped onto his back and closed his eyes.

"Yeah, it was... fun," I attempt to say with enthusiasm, because it did start out reasonably well. I'd forgotten how much I missed the sound a man makes when you kiss him, all low grunts and helpless groans that make you feel powerful, or at least competent. But presumably I put too much effort into showmanship and not enough into expediting my own arousal.

"Mm." Will turns to look at me. "You can stay if you want," he says, "but just so you know, I gotta be up real early for a meeting. No rush, though," he adds.

"I... oh." That's an invitation to please leave immediately if I've ever heard one. "Right, yeah, that's fine."

"We should hang out again sometime," he offers noncommittally.

"Erm, sure," I say, not that it matters. "I'm just gonna, you know, clean up..."

He's not listening. He's definitely asleep.

Men. The post-orgasm coma is among Andrew's favorite things, which reminds me that I either miss him desperately or miss the fact that he could make an effort to engage with me clitorically. No, no, it's the first one.

I squint for my purse and feel around blindly for my underwear, which is obviously kicked somewhere under the bed. Gathering my things in both hands, I locate my dress and shoes, fumbling into the bathroom and surveying the toilet doubtfully before deciding to go the route of awkward squat. I manage with some difficulty to remove my phone from my purse simultaneously, pulling up Andrew's message box with my free hand.

Miss you. We should talk soon. xx

The message shows a read receipt, and then three dots. I wait, setting the phone on the sink while he types his response, but then the dots disappear. I wash my hands carefully, drying my fingers individually, with meticulous attention. Nothing.

Goddamn it. He's leaving me on read, and to make things worse, I'm missing a sock. That's what I get for not wearing better escape shoes.

I resign myself to the necessity of returning to Will's bedroom with a stifled groan, spotting the recalcitrant sock near the door. I snatch it up, glancing at the bed, but to my surprise Will is no longer in it.

Hm. Odd.

I step into the living room, peering skittishly around until I spot him standing beside a vintage bar, fully dressed. I hadn't noticed the bar earlier, but it's built around a surprisingly gorgeous piece of furniture, a mahogany mid-century sideboard with brass fixtures that I wouldn't have guessed to be to his taste. Clearly it's well-stocked, too, though that also seems odd. At dinner, Will only drank light beer, which I attributed to his six-pack (that, at least, was not misrepresented in the slightest).

"Oh," I say, and Will looks up, the expression on his face unreadably placid as he gives a silver cocktail shaker a vigorous turn. "I... thought you were sleeping."

Will's wearing a pair of expensive-looking joggers now, though he wore jeans to dinner. Still, he looks... cleaner, oddly. More put together somehow, though I can't identify why.

"You're a bit different from the usual, aren't you?" says Will, his voice somewhat deeper, and accented by something slightly foreign that definitely wasn't there before. "I suppose it's too much to hope that he's actually gotten more discerning."

This from the guy who mispronounced *arugula* twice. "I beg your pardon?"

"Are you really a bartender?" Will pours the contents of the shaker smoothly into the glass, not looking at me, and I feel a familiar bristle of distaste for the way my accomplishments are so easily undercut by the way I earn my living.

"I bartend, yes," I force through my teeth, "though as I said, I'm also a doctoral candidate—"

"Ah, so that's why he thinks you're some kind of librarian. I knew that seemed odd." Will looks up at me, gauging me for a moment before asking,

"Would you like one? Though I should warn you, I am particular. I prefer my martinis with equal parts sweet and dry vermouth."

There's absolutely no way the man I just slept with knows how to make a perfect martini. No man who does can ever prevent himself from saying so, much like men who are scotch drinkers, or crossfit enthusiasts, or vegan. "Since when? And wait," I realize belatedly. "What do you mean some kind of librarian?"

"Don't take it personally," Will says with a shrug. "There's very little he understands, and admittedly he did not have the requisite interest to contemplate it further. I'm afraid you'll likely not be receiving a call, if in fact that's what you want." Will removes a second martini glass, which appears to also be 1950s vintage, and offers it to me. "Are you staying for a nightcap?"

"I thought—" This is very bewildering behavior, considering he seemed eager for me to leave just a matter of minutes ago. "I thought you, um—"

"What is your actual area of study?" Will asks me, pouring a second glass. "Something to do with books, obviously, but that could be anything. Especially given his general comprehension about the world. By the way, whatever he told you about his start-up, you should know it's rather a non-starter," Will remarks with a low chuckle. I still can't place the accent, but it's definitely there, which makes no sense for a man who was born in Denver. "It's a clever way of saying his wealth is inherited. It used to be the artists," he adds, ostensibly to himself. "The bittersweet torment of relying on mummy's money, that sort of thing."

"Who is 'he'?" I ask, and Will offers me the martini he's poured for me.

"My host," he assures me.

I stare at him but accept the glass, probably out of habit.

"Are you saying...?"

"Not to rush you," Will says, "but either we can dwell on it or we can move on." He scrutinizes me for a moment, taking a slow sip. "Judging by the look on your face when you walked in," he murmurs, "I have my doubts you'll be leaving here satisfied if you do so now. So, we can have a friendly drink that turns... perhaps more friendly," Will suggests, "or you're welcome to go home and wait to see if he responds."

"Who?" I ask against my will.

"Whoever you're expecting to return your message," Will says, pointing to my phone. The screen has gone blank, and dizzily I frown at him. "He won't, but I doubt you need me to tell you that."

"Are you mansplaining my life back to me?" I say with a distant sense of indignation, though discomfort prompts me to sip the martini in my hand. It's actually profoundly good, top shelf gin for sure, which gives me the odd sensation of wondering (again) where I might have been tonight if not for Vile Damien, Meredith's obscenely hot boyfriend. He's always at our place rifling through our food supply, although ha, joke's on him, we never have any unless Meredith's made some. We're all just savages subsisting in the same dilapidated ecosystem, but anyway he was shirtless and the die was cast.

"Technically I don't subscribe to any gender, but point taken," says Will, observing my reaction to his cocktail. "Anyway, may I presume classical studies? I can't imagine why else anyone would be so taken with Menander."

I choke on my martini at the reference. "What?"

"It's not mansplaining so much as unavoidable observation," he says, and takes a seat on the sofa, patting the spot beside him. "Sit, would you?"

I can't possibly be drunk enough to have hallucinated this. Can I? I sniff the martini with some degree of belated suspicion, but why would a man who's already slept with me feel the need to drug me?

"I'm drinking from the same shaker," Will reminds me, pointedly taking a sip from his own glass.

I collapse numbly beside him. Is he reading my mind? Impossible. "There's no way you know Menander," I say.

"Why," Will asks, "because all but one play was destroyed? He was rather popular in his time."

"I mean, I *know* that," I mutter, because vocationally speaking, I do. I sip the martini again, astonished anew at how smooth it is. "But you... you're—"

"An idiot, I know," Will laments with a sigh, crossing one leg over the other. He didn't sit like that at dinner, preferring instead to spread out so that his feet shoved into mine beneath the table. "But unfortunately," Will adds, "his other attributes are so very compelling."

"How often do you go to the gym?" I ask him, still nose-first in my rapidly emptying glass. It's a very, very good martini, and I don't normally even like vermouth.

"Oh, daily. You can touch if you'd like," Will says, lifting his shirt so that my gaze drops instantly to the contours of his abs. "Seems like maybe you didn't get your fill earlier."

"Not really," I admit, reaching out to run the tips of my fingers over his muscles, which contract gently at my touch. "It's," I begin, and swallow. "Very... impressive."

Will looks at me, amused. "Your pupils are dilated."

"Well, I don't know what you expect," I mumble, indecipherable thoughts of longing beginning to populate my addled mind as I stroke the lines that shoot up from his hips. The motion floods me with a carnal form of glee until I'm reminded, sourly, of my *many* inadequacies. (The circumference of my thighs, my general addiction to cereal, the disdain from Vile Damien and of course the ambivalence from Emotionally Distant Andrew. The time stamp on his unanswered message mocks me from my palm, which is now clutching both my phone and the base of my martini glass. Fucking Andrew.)

"Interesting." Will turns to face me, eyeing my expression with abject curiosity—the first genuine interest I've seen from him all night, come to think of it. "You think your desire is some... perversion to be ashamed of?"

"Hm?" I look up, dazed. "No, it's just that's... no, men are, you know, allowed to feel, um. The point is I'm obviously a feminist, so—"

He shifts to his feet so suddenly he startles me into gasping. "What," I half-squeak, floundering once again when he positions himself in front of me; very nearly on top of me. "I," I attempt, but when no further vocabulary comes to mind, he reaches out and removes the glass from my hand, placing it on—gasp—a *coaster.* Then he does the same with my phone, lowering himself slowly to his knees.

"May I?" he asks, trailing the tips of his fingers from my calf to the hem of my dress.

By this point words have long since failed me, so I give a voiceless nod. He peels back the fabric, brushing his lips to the inside of my knee while his eyes find mine.

"I promise you will enjoy this," he says. "Conveniently, so will I."

And though I should have every reason not to believe him, the sound I make when his mouth puts itself to use is hardly recognizable as my own.

†

My eyes snap open to find I'm once again in Will's bed; an uncanny episode of déjà vu. Briefly I contemplate the likelihood of some sort of time loop, only that wouldn't be possible. Light leaks in from the blinds, and this time my body is noticeably heavy, positively boneless. I am, as the poets say, well-fucked.

"Oh," says Will from beside me. "I thought you'd gone home."

I squint at him, struggling to sit upright. "You... what?"

"It's just that I have an early meeting," he says, rolling out his neck and letting what I can only call a belch escape into his fist. "Sorry," he says, turning to look at me. "Damn, I'm exhausted."

I would imagine so; he certainly kept me up. "We had a late night," I offer in semi-apology.

He looks at me quizzically, frowning. "What time was it? Like, ten?"

"Umm..." At the point he had me on the kitchen counter it was already well past two in the morning, and that was hardly the evening's denouement. "Well—"

"Sorry," he says again, conveniently losing interest. "But I gotta take a shower, so..."

"Right. Yeah, sorry." I reach out for my clothes, but they're in the living room. "Right, well, all my stuff's out there, so—"

"Nothing I haven't seen before," he calls over his shoulder, disappearing into the bathroom as I unexpectedly wince. Not that I've never done the walk of shame (or whatever this is) before, but it's still a bit of a shock.

I creep into the living room, half-expecting to find some sort of cyclone of destruction in the wake of my debaucherous aims, but the martini glasses have been washed, dried, and carefully replaced. My dress is draped neatly over the back of the living room armchair, my shoes paired beside it, my underwear and socks discreetly placed beside my purse. There's a note with a line of spindly handwriting: *phone is on the charger.*

I glance around, bemused, and spot my phone plugged into the outlet, sitting cheerfully on the kitchen counter. I dress quickly, a little stunned by all this unprecedented thoughtfulness, and then the toilet flushes, the bathroom door opening behind me. "Hey, thanks for this," I call to Will, who doesn't pause to see that I'm referencing my fully-charged phone.

"Yeah, for sure. I'll call you," he yells back, then the bathroom door shuts again, the shower running by the time I slip out the front door.

✝

"Babe, we discussed this," says Meredith. "One night stands are *not* a cute look anymore. We're not getting any younger, and I mean, let's be real," she sighs, lips pursed. "If he gets it too easily, he won't want it anymore."

"She's right," says Damien, that too-handsome ghoul, and of course he's shirtless. Not that I didn't get my fill of gentlemen abs last night, but still. It's really uncharitable for him to exist like this when the last conversation we had was about how female comedians are annoying. ("I don't know, they're just not funny," he said, unlike—presumably—him. Vom.)

Damien's in the academic sphere as well, as he's just gotten an MFA in creative writing and, worse, an award for his paper on otherness. He is Korean and Italian and believes the Asian male deserves a more prominent place in the Suffering Olympics. (He is probably not wrong, but I just honestly hate to give it to him.)

"This one made me wait five dates," Damien adds, smacking a hand on Meredith's rear. She giggles, as romantically delighted with this as if he's presented her with a flower crown of wild daisies. Or a sonnet. Which he technically *can write*! But I digress.

"You'll notice that Mer here is neither engaged nor married," I point out, because Meredith will be annoyed and forgive me while Damien will be annoyed and leave, which are consequences I am overwhelmingly fine with.

"Well," Meredith leaps in frantically, "nobody's in a *rush*. I'm just saying that commitment takes practice. Right, babe?" she says to Damien, slipping her arm around his waist. He allows it, but I can tell his eyes are frantically searching for an exit while he takes a final sip from his coffee cup. (The milk foamer is out, which means Meredith made him that latte. It's probably filled with maple oat milk and love. God, he repulses me.)

"Yeah," Damien says vacantly. "Well hey, I better get in the shower if I'm going to make it to that meeting with my advisor."

Oh no, how sad. "Bye," I say, reaching for his cup once he disappears into the bathroom and taking a sip, groaning a little at how good it is. For someone who makes beverages as often as I do, you'd think I'd have a talent for this. And maybe I do, but what I lack is Meredith's effort. "Why does he always shower at our place?" I ask her, savoring the last dregs of the latte despite Damien's probably vile backwash. "Is he homeless?"

"Okay, *you* are a dick," Meredith hisses, rounding on me once the shower is running and Damien is in no danger of overhearing her real personality. "I *told* you, he's got a whole thing about marriage, okay? His parents divorced and then got back together and, like—" She cuts herself off, sputtering in barely suppressed hysteria. "I'm *working* on it!"

"Meredith," I begin sagely, "if Damien doesn't know your domestic aspirations by now, then he clearly doesn't know you at all," because aside from Meredith being a nanny who genuinely loves children, she also has several vision boards on Pinterest: The Ring, The House, The Dress... you get it. Meredith's dream is for someone to run away with her to the suburbs and impregnate her several times in a row until she finally gets a bob and fills her home with macaroni finger-paintings—and honestly, I don't blame her. She has a lot of the skills I would want in a mom. Plus I think I'd marry her myself if it meant I could have her lattes every day.

"What are you guys shouting about?" moans Lea, wandering into the kitchen barefoot and still in a bright red cocktail dress from last night. Her older manfriend, Simon, is one of those Very Rich types who can afford to take his mistress around town without a word of it reaching his wife, or so we assume given Lea's lack of hate mail.

"Nobody's shouting," Meredith says, disapprovingly shoving some coffee (sadly just the ordinary kind) at both of us. "I'm just telling *her*," she says with a rather impolite gesture to me, "that she needs to stop all this messy behavior and actually settle down."

"That's true," says Lea, who is a literal mess. "You really should start to think about your future. Like, okay, when things first got serious with me and Simon—"

"He's not leaving his wife," Meredith and I reply in unison, which of course Lea waves away.

"Okay, whatever, you guys can be cynical all you want, I know what we have. And the point is you can't just keep pointlessly slutting around," says Lea, who doesn't even have a real job. (Okay, she does. She's a part-time spin instructor, part-time physical therapy assistant, and I'm sure I don't need to tell you that's how she met Simon, who has a bum knee from a condition the experts call *advancing age*.) "What happened with Andrew?" Lea asks me optimistically.

Oh god. I wish Rae were here. She's very sensible, and more importantly a lesbian who takes no interest in my heretofore tragically hetero sex life. "Andrew is not a viable option," I say, hoping that might be the end of it, although historically I have a very good chance of being wrong. "He left me on read."

"Maybe he's just busy," Lea says reassuringly, albeit delusionally.

"Look, not everything I do has to be about some eventual marriage-and-babies endgame," I remind them. "And anyway, Andrew's a Pisces."

"Ew," say Lea and Meredith in unison.

"Exactly," I say, just as Damien re-emerges from our bathroom, which now smells incurably (and supremely unhelpfully) of Old Spice.

"Babe," Meredith calls to him, "what's your take on Andrew?"

He walks into the kitchen with the towel slung around his waist, droplets still gleaming on his back and shoulders. "Who?"

"Nobody," I mutter as Meredith presses, "Andrew, remember? We've met him like, several times."

"Oh." Damien looks at me. "What about him?"

"He left me on read," I mumble, staring at the kitchen counter.

"Oh yeah, no," he says, turning to leave the room as I shoot daggers at Meredith. I'd forgotten that her forgiveness of me usually comes at a price, because she smirks at me, satisfied.

"Oh, ignore him," sighs Lea, whose love life would belong to a fairy princess if it weren't for the whole older married lover thing. "Look, you *felt* a connection, right? That's all that matters."

Actually, I did feel a connection. But not with Andrew.

And technically not with Will, either, although that part still remains to be seen.

†

I check the conversation with Will on The Apps several times over the next couple of days, but of course there's nothing. I guess it's true what they say about men being more themselves in the harsh light of day, unless that was about vampires. No, they're not mutually exclusive.

Anyway, I don't expect to hear from him, although a few days later I do. *Let the die be cast,* reads a text from a number I don't recognize.

I inhale sharply, my pulse quickening a bit at the message, and Rae, who's just finished paying her bills with what I can only assume to have been her very lucrative burlesque series, looks up with a frown. "What's up with you?" she says, eyeing me. "You look weird."

"Oh gee, thanks Rae," I say, texting back.

More Menander?

The reply is instant. *Initially I thought of opening with Euripedes. Bad company corrupts good character.*

Which of us is the good character and which is the bad company? I ask.

Perhaps we ought to find out, he replies.

"Okay, who is it?" says Rae, just as Meredith finally sits down beside me.

"Damien's writing," she says in that annoying double-tone of *my boyfriend is a Great Artist and aren't I so lucky to be his muse but also how rude of him, ha ha, men are the worst.* "So I guess it's just us," she sighs.

"Evidently not," Rae says, gesturing to me. (I have just texted back in what I hope is a coyly playful tone: *Meaning?*)

"Oh my god, it's like, eleven," says Meredith with a frown. "Is this a booty call?"

Come join me for a drink. I have more in my repertoire.

"Didn't Damien used to text you late all the time?" I ask Meredith without looking up, typing back: *Thirsty?*

"That's different. He needs the daylight hours to write," Meredith insists.

Yes. Very.

"Wait, who is this?" asks Rae. "Mr. Friday Night?"

"I told you it's time to start getting serious," Meredith interjects without waiting for my answer; she's too busy looking maternally disappointed in me. (Told you she would make a great mom.) "You can't just go over to his place now. He's practically 'you up'-ing you!"

"Who says *he* doesn't work during the day, hm?" I ask Meredith. "Start-ups are very demanding," I say, flouncing to my feet.

"That sounds fake as shit," says Rae, so I kiss her forehead.

"Can I use your good lip balm? My lips are dry."

"We really shouldn't share that," she says without looking up.

"Okay cool, I'll just take it then—"

"This is, like, super not what I meant when I said you needed to take things more seriously," Meredith says, but it's too late, as I am already trying to remember whether my most butt-hugging jeans are clean. Actually, it doesn't matter, who washes their jeans?

"Okay, well, I'll be back in the morning probably," I say, patting Meredith's feet. "Don't watch any true crime without me."

"Bye," says Rae, her eyes not moving from the screen.

"If he just wants to sleep with you, this really isn't going anywhere!" Meredith calls after me, but even if I wanted to listen to her, it's too late. I'm already out the door.

†

When I wake the next morning, I'm practically catatonic with satisfaction. There's no other way to explain it, but I swear, all my joints are moving fluidly, my skin is clear, my hair is bouncy and vibrant, and I don't need to look in the mirror to prove it. Not that Will is some kind of miracle worker, but he kind of... is? Last night he poured me an extraordinarily good old fashioned and then sat down to work out the knots in my shoulders, eventually undressing me for a full-body massage that escalated, and then escalated again. And then again for good measure. I don't know if it's all that time in the gym, but he has quite an impressive stamina.

"What the hell," says Will, startling me into opening my eyes despite the gentle waking I had previously been enjoying. "How did you get in here?"

"What?" I blink, struggling to sit up as Will bolts upright, then swears. "Are you okay?"

"My head is killing me," he says, turning groggily to me. "Feels like I was up all night."

He was, but that doesn't seem worth pointing out to him. "Did you drink last night or something? You texted me," I remind him. "You're the one who asked me to come over."

"Oh." I can't tell if it's better or worse that this seems like a sufficient explanation for him. "I mean... yeah, I guess I must have just been blackout or something. Weird." He shrugs, rising to his feet and reaching for a pair of sweatpants.

"How often does that happen to you?" I ask him, suddenly relieved I didn't have to insist on condoms.

"I don't know, not often, I just..." He trails off, frowning. "I texted *you*, really?"

Well, that stings. "Is that so hard to believe?"

"No, no... I just didn't really think you were that into it last time." He cuts me another doubtful look. "Sorry if I freaked you out."

"You didn't." But he kind of is now. "So you don't remember last night at all?"

He hesitates, and then he leans toward me, looking like he's trying to bring himself to kiss my lips and then swerving at the last second for my forehead. "I remember I had a great time," he says. "But uh, I've got an early meeting, so—"

"Right," I say, trying to mask my deep exhalation of disappointment at what is clearly just another convenient dismissal. "Got it. I'll be out in a sec."

✝

My lunch shift at the Olympia Club is well-timed, because it allows me the convenience of resenting my job to a degree that successfully drowns out any romantic anxieties. Mrs. Harrison, one of our most persnickety regulars who is unfortunately too rich to drink tap water but not rich enough to have a second residence outside of the city, is in a particularly foul mood. "This champagne tastes off," she informs me. "Are you sure this is a fresh bottle?"

"Yes, Mrs. Harrison, I'm sure," I tell her. "Would you like me to pour you a fresh glass?"

"Why, so I can just suffer again?" she snaps. "This club used to have *standards*."

Considering that the bartender currently on staff (me) is a highbrow scholar in some relatively distinguished circles, I choose not to challenge her on this. "If you want I can sweeten it up a bit? Make it a nice mimosa or a bellini, if you'd prefer."

"So you can water it down with some cheap off-brand juice? No, thank you. I'll be getting my money's worth," she says irritably, though not before making further conversation about the tragic state of the club's tennis facilities.

By the time I make it home (with no further messages from Will), this morning's awkward waking returns to me. I walk in the door to find Meredith in full housewife mode, complete with a frilly apron from Anthropologie.

"Oh good, you're here," she says, sort of half-looking at me. "Would you check on the coq au vin?"

"I don't know what I'm looking for, but sure," I say, lifting the lid as Lea comes in, curiously sniffing the air.

"Is that dinner?" she asks, settling herself at one of the countertop stools. "Good, I'm starving."

"Not for you," Meredith informs her, swatting me away from her fancy French stew. "Damien's going to be here any minute. How's my hair?" she asks me hysterically, as if the man she's been dating for the last two years has somehow never seen it in a ponytail before.

"You look great, Mer," I assure her, and she gives me a wild-eyed smile in relief. "What's all this for?"

"Oh, he's gotten approval for his dissertation," she says, distractedly checking on her balsamic-glazed brussels sprouts. "Something about, I don't know, Proust."

"Jesus," I say, looking over the extravagance of what appears to be ramekins of crème brûlée setting in the fridge. "What are you going to do when he actually finishes it?"

"Say 'hi honey, welcome home, the baby's asleep,'" Rae says when she comes in from our bedroom, earning herself a glare from Meredith and a smothered laugh from me.

"Hey, question," I ask them, since I may as well make use of the village I have and spare us all the trauma of speculating about Damien's virility, "is it possible for a guy to be one way with you and then just... completely different later, for no reason?"

"Girls are like that," says Rae with a shrug. "Bitches be crazy."

"Oh my god, I know you're joking but stop," says Lea.

"It's because you haven't made a genuine connection," Meredith chides me again, brandishing a pair of tongs in my direction. "I told you that you can't just make everything about sex! He just wants to get off and get out, that's all."

"It doesn't really seem like it," I say, because never in the history of time has a man ever taken such care to massage my feet before, and certainly not before going down on me for what I can only call a substantial period of euphoria.

"You don't actually think things are going to get serious with this guy, do you?" asks Rae.

"Oh, stop," says Lea, pouting as she does whenever her optimistic view of love is trampled. "So what if it starts with sex? Plenty of relationships are physical first."

"Just because Hollywood says something does *not* make it true," Meredith says, nudging me backward and out of range right before she starts her handheld chef's torch. (Safety first with Meredith, always.)

"It's only if he's not being honest with you that there's a problem," Lea tells me. "Like with Simon—"

"Yo, that's not happening," Rae says.

"—like with *Simon*," Lea emphatically continues, "he's always really upfront with me about everything. Where he's going, what he's doing—"

"Whether he's screwing his wife," Rae contributes at a sing-song.

"It's a *loveless* marriage, okay? And she probably has affairs too!" Lea snaps irritably.

"So you admit it's an affair?" says Meredith, who's now wearing safety goggles.

Lea looks at me to see if I'll contribute to the heckling, but I shrug. "It's all been said already," I assure her, and she rolls her eyes.

"Okay, well, I think you should just see where it goes," she says. "Like, does he do what he says or not? That's all that really matters."

Sure, I think with an inward sigh, watching Meredith light her fancy custards on fire. Sure it is, of course.

†

Later that night, I get a text message. Well, two.

Hey, sorry, been crazy busy compiling my syllabus, Andrew texts me. *Just wanted to let you know I'll be back in the city next week. Drinks once I'm settled?*

The other, which I admit I was slightly more excited about, was this:

Thoughts on brandy? A sidecar can be gauche I admit, but a good Cognac is worth its weight in tawdriness.

I type *sure, lmk* back to Andrew and return to the window.

You certainly know how to keep a girl on her toes, I say.

Not my intention, he replies. *Unfortunately my schedule is rather limited.*

Limited to booty calls?

Ah, now you've cheapened it. But I suppose if that's what you want, I'm happy to provide it.

I don't think I've cheapened it. It just is what it is, right?

Perhaps you still misunderstand my intentions.

Which are?

I enjoy your company. I find your thoughts exceedingly stimulating.

Until morning, you mean.

I am... not a morning person, one might say.

Why should I believe you have any interest in me if you're going to be two completely different people from day to night?

Well, that's just it, isn't it? Would you expect two completely different people to have equal interest in you?

I look up with a frown.

"It's him, isn't it?" asks Rae, who's watching something on her phone. Possibly herself, which I think is very bold of her. I've always admired Rae's ability to not hate her body, which consists of a beautiful self-acceptance I could never dream of achieving. Not that she has reason to, obviously, as I and plenty of her subscribers think she's gorgeous, but Meredith is also lithe as hell and still perennially desperate to lose five pounds, so it doesn't seem connected to reality in the slightest.

"Yeah, it's him," I say, though in my head I think sure, it's *one* of him. Hm.

If you've some opposition to the way we spend our time together, I understand, he adds. *I was under the impression that I'd spent our evenings together giving you exactly what you wanted.*

You are, I say with an inward grumble. *That's the problem. What happens in the morning?*

You never said you wanted mornings, he replies, and although I know I should have suspected it sooner, it doesn't fully occur to me until I'm already in the cab.

"You're not Will," I blurt out when he opens the door, half-panting with the surreality of it.

"No," the thing in Will's chiseled body agrees, beckoning me inside as he gifts me a solemn smile of approval. "No, I'm rather not."

PART II: YOU GOTTA GET WITH MY FRIENDS

My phone buzzes behind the counter as I pour bellinis for my roommates Lea and Meredith, who under normal circumstances would not be allowed into the Olympia Club without exclusive membership. Unfortunately for the more scrupulous Olympias of yore, exclusion does have a cost; recently, in accommodation for certain losses of income/mass absconsion by preeminently wealthy patrons, the board has decided to start a Tuesday brunch (Tuesday being an otherwise dismal sort of day) specifically for non-Olympias. It makes very little difference to me, since I'm once again a patron of the holy church of Zoom for my doctoral program this term, but was thrilling news for Meredith, who wants very badly to be considered a sort of Junior Olympia, or perhaps an Olympia in training. I've told her several times that her boyfriend, the handsome but abominable Damien, is not in finance or the markets but rather in literature, and therefore the possibility of her being embraced by any sort of social club is almost impossible. She does not listen to me.

Anyway, my phone. I'm waiting on a response from my latest endeavor on The Apps: the ever abdominal Will, whom I texted rather lasciviously to no response as of yet. Meredith, that hawk of a girl, spots my face when I flip the screen and hide a frown, because of course it is no one of sexual interest. (It is my bank, wanting to know if it was indeed I who purchased a new vibrator despite having very little disposable income at present.)

(It was.)

"I see you're still waiting for him to call," Meredith says snidely, which is absurd. Nobody calls anymore, as it is not 1993. And also, she hasn't the faintest idea what she's talking about. "Whatever happened with Andrew?" she presses me. "I thought he's back now, isn't he?"

"My god, that's Simon's wife over there," says Lea, who isn't paying the least bit of attention to our conversation. Bless her. By Simon she is of course referring to her Elderly Gentleman Lover, who is never going to leave his aforementioned wife. Not that such things would ever cloud Lea's natural embrace of star-crossed romanticism, however aging it happens to be.

"Where?" I say.

"Hello?" says Meredith. "I asked a question."

"Over there," says Lea in a breathy sort of voice. "Wow. She's actually quite beautiful, isn't she?"

I look up to peer onto the balcony seating at a queenly sort of woman in perhaps her mid or late forties, who does indeed look magnificently well-preserved. There's no sign of Botox or fillers, which is very unusual for an Olympia. "Have you never seen a picture of her before?" I ask.

"Hello?" says Meredith. "Remember me?"

"Only faintly," I tell her as Lea continues to stare, mesmerized, over her shoulder at Mrs. Whatever Simon's Last Name Is, which I suppose I'll simply have to shorthand as Mrs. Whatever until such time as... Well, probably forever.

"Of course I've seen a picture of her," Lea informs me, missing her mouth by an inch or so and dribbling a bit of bellini onto the front of her dress, "as that's how I know it's her, don't I? Oh drat," she adds, dabbing at her breasts with a sigh. Even this she can't do without looking at Mrs. Whatever, who seems to also have beautifully constructed decolletage. "She just looks so much more elegant in person," Lea sighs wistfully.

"Isn't Simon some sort of septuagenarian? Even she's at least three decades younger than he is," Meredith says scornfully, so perhaps she's forgotten to continue harassing me about my love life. What a time to be alive!

"Well, I believe she's his second wife," Lea says, and frowns. "Or possibly third?"

"And you're angling for fourth wife?" I ask.

"That's quite a bit of attitude coming from you, Miss Booty Call," says Meredith, which means unfortunately I've not gotten off scot-free. "What's going on with Andrew?"

"Oh Mer, please don't," I say, but it's too late, because my mind is already revisiting the last time I saw my erstwhile paramour, another doctoral student in my program with whom I was heavily involved, to the point where perhaps a normal person might say we were dating.

Andrew is, like most academics, very much not a normal person, though I go in and out of my awareness of that fact. He abandoned me to care for his mother upstate for nearly a year without a word, instead leaving a message on my office phone—my *office phone*, which of course I only check AT MAXIMUM once a week, which he surely must have known because he harangues me for it regularly—to say that he didn't know when he'd be back and so to please forward his correspondences. A year ago, I was confidently referring to Andrew as my boyfriend. These days, I'm not so sure.

The trouble with Andrew is he's one of those men who are not very attractive—certainly not in any conventional manner—and therefore his inattention creates a bit of a personal maelstrom, despite what I believe to be my general soundness of body and mind. I am objectively better looking and smarter, and yet for some reason Andrew is intermittently resistant to both me and my charms. True, there are times when I'm strongly aware that we're very compatible and perhaps might even like each other a great deal, and although my friends have all met him and agree that he's "not to our taste, although he makes perfect sense for you" (harsh), he does create a sort of desirably predictable future: a Brooklyn brownstone, perhaps, with two bookish children, plus joint university tenure and eventual holidays in the Keys.

Also, he did make a point to see me when he returned from coalescing with his mother, although not until after he saw his advisor and apparently the new exhibit at the Met as well. Which I had specifically told him I wanted to see, but let's not get into it.

"Andrew is a much better option than Will," says Meredith. "He has an actual job, for one thing."

"Andrew's got exactly the same job I have," I remind Meredith, waving a hand to indicate that my current position standing behind the bar is my actual source of income, and therefore a person can't be so quick to laud a life of highbrow academia, whatever the poets say.

"Well, he'll grow into it, same as you. And obviously he has some inherited wealth," Meredith says. "He seems quite stable."

"Will is also rich," I point out, and Lea, who has yet to take her eyes off Mrs. Whatever, makes a face in opposition.

"Can we not discuss money like this?" Lea says. "It's so crass."

"We'll use a codeword," I suggest, adding, "Will has plenty of kangaroos."

"Maybe so," Meredith sniffs, "but it's where the kangaroos come from that matters. Not to mention how one goes about managing one's forthcoming source of kangaroos," she adds, sipping her bellini and sliding it back to me. There's no one above me on staff today (it is, after all, Proletariat Tuesday) so I slip her a bit more prosecco. "And didn't you just see Andrew last week? I doubt he'd take kindly to knowing you're sleeping with another man as well," she tells me, lifting an admonishing brow.

"But I didn't have sex with Andrew," I say, because I didn't, and Lea sighs again. (She isn't *not* crass, but I suppose the Olympia Club countertops are getting to her.)

"In public, really?" Lea says.

"Fine. I didn't *jump rope* with Andrew," I correct myself. "If anything, we got a bit tangled up before things got anywhere." He took me to lunch but was in a bit of a rush, and then he told me that if I wanted to come over to his place he had about half an hour, and for some reason it made me quite sad to think that the version of me that Andrew thought he was lunching with would have simply said yes and gotten on with it as if he hadn't been gone for several months. I told him that I also had a meeting (I got frozen yogurt) and then sulked by myself in the park, wishing I'd just had the sex. (My fault for choosing frozen yogurt, which is about as orgasmic as a sneeze.)

"But I should think tangling up would be a promising start," says Meredith, frowning.

"For theoretical jump roping, maybe. But not for actual jump roping," I say, and she nods with clarity as I explain that I wanted a bit more than twenty minutes of very bland missionary.

"Still, I think you ought to put this Will business away and focus," Meredith says. She made me show her pictures of Will from his profile on The Apps after a week of me being "entirely glued" (her words) to my phone each night, and she's disapproved of him ever since. She is convinced that a person with abs like Will's cannot possibly possess any other redeeming qualities, which is both true and unfair, since her own boyfriend is both sculptedly divine and an egregious cad. I suppose it's a bit of a "do as I do, not as I say" situation in the end, which in my experience is yet another testament to Meredith's proclivity for motherhood.

"He only texts you at night," Meredith reminds me, "and he never actually takes you anywhere during the day. I mean, doesn't he even want to meet *us*, for god's sake? We're your friends. If Damien had been resistant to meeting any of you I'd have dumped him on the spot," she proclaims, swaying a bit from the force of her self-righteousness (and the ungodly ratio of booze-to-juice in her bellini).

I wouldn't call that a very fair assessment on Meredith's part, since Vile Damien meeting us had more to do with him constantly coming over to eat the food in our apartment than it did any genuine interest in what any of us think. But there's no point saying that, since Meredith will never hear a word against him.

"Well, we've never met Simon, either," I point out with a gesture to Lea, who shushes us half-heartedly. She's watching as Mrs. Whatever continues her very leisurely conversation with a female friend, which admittedly does look very cool and serious. As if they might be discussing scientific advancements in the study of time loops or something of that ilk, or perhaps they're exchanging notes on abstract modernism.

"I just think you ought to really consider your priorities," Meredith informs me with a delicate hiccup, draining her glass and sliding it wordlessly to me for a refill.

✝

Will gets back to me around midnight, which wakes me from where I've fallen asleep over my notes on Sophocles. I'd kept my phone on loud for this precise reason, so I snort myself awake and then drag myself into a cab, pulling up to his apartment to find that he looks, as always, fresh as a fucking daisy. He's in what I can only call Gatsby loungewear, which admittedly does look very cool.

"You're a sight," he says with a bit of a fond laugh, kissing me firmly as I hobble in the door. He's a very generous kisser, which I would appreciate more under other circumstances, though I have some other things on my mind.

"My friends want to meet you," I say.

"Do they?"

"Well, more accurately they want *you* to want to meet *them*."

"Ah yes, one of those pesky mortal social conventions." He laughs, tickled pink. "Well, if it helps, he's been thinking of you."

"Who?"

"My host," he reminds me, placing me delicately on the arm of the sofa and tipping my head back to explore the column of my neck.

"Has he?"

"Well, you're often there when he wakes up disoriented, aren't you? And you're very amenable," Will-who-is-not-Will radiates to the hollow of my throat. I flinch, and not-Will pulls away, frowning. "Does that upset you?"

"I don't want to be *amenable*," I point out, a bit stung. "If it weren't for you coming out at night, I wouldn't bother to see him again at all." After all, I *do* have some self-respect, whatever Andrew or Meredith happen to think, or Vile Damien for that matter. It's not as if I *aspire* to be tangled up (Meredith's right, that is confusing) with a man who doesn't give a damn whether I live or die!

Only it does seem to be a leaf from my usual playbook, so hm.

"I do apologize for the inconvenience of our... dichotomy," not-Will says, looking meaningfully at me. To his credit, he does look very sorry, and not only that, but he also seems to grasp the extent of my inconvenience in this case. I feel as if I would not even have to explain to him why it matters that my friends should approve of him—he grasps it intuitively, no explanation needed—and that alone feels rare enough that part of me wants to assure him it's not a problem. It's really no problem at all.

Except it *is*, isn't it? This is the thing with him. Am I aware that he's some sort of demon who requires a human host? Yes. Come to think of it I may have forgotten to mention that earlier and anyway, we'll come back to it. But as I was saying, there's so many things that *could* be wrong with him. For one thing, he's a man, so he could easily be a misogynist or politically conservative, two things I couldn't possibly abide, or he could even just be addicted to porn or generally very disgusting, which he isn't. At this stage in a relationship, I could forgive a man for not returning my calls and texts or for sleeping with other women who aren't me, which is, as not-Will has pointed out, part of the mortal social construct of dating, particularly on The Apps. It's too early to expect a man to be serious or exclusive—and I'm still at the point of a relationship where most women would say I ought to give him a chance—so am I supposed to just *walk out* on a clean, intelligent, well-spoken man who has yet to fail to satisfy me sexually just because he isn't technically accessible during daylight hours?

And really, the trouble with not-Will is that he *listens*. It's incredibly gratifying, and dare I say more stimulating than any dick pic I've ever received. There's something about being heard and acknowledged that practically makes my mouth water just to think of it.

"Can you explain the demon thing to me again?" I ask him dizzily, and not-Will chuckles. "I should probably stop calling you not-Will, for example."

"My true name is unfortunately very powerful," he tells me, "so if you were to say it aloud, my host would most likely crumble to ash."

"Oh," I say, a bit disappointed.

"I'd be willing to, of course," he assures me quickly, "if that were very important to you. I only wanted to give you fair warning in advance."

"Well—" That's fair. "I suppose I just... want to be sure my conscience is clear," I clarify. "For example, my roommate's boyfriend is married—"

"Oh no, that won't do," tuts not-Will with disapproval. "Blood oaths are really very volatile and should not be undertaken lightly."

"—right, I agree," I say enthusiastically, skirting the questionable bit about blood, "so I suppose I just want to make sure that you're not, erm. Going to try to... possess me, or something?" I pose as a hypothetical, and when he chuckles, I admit with a sigh, "I'm afraid I don't know very much about what demons do, realistically speaking."

My Classics education has not been absent demons (or daemons) by any means, though the reference has always been very abstract. In Greek mythology and philosophy most demons are benign, intervening nature spirits or a generalized occult power, but there definitely are some malevolent ones who exist to mediate the good fortune of human life.

Not-Will takes my hands and kisses them, shifting so that we face each other on the sofa. "I'm not exactly benign," he says. "I do drain my hosts considerably. They will become dust one way or another, whether I exit them or am evicted by some external force."

"Oh," I say. Very discouraging.

"Though, while I require a body for survival purposes," not-Will adds hastily, "you are not at risk, of course. I already have a host."

"So you're not using me?" I hadn't been overly concerned, but it did linger as a possibility.

"Oh, I'm definitely using you," he confirms, "but in rather a similar way to you using me. It's..." He considers his words carefully. "Mutual subsistence, perhaps? I'm told this is called love."

"Love and ownership are very different," I say, and not-Will snaps his fingers.

"Yes, exactly," he says. "But love is a comfort to you, is it not? Safety?"

"In some sense," I say warily, and he nods.

"For me, you are similar," he says. "The more I interact with you, the more of your spirit I come to share, the more we become a sort of... harmonious union; one that allows me to thrive outside the limited constraints of my host. As you know, my current host is a bit of an idiot," he says with a pursed look, "and I am not as stimulated as I might be in, say, Kit Marlowe. Or Van Gogh."

"You didn't actually live inside Van Gogh, did you?" I ask.

"The point is, everyone has their demons," not-Will tells me, our knees comfortably placed beside each other on the sofa. "And while I'd be happy to meet your friends—because socialization is very stimulating," he confides to me as an aside, "I do not know that they will be willing to meet me in the dead of night. Nor can I make any promises for my host." He and I both exchange a look at the idea of me broaching this subject with Will, whom we both know is only lukewarm about me at best.

"Is it possible for you to change hosts?" I ask, mostly out of curiosity. Call it my academic nature, but I do like to understand a situation from many possible angles.

"Well, I'd need a bit of help," not-Will says, "with the rituals and such. And my current host would die, and I'd be conscripting another mortal to an early death. Which to be clear makes no difference to me," he clarifies, beginning to massage my feet. "I'm never very attached to my hosts, although I do prefer them to have a certain..." He considers it.

"Attractiveness?" I supply.

"Virility, yes," he confirms. "Optics are not so crucial for transference, although they can be excellent symptoms of general health. And for your purposes, it would have to be someone you found equally compelling as this body," he adds, kneading my arch while resting it atop one of his abdominals.

"This all sounds very complex," I say, suddenly drowsy with relaxation, and not-Will shrugs as he works the tension out of my heels.

"Not especially," he says. "I've done it several times, although never with assistance, which presumably would be easier. If you could stand it, of course, within your own constraints," he adds meaningfully.

"I suppose I'd feel badly about sentencing some poor man to death," I sigh in concession, closing my eyes.

"I thought you might. And your conscience matters a great deal to me," not-Will says.

I crack one eye, frowning at him. "Really?"

"Well, it's one of your foundational parts," not-Will says. "In fact, Plato—"

"Said that a daemon was a form of the human conscience, tantamount to a higher self," I grumble to myself, and not-Will smiles brilliantly. He leans forward to kiss my lips, pulling away, and then returns again for another, more roughly.

"Have I told you lately how very magnificent you are?" he breathes to me, my legs falling around his waist as he leans over me, fingers brushing the hem of my shirt and guiding it upward along the length of my bare waist. "Your mind is so very refreshing. I find I cannot help but crave you," he says, "indecently," and I shiver a little, lifting my chin for him to deepen the kiss.

In the morning I wake in Will's bed. Will is of course a bit panicked, poor thing.

"How—?" he begins to say, and I sit up with a yawn.

"Morning," I tell him, leaning over to kiss his cheek. He balks, but relents. Not-Will told me that Will is very susceptible to affection and craves it, secretly. A very helpful piece of intel. "I'm so glad you called yesterday," I add, and slip out of bed, stretching luxuriously. "I'll have to let you know about tomorrow."

"Oh, uh. Tomorrow?" echoes Will, scratching his chest.

"Well, you said you wanted to meet my friends," I remind him, or rather, say in a tone as if I'm reminding him, as this is the first he's hearing of it. "I'll have to see, but I think it can be arranged."

"Oh," Will says, looking as if he's been hit over the head with an ax. "Well, if it's too much trouble—"

"Not at all. Anyway, I'll be out of your hair," I tell him with a sunny smile, pulling on my sweatpants and deciding to take the long way home, just to enjoy the loveliness of the day.

✝

I arrive home to find the kitchen in shambles. This is unusual, owing to the fact that only Meredith cooks with any nutritional aims and/or complexity, and she is also inhumanly neat. She's one of those cooks who cleans up after herself as she goes, which is madness. At the moment, though, there's a shattered porcelain platter in the sink and what appears to be eggs benedict strewn within it. I dip a finger into the sauce on the stove and yep, Hollandaise. Hm.

"Mer?" I call.

"In here," is Rae's reply, which is an additional surprise. Since she's a DJ with a thriving OnlyFans page, the morning hours are usually her prime sleep zones.

I wander into Meredith's bedroom to find that she's lying on the floor looking quite dead. Rae and Lea are standing on either side of her, Rae still in her silk sleeping cap and Lea with one of her delicate little nighties skimming the tops of her thighs.

"What's this?" I ask, bewildered.

"Damien has decided that it would be best for us to take separate paths on our journey through life," says Meredith.

"Oh." The first oh is a what? " *Oh.* " The second one is an oh, shit.

"I'm fine," adds Meredith from the floor.

"She's not fine," says Rae. "I woke up to the sound of her screaming."

"I thought she was being murdered," Lea adds, one hand worriedly over her mouth.

"Don't be ridiculous," says Meredith. "I'm obviously fine."

"Yes, obviously," I say, gingerly tiptoeing into the room to get a better look at her. She doesn't appear to be hysterical, although her lipstick is smeared in what I can only call a carnal sort of way. "Well," I say, unsure what to tell someone who was up until now planning to have Vile Damien's vile children. "Would you like me to say very hurtful things about him?"

"No," says Meredith, forcing herself listlessly upright. "I don't care about him. I'm fine."

"Oh *yes* babe, of course you're fine," I coo reassuringly to her, watching Lea creep backward as if she's worried Meredith's head might suddenly spin around or something. "But would it help if we took you out for coffee, or did a bit of shopping, or...?"

"Where were you?" Meredith sniffles, wiping her nose with the back of her wrist. A very un-Meredith thing to do, but here we are.

"I was at Will's," I say, and before she can say anything, I add, "And he wants to meet you, by the way. I thought tomorrow, but given everything—"

"Nonsense. I'm fine."

"Yes babe, obviously—"

"And tomorrow at noon would be perfect, since I no longer have standing lunch plans with Damien." Meredith shifts forward, lurching as if she plans to stand up, but then changes her mind, or perhaps gravity changes it for her. "Actually, there's one other thing you can do for me," she tells me, and I fight a groan.

"If you're going to tell me to call Andrew again, I keep telling you, he can just as easily call me first—"

"Well there's no need for you to be so stubborn, is there? And no, I just need you to take Damien some of his things," Meredith says, crisply rearranging her skirt, which I can see now is smeared with something that may well be the Hollandaise.

"Oh, goodness Mer, of course," I say, having been briefly concerned it would be something far worse. "You shouldn't have to see him again."

She nods, her eyes looking slightly more lucid.

"Yes, I think that would be best. Better for everyone, really. Anyway, I'm going to have a shower," she says faintly, trying again to stand, and this time Rae and I both manifest feverishly beneath her elbows, catapulting her up from the floor. "Thank you," Meredith says, a bit dazed as she wanders to the bathroom.

In her absence, I turn to the other two. "What exactly happened?"

"Don't know. He called this morning and ended it, I guess." Lea chews her lip.

"He *called* her?" I echo, disgusted. "As if he doesn't practically live here!"

"Speaking of, he has a key that he never actually uses," Rae reminds me, and Lea rolls her eyes, because Damien has definitely buzzed all of us individually for entry before. "You'll have to get that back."

"Ugh. And here I'd hoped never to speak to him again," I sigh.

The other two offer sympathetic looks in reply. Granted, we've always wanted Damien out of our lives, but I doubt any of us thought it would actually happen. And certainly not this way! He may be criminally handsome, but surely even he could do no better than Meredith. Meredith, a true queen! And to think he never even knew the true extent of her neuroses. For him, she was just an incredibly doting woman with absolutely no lunacy or flaws. Does he expect to find a better version of her out there in this heinous world? No doubt he'll come crawling back.

†

I mention this to Meredith after her shower, though she seems resolutely done with it. She simply hands me a box with a variety of Vile Damien's vile things and tells me to be sure to get *both* keys, not just the apartment key. It's astounding how calm she's being about all this, which leads me to wonder if perhaps she always knew he was a pile of asshats wearing a trench coat? Maybe all that work she did to keep him was just a distraction from the misery of having to pretend that any of it was love.

I knock on the door of Damien's apartment, which I'm upset to find is in a building with a doorman and by the looks of it, plenty large. What on earth was he always doing at our place, which is essentially a brothel?

"Oh, come in," he says, and naturally he's shirtless and freshly showered. It smells absolutely incredible inside, spurring both my recalcitrant loins and my eternal hatred of him.

"I've just come to drop this off," I say, gesturing to the box in my hands. "And to pick up our keys."

"Ah, they're in here somewhere." He ushers me inside like some sort of beautiful hairless sheepdog, and against my will I find myself stepping into his apartment. It's fantastically furnished, which makes me furious. One wall is a gorgeous navy that sets off the chestnut accent pieces, and his brown leather sofa is an idyllic mix of comfortably used and noticeably expensive. Meanwhile, most of our furniture is Ikea, taken off one of our neighbors for free, or broken. Some of it all three.

"It's in one of these drawers," Damien says, rummaging through his kitchen—which is one of those open plans, my god, am I drooling? I quickly check my mouth and then obscure the motion. "Sorry for the mess," Damien adds vilely, and truly, would anyone blame me if I punched him? He's neat as a pin, the little shit, and the only thing I can even think to consider a mess is whatever he's left out on the stove, which seems to be some kind of breakfast casserole. So he can cook, too? Then why was he always eating our hummus? And why on earth was Meredith slaving over him!

My blood boils and I drop the box on his coffee table. (Which! Is! Transcendent!)

"Maybe if you can just drop them off la—"

"Here we go," Damien says, and cuts me off as I move to leave, pausing me with a hand on my arm and startling me so thoroughly that I wind up whirling into him.

His eyes drop to my neck, pointedly, and then rise to my face, which probably looks surprised instead of positively incendiary, owing to the sudden shock of his proximity.

"You know," he comments in a soft, low voice, "I always thought there might be a little something between us."

"What?" I say indignantly, only it comes out a rasp. I clear my throat, but that only makes it worse. His closeness is pressing in on my vocal chords or something.

"She's your friend, I understand, but you can't pretend there isn't something here," Damien says, smelling like clean laundry and nefarious indiscretions. His eyes are very luridly on mine. "I've seen the way you look at me."

To this I cannot fathom a response. "You're an absolute idiot to let her go," I say, wrenching myself free, but of course I stumble and he catches me, and now we're even closer than we were before.

"You know where to find me," he says, his hand lingering on the small of my back, and have I mentioned how positively *vile* this man is? I find it insulting that my body should respond in such a keen and disgusting way when my mind is adamant that I could easily stuff him down the rubbish chute. (Can't believe he has one, by the way! What kind of sorcery could have put him in this apartment? Meanwhile the rest of us have to carry our trash down the stairs like peasants.)

The wind whips in from the balcony (my GOD this man has a BALCONY) and I regain my sense of awareness, shoving him away.

"You should be ashamed of yourself," I say.

"Mm," he says unabashedly, and by then I'm so enraged I simply make it to the door and walk out, realizing with a surge of fury that I didn't actually get the keys.

Well, so be it. We're never getting out of that apartment anyway.

✝

Shock of all shocks, Will agrees to lunch and arrives close to twenty minutes late, which Meredith pretends not to mind. She's been doing quite a lot of pretending since her breakup with Loathsome Damien, although it's possible she really is fine. Either way, grilling Will winds up taking most of her concentration.

"So you have a start-up?" she says aggressively. If I worried much about what Will thought, I might be irritated that Lea seems distracted and Rae's too busy eating to keep this from devolving to a sitcom-ian circus act, but as it is I can't see this happening again.

"We're still in the early development stage," Will says, evasive. "We're really trying to perfect our pitch before we move forward."

Meredith doesn't back down. "Are you relying on institutional funding? Angel investors?"

Will turns his water glass, adjusting it where it sits for a moment.

"What did you say you did?" he asks, and her expression flickers.

"I'm a nanny," she says, "but my degree is in marketing, and—"

"Oh, cool," says Will. "Yeah, kids are great."

Meredith is silenced by this, which reminds me that while Will is genuinely an idiot, Noxious Damien was intentionally not very kind about Meredith's job. She edited quite a few of his stories, and I remember him dismissing her comments on the basis of not knowing what his professors were looking for or some other thing that professed to be her ignorance rather than his error. She always backed down then, too, which makes me feel suddenly quite murderous on her behalf. I stab a cherry tomato with my fork, wishing for worse.

The rest of lunch goes similarly poorly, although to my surprise Will invites me over afterward. I agree, mostly out of having very little else to do. Part of me feels like Will is trying to imagine what it might be like to actually date me, which I hate to inform him is something that would never happen. After all, Will doesn't have a real job and I'm not fully convinced he can read. But I do want to see not-Will, so I "accidentally" fall asleep on his couch after a bit of Netflix scrolling and such.

"I have a question," I remark to not-Will later, who is in the process of baking me a lovely focaccia. "What would happen if you took over more of a body? Like, say, all of it," I pose with something I hope is innocence, or at least plausible deniability. Not that I expect a demon of all people to judge me.

Not-Will lifts his head from the oven, brow knitting as he considers it.

"You mean if I didn't allow the consciousness of my host to coexist alongside mine?" he asks, and I nod. "Well, it's a matter of longevity, really. Any percentage more of me would kill them that much faster," he explains. "Since I am essentially a poisonous parasite."

"Well, say that hypothetically that would be fine," I suggest, and he smiles, ducking in for a quick kiss before attending to his olive oil filigree.

"Are you hoping I'll take over more of my current host?" he says. "I suppose it's not a terrible idea."

"Actually, I had someone else in mind," I tell him, and go on to explain the existence of Vile Damien, who is actually much more suited to not-Will's aesthetic than Will, mid-century furnishings included. "I hate him," I conclude vitriolically.

"But you wouldn't mind if I looked like him?" not-Will asks.

"It pains me to admit it, but not particularly," I say with a grimace, because as Damien himself seems to have noticed, it's only Damien's vile insides I can't stand. "How soon would you... you know. Use him up?"

"Depends on his resiliency," not-Will says. "Three mortal years? Five?"

Hm. I could keep him away from Meredith for three years if I had to, probably. I know it sounds inconvenient, but I think I'm mostly assuming that in a week or two when the initial grieving has passed, I'll be able to tell her that a demon has taken residence in her ex-boyfriend and she'll consider it to be a suitable revenge. "Great," I say, pulling out my phone. "What do you call it, anyway? The swap?"

"The ritual of transference?"

"Sure."

"The ritual of transference."

"Yep, right, got it—" I type a quick message to Damien telling him I want to meet him tomorrow night at his apartment. "You're sure you don't mind?" I ask, realizing I should probably clarify that first.

"Me? Not at all. Whatever you want," not-Will says, and then he kisses me, and I feel fine.

†

The next day we schedule a girl's day in solidarity with a still-silent Meredith, for which I meander mutely through my Zoom lectures and Rae puts her burlesque content on pause. We settle in for a day of pizza, face masks, and gossip, although it goes sideways almost immediately.

"I've started sleeping with Simone," Lea bursts unexpectedly, and I choke on my swallow of cheap champagne.

"What?"

"Nice," says Rae, toasting her. "Welcome. Would you like a badge? We have badges."

"Who is Simone?" asks Meredith, bemused. Which, to be fair, is a very good question.

"Simon's wife," says a rosy-cheeked Lea.

"Wait," says Rae, cutting in with a frown before the rest of us can react. "This dude married a woman with his own name? Actually, never mind," she informs her glass with a shrug, "that tracks."

"So now you're sleeping with a married man *and* his wife?" I ask, more incredulous than anything else. Not that I'm generally very judgmental, but this makes my sleeping with a demon seem slightly better by comparison, which is a plus.

"Not *both*," Lea says, and sighs. "Well, both, but not simultaneously."

"Why not?" asks Rae.

"Stop," wails Lea.

"But I thought you were in love with Simon," I say, because to my understanding, that was the only reason we weren't forcefully intervening in the first place.

"Yes, of course I am!" Lea insists. "I just might also be in love with Simone," she adds pitifully.

"But you only just saw her two days ago," I point out.

"Life comes at you fast," says Rae through a mouthful of pizza, and Lea wails again.

"Obviously I didn't *mean* to," she says imploringly. "But she was just so beautiful and I thought... maybe if I just *spoke* to her I could give it up with Simon, since you're all always tormenting me about him, and then one thing led to another and..." She trails off, cheeks flushed. "Well anyway, I'm supposed to see her again tonight. And I know I should break it off," she says, letting the sentence dissolve to a wisp of nothing.

"Yes," says Rae. "You should."

"Right, of course," Lea assures her. "But then again...?"

She looks between us hopefully.

"Sorry," Rae says. "I know my morals are typically the flimsiest, but even I have trouble processing this one."

"I just don't understand how this ends," I say, frowning. "Best case scenario, what happens?"

"Does it really have to end?" Lea sighs wistfully, and to this I have no choice but to scoff.

"Okay, so when *I* have an extremely suspicious romantic partner it's all about how irresponsible I'm being," I remark with a certain unbecoming air of gloating, "but when you have *two—*"

"Just leave her alone," says Meredith quietly, whom all of us have forgotten up to this point. We all turn with surprise to see a tear slipping down Meredith's cheek, followed by another. "Love is hard enough as it is," she suddenly sobs at us, rising sharply to her feet and leaving the room, shutting her bedroom door behind her.

All of us feel a bit shamed, as Meredith has a tendency to do. I am very susceptible to the acuteness of her disapproval, and for a moment it occurs to me that actually, perhaps Meredith really did love that vile monster Damien, and so perhaps she doesn't want him to die. It's a conclusion that fills me with regret, but there it is.

"I guess she's not fine after all," comments Lea in a small voice.

Unfortunately, I have no choice but to agree.

✝

In the end I bail on Damien. Not-Will says he doesn't mind not doing the ritual of transference; whatever makes me happy, he says, which in this case is a lovely fondue. I sigh and ask him if a curse on Damien's bloodline can be arranged instead and he says yes of course and kisses my forehead, which leaves me feeling boneless with happiness. As I'm falling asleep, I accidentally say aloud that perhaps I might be in love with him, to which not-Will tells me that love as mortals feel it is not technically within his capacity but he reciprocates with his equivalent, which is really more similar to loyalty.

Andrew calls, finally, and I ignore it.

In the morning I wake up to find Will looking at me with his usual expression of concern, though he seems to be adjusting. He isn't making any sudden movements or trying to kick me out of bed, so that's an improvement of sorts.

"Can I tell you something?" he says when I open my eyes.

"Go for it," I reply.

"I think something might be really wrong with me," he tells me.

"Hm," I say.

"I know," he agrees, probably for different reasons. "But anyway, I was thinking that maybe we ought to make this official."

"This?" I echo.

"Yes. Us," he says.

Oh good, I think to myself. So just another ordinary day in my life, then.

"Erm. Sure," I say, and Will kisses me, and somehow I manage not to squirm.

PART III: IF IT COMES BACK TO YOU, IT'S YOURS

Today's interminable Zoom lecture is about the Aristotelian approach to melancholia, which is a subject I am thankfully not teaching although I can't honestly say that I'm learning, either. The point is we're conveniently discussing sadness and black bile while my roommate Meredith drapes herself across my bed and moans to herself—about what, unclear. From context it seems a bit "look upon me, cruel gods! Feast thine eyes on thy woeful progeny," but in reality it's probably just something-something Vile Damien (as usual) and therefore unrelated to the divine. I stroke Meredith's head absently, because such things are required of roommates and friends, but also because if she doesn't quiet down she'll wake Rae, who is normally a very peaceable sort of person with the exception of when she's rudely awoken.

We have progressed through denial and anger and bargaining and have finally made it here, Meredith's weepy breakup phase, just shy of the three-week mark from Damien's unconscionable absconsion. The four of us (including Lea, part-time physical therapy assistant, full-time polyamorous sugar baby) held one of our brothelly flat summits and agreed to swap rooms for the time being, ostensibly due to the fact that Meredith and I function as relatively normal human beings whereas Rae, with her booming OnlyFans page and vampiric hours of DJing and parties, sleeps during the day, while Lea is of course never home, being the inamorata of a bustling elderly gentleman and his Very Distinguished wife.

This has worked out very well to the benefit of the two absentee roommates, and not so much for me or Meredith.

Beside me my phone buzzes and I glance at the screen, sighing internally or perhaps also externally. During the daylight hours there's only one person it could be, and of course because it is a predictable world in addition to an unjust one, it is. I glance at Will's name and contemplate ignoring the message, only I already know it'll be some sort of desperate attempt at normalcy. Eventually I grit my teeth and reply to his message ("come over?") with a heart emoji: the pink one with sparkles. It's very "live, laugh, love" as far as emoji hearts, and therefore a bit spooky to men. (Beautifully ambiguous and yet barbarically delicate, as we the fairer sex tend to be.)

I know it seems a bit problematic for me to say things like I'm only dating Will for access to the demon who lives in his body, but is it really all that different from the men who've only been with *me* for sex? After all, below Will's series of messages is only more whining from Andrew, an erstwhile situationship with which I'd been relatively content until it became clear that bending to his needs for the benefit of his convenience was not quite the dexterity I aspired to as a contemporary feminist/verified human person. I've been ignoring Andrew steadily for a week, which I know Meredith looks upon with her usual matronly disapproval. In fact, as I say this, I notice the moaning has stopped, and she's watching me very closely. Unnervingly closely.

I check that my mic is muted (an eternal paranoia) and glance at her, obscuring the motions of my mouth whilst nodding sagely about the finer points of *Problemata*. "Yes, babe?" I ask with beatific patience.

Meredith opens her mouth to say something, which is probably going to be either her dislike of Will or her certainty that I should invest myself once more in Andrew, a man who is growing wildly desperate only now that I'm no longer at his beck and call. Meredith is unfortunately very susceptible to the propaganda of romantic movies written by men in which the male love interests take a great amount of time to sort out the intensity (?) of their feelings.

"It's not Andrew's fault," Meredith once remarked when Andrew was conveniently (for him) being inconvenient (for me). "What he really needs is a tragic loss, you know? Men never know what's in front of them until they go through some sort of trauma," she determined, tearing into the flesh of a grapefruit. "Everything was different between us after Damien's grandma died," she added matter-of-factly. "He needed me 24/7 just to cope with it, and look how close it made us." (This conversation, of course, preceded the aforementioned Vile Absconsion.)

"Andrew's grandparents are already dead," I informed her, to which she shrugged.

"Well, there's always his mother," she said matter-of-factly. "Isn't she in poor health?"

"Jesus Christ," was my very reasonable response to that, because Meredith is not someone I'd call anything short of terrifying.

But back to the moment at hand. Before Meredith can open her mouth to begin ill-wishing Will's parents, there's a knock at the apartment door. I sigh, gesturing to the lecture I'm currently sitting through, and Meredith reluctantly drags herself upright to attend to the UPS man or whoever it is that I'm much too plugged in to address.

I am reminded as Meredith glooms to her feet that she has become somewhat un-enamored with showering of late; she's also wearing a garment of Rae's that she once referred to as "those abominable sweatpants, like a sign on your forehead that says 'I prefer public television to sex.'" The bun sitting atop the apex of her head topples sideways as she oozes glumly into the living room.

I begin contemplating once again how I'm going to shake Meredith free of her post-Vile Damien funk. It's not as if Meredith and I have not coaxed each other through romantic difficulty before, but it seems particularly traumatic this time, either because I'm not being honest with her about my own life or because she's especially distressed over the loss of whatever strange Stepfordian future she'd been manifesting for herself. My lack of sympathy on this matter is not helpful, and the older we get, the more she seems aware of some impending finish line; a ticking clock she's losing to. In that sense I suppose I can understand her intangible sense of doom, even if I can't quite interpret her methods.

"Mortality is a drag," as not-Will agreed with me recently, once his host finally nodded off during our third consecutive watch of *Borat.* "The constancy of peril. And biological limitations aside, there's still the existential. It's all very lose-lose."

He told me that Will, his host, is experiencing some form of psychological decay. "Unavoidable," he added, with something I would call a healthy modicum of decency. "Though your presence does help to slow the otherwise careening regression."

"Is it really that bad?" I asked, perhaps a bit guilefully. Call me selfish, but I'm beginning to find it annoying that Will's sublimating consciousness is interfering with my otherwise perfect relationship.

"Well, he's not entirely aware of me yet," said not-Will. "But there will be little to prevent a full psychological collapse once he becomes aware, irreversibly, that his actions and thoughts are not his own. And he is beginning to suspect that something isn't right."

"Only *now?*" I ask, dismayed. I know I'm an overstuffed leftist academic even on my best days and therefore a substantial degree of useless, but I'd like to believe myself capable of noticing if something had breached my metaphysical gates.

"He's not the brightest bulb," not-Will reminds me. "And there's something to be said for the persistence of toxic masculinity, which of course prohibits my host from any sort of intimate self-reflection," he adds, as he and I nod in solemn anti-patriarchal conspiracy. "Emotionally speaking, he's unlikely to ponder much about his circumstances. It's why I prefer to occupy the bodies of men—altogether more convenient for me," he concluded, pouring me a fresh glass of Bordeaux.

I think again about the frothing desperation in Will's increasingly frequent messages and feel another twinge of guilt. Handsomely vacant though he continues to be, there's a shadow of exhaustion to him now, and a certain detectable but unconfessed need for validation. Sometimes he looks at me a bit jumpily, as if to reassure himself that I'm seeing what he's seeing, too. And his demonic half isn't wrong; he is desiring of something— support or comfort or intimacy—although whatever it is, I'm certainly not the person to give it to him.

Unfortunately, the limiting circumstances I so enjoy about our pseudo-relationship prevent anyone else from showing up to do a better job. Bit of a "chicken and egg" thing, albeit a touch more "demon and demon-enamored girlfriend."

Once again suffering my fragile mortal impulses, I follow up on my previous text to Will, this time with "see you after my lecture" and then, following a moment's pause, an exclamation point for pep. He responds immediately, typing, and then a pause, then more typing. "Can't wait" is what he's decided to go with, which is really kind of sweet even if I know it's being said from a place of desperation, as per his mounting psychological breakdown.

Not-Will is right; to be mortal is to be forever deconstructed as the playthings of ambivalent gods. Or something. It certainly sounded right when he phrased it that way.

"Babe?" calls Meredith, appearing in the doorway and motioning for me to remove my headphones. I do, frowning a little as someone comes into view behind her. "You have a visitor."

For the love of god, it's Andrew. "What on earth," I manage to emit in a sort of squeak, sitting hastily upright before checking once again that I'm on mute. "What are you doing here?"

"I knew I'd catch you," Andrew says with profound gravity, gesturing to my monitor. I look down and realize that while he is also supposed to be attending this class, he's currently signed in as a black screen. "You've been ignoring my calls for days now."

"Hm, I wonder what that might mean," I reply sarcastically, noticing that Meredith is still lingering in the corner. She has removed her wobbly top-knot and is now self-consciously petting her hair, entranced by what appears to be Andrew's version of a grand gesture. I tear my attention from her very suspicious body language and return to eviscerating him with my devastating rhetoric. "It's not as if you were very responsive to me while you were away, were you?"

"I was caring for my mother," Andrew insists yet again.

"You were gone for nearly a year! Was she in hospice, Andrew?"

"No, but—"

"She's got a vacation house in the Keys, for Christ's sake!"

"I hardly see how that's relevant," Andrew informs me, nudging his specs up his nose with all the wounded vulnerability of a toddling orphan. "So that's it, then? Everything we had suddenly means nothing to you?"

Unbelievable. I ought to have said the same thing six months ago. "What we *had*, Andrew, was the occasional episode of convenient but unremarkable sex, the quality of which I could easily surpass with any two fingers on my right hand," I erupt hotly, to which there is a sudden outburst in my ears.

I glance down, realizing that in ascertaining my situation on mute, I have (of course) un-muted myself instead, and now a series of doctoral scholars plus a guest lecturer on loan from Athens are giggling at me from their screens like a bunch of randy schoolchildren.

"As if half of you aren't currently involved in the *exact same* problematic tango," I snap, promptly shutting my laptop screen and returning my attention to the empty space in the doorway where Andrew once stood.

To my surprise, though, he's gone, as is Meredith. And having already abandoned my scholarly efforts for the morning, I sigh and pick up my phone, texting Will that evidently I will soon be on my way.

†

"I did have a difficult childhood, you know," Will informs me over a fourth or so glass of scotch. Nice scotch, but still, it's notably three in the afternoon. "My father was always very overbearing. And my mother preferred my sister." He sloshes a bit of liquid onto his hand and stares at it, heartbroken, before sighing aloud. "And imagine how hard it is now," he continues, waving his glass around until it dribbles on the floor. "Imagine being a straight white male amid all this 'diversity this' and 'diversity that'! I understand the logic but my god, where does it end?" he woefully informs me, pining for imperialist times gone by. "Apparently it's not enough to have a solid pitch if I don't *also* tick some minority box."

"Wasn't your game inspired by someone you went to school with?" I ask.

"Well of course—her version was a mess—but the point is it's madness. It's no wonder the whole country's got an identity crisis on their hands."

"Well," I say, forcing a smile, "at least there's that generational wealth to fall back on, isn't there?"

"What?" Will barks, the glass in his hand slipping into his lap, landing on his abs. "The money's not inherited. My family's essentially middle class—Dad's a stockbroker and Mom's a housewife. They paid for college and the apartment but nothing else."

Oh yes, of course. Middle class. "So where does the rest of your money come from, then?"

He gives me a questioning (drunk) look and then leans toward me, smelling vaguely of bacon. "If I show you," he whispers loudly, "do you promise not to tell?"

Even the freckles below his eyes look different when he's not occupied by his more interesting half. "Will, believe me, I'd never tell a soul," I swear with the ceremony of a Girl Scout.

"Okay. The thing is, I've got to be much more drunk," he informs me, and dutifully plucks the glass from where it's been resting on one of the contours of his stomach.

What follows is something I can only call a weaponized frenzy of mildly troubling alcoholism, plus a few more lectures about how difficult it is to be so Caucasianly off-trend and a clumsy, open-mouthed kiss that eventually ends with him slumped across my breasts in a state of apparent unconsciousness. I pause beneath him, uncertain. I can't say I've ever tried intoxication as a money-making scheme, but if it works then I would certainly like to see it.

After a moment Will sits up; only it's not Will, of course. "Hello, darling," says Will's demon, looking positively invigorated. "You're here early, aren't you?"

"Oh, hi—yes a bit, I suppose," I say, leaning forward to kiss him until I remember that corporeally, he'll need to brush his teeth first before I do any such thing. "I didn't realize *you* were the one who made the money," I remark as not-Will registers his own putrid breath and immediately gets up to gargle some mouthwash.

"I do prefer a certain lifestyle," not-Will calls from the bathroom.

"Understandably," I agree, rising to follow until I meet him in the corridor. "So is it stocks, then? Some time-travel-y mumbo-jumbo? Secret stash of Egyptian gold?"

"Oh darling, you know as well as I do that the mortal economy is an altogether imagined concept," says not-Will, stroking my hair. "Hungry?"

"Starved. Pizza?"

"Of course."

"And does that mean you just... make money? Like magic or something?"

"Magic is a somewhat prohibitive term, but yes," not-Will tells me, then adds, "What do you think, a bit of cunnilingus before the food arrives? You seem stressed." He scrutinizes me closely, holding my face between his hands. "I'll get you a fresh glass. How did you like the Chateau Latour?"

"It was lovely," I say at once, fumbling to slip out of my underwear on the spot. "And I suppose I *am* feeling a bit... taxed," I add, as not-Will nods in sympathy. "I think I see what you mean about him devolving."

"You're handling it beautifully, though," he assures me, tucking a curl behind my ear. My hair is always so bouncy and shiny around him; whatever "prohibitive term" he's using to do it, it's magic enough for me. "And if I could spare you the worst of it, I would. Do you want the burrata? Of course you do," he answers himself, chuckling while I enjoy the usual rush of absolute pleasure at being so seen. "Take this," he instructs me, handing me the glass of wine. "Be sure to savor it."

"And what will you do while I'm savoring?" I ask, taking a sip and letting it sink, honeyed, onto the recesses of my tongue, the scent of it wafting into the eager caverns of my nose.

"Make myself useful," the demon assures me, lowering himself to his knees while I close my eyes, elated.

✝

The following day I come home to find Meredith waiting for me, perched daintily on my bed as she might have done pre-Vile Absconsion. Her hair is glossy again, which is interesting. She's also wearing what appears to be a new dress.

"Come sit with me, babe," she says in her very Meredith way, and I do. "Now, you know that I adore you," she says very solemnly, and in a way I suspect she rehearsed earlier in the mirror, "and I always want us to be honest with each other."

"My god, where have you buried the body?" I joke, though she doesn't crack. "Mer," I sigh, "if this is going to be yet another speech about how I've been spending too much time at Will's—"

"I'm seeing Andrew," she says calmly.

"—I don't think I can... what?" I ask, trailing off. "Andrew who?"

"You know exactly which Andrew, you dolt. It's just... he absolutely fell to pieces yesterday after you embarrassed him like that in front of your whole class," she says, stone-faced. "I never really intended it to go anywhere, but after we spent the afternoon chatting over coffee about our respective break-ups—"

"What?" I demand with a certain lack of dignity. "Is he actually comparing me to *Damien*? My god, I'll run him through with a spear—"

"—and ultimately, babe, I just think there's something between us that I would like to explore," Meredith continues, "though of course I won't if you'd find it too upsetting." Then she pauses, ostensibly to see how the news sinks in.

Truthfully, I have no idea. Part of me is absolutely astonished by how completely unsurprised I am by this information. After all, Meredith has always liked Andrew to a certain degree of irrationality; Lea and Rae, hardly more sensible but certainly belonging to slightly different delusions, always felt that Andrew was a bit of a dork they could take or leave, whereas Meredith was devoted to the idea of him as the object of my affection.

"You and Andrew?" I ask, still trying to process this.

Rae, speak of the devil, walks in at precisely that moment. "Can you keep it down?" she says, glaring at me. Unsure how she finds this more disruptive than Sad Meredith's melancholic moaning, but I suppose I may have become quite vociferous in my shock.

"Meredith," I say, turning to her and ignoring Rae altogether. "You cannot date Andrew."

She exhales deeply. "I thought you might say that. And listen, if you've still got feelings for him—"

"No babe, that's absolutely not what I mean. Andrew's a six-foot tall infant," I inform her. "He's incapable of processing anyone else's feelings."

"He's an academic," Meredith says, as if this and "misunderstood" or "tragic" mean the same thing. She is once again willfully choosing to ignore the fact that Andrew and I are in the same program—studying the exact same courses, declining the exact same dead nouns. The fact that I am a part-time bartender getting most of my ecstasy in life from a demon while half-starving alongside my three brothelly roommates is extremely relevant to the situation at hand, though I'm struggling to find a way to shorthand that.

To me, the problem here is terribly obvious. Meredith's pride is hurt and so is Andrew's. The difference is that Andrew brought this on himself and will definitely bring it on himself again. Meredith *devotes* herself to the person she's with, and like all men and vampires, Andrew will drain her. She'll call it happiness but it will only be Vile Damien all over again, and if I let it happen without intervening I will be complicit in a great and terrible evil, amen.

"Mer—"

"What's going on?" asks Lea sleepily, wandering into our room in what appears to be very expensive polyamorously-purchased lingerie.

"Not now," I inform her and a curiously onlooking Rae, who is apparently no longer interested in sleeping. "Babe, listen to me," I continue sternly, turning to Meredith. "You can't waste another two years of your life on Andrew. Or more!" My god, he'd probably marry her. If he doesn't choose to string her along for a decade—which is at the top of the list of plausible outcomes—then he might actually decide to give her his entitled, hypochondriatic, tendinitis-prone children. When this was *my* potential outcome it was reasonable, because I am a series of flaws tied together by dental floss beneath a stolen trench coat, and I would absolutely abandon me if I could conceivably find a way to do so—but this is *Meredith.*

Ultimately, this would mean a lifetime of watching a man like Andrew wind up with a goddess whom he firmly does not deserve.

"I always thought you needed to give him more of a chance," Meredith reminds me.

"Why? What for?" The words come stammering out of my mouth, all my more philanthropic thoughts receding.

"Look, babe," Meredith sighs, "you know I never want to be critical of you"—a bald-faced lie—"but you've always been so unreasonable about relationships. And really, how can you say those things about Andrew when you're in yet another dead-end cycle with Will? Your expectations for Andrew were always *way* too high—"

"Did you perchance consider, oh Romance Guru, that if Andrew cared about me at all he might have found a way to rise to them?" I snap, and while Meredith's first response is to become doe-eyed and damsel-esque with shock, she conceals it very quickly.

"Fine." She rises to her feet. "I can see you refuse to be reasonable about this. But if you're going low, then I suppose I'll just have to go high."

She's trying to Michelle Obama her way out of this? Over my dead body! "You're terrified of being alone!" I fling at her back, shooting upright and lunging after her in a fit of tantrum-y fury. "Why, Mer? Why is that the worst thing you can imagine?"

I realize I'm pleading with her a bit, which is admittedly not a cute look. Nor did I intend things to get so vulnerable. I assume she hears it, because when she pauses to look over her shoulder at me, her lips are pressed so thin there's a fine mark of pale between them.

"I could ask you the same thing," she informs me tightly, then exits the room.

For a moment there's a dull thud of silence, and then Rae and Lea exchange glances. "Now seems like a bad time to bring it up," Rae says, "but I've been thinking I need my own place. There's my schedule, plus it's getting harder and harder to bring girls home. Too much of whatever this is," she clarifies with a lofty wave to Meredith's absence, "which really offsets the vibes."

Well, this might as well happen. Why not, honestly?

"And Simon and Simone have asked me to move in with them," Lea adds in a small voice.

I sigh. There never was a world where four women in their twenties lived together happily into perpetuity, was there? Someone was always going to leave, and it was never going to be me.

With a pang, I remember that it was always supposed to be Meredith. But while I can imagine life without Lea and Rae—they're hardly ever here to begin with—I can't imagine my life unbeholden to Meredith's mercurial moods and arbitrary falsehoods and the terrible little truths that only we got to see.

Demon sex aside, I can't imagine anything more me than... her. Even at her most terrifying.

"Fine," I say raggedly, just as my phone begins to ring.

✝

I walk into Will's hospital room to find an attractive older couple and a girl about my age, all of them weeping. I suppose these are his family members, which makes it all the more bewildering that he seems to have named me his emergency contact. Obviously I should have chosen a more rapid form of transport, but here we are.

"He's told us so much about you," says Will's tearful mother, who seems perfectly devoted to him. Not that anyone can ever truly know another person's experience, but even after hearing him bemoan his situation, it's difficult to imagine Will's childhood being much less than charmed. "He said you were the first person who seemed to really understand him."

"Oh, how... sweet," I manage to conjure from somewhere.

"I just don't understand how this could have happened," his sister says, sniffling. "He was always so happy and friendly. Everybody loved him. Everyone!"

"Oh, of course," I say meekly, glancing at the machines charting his steady pulse and shallow breathing. "Well he's not... *dead*, is he?" I ask, purely for clarity, though the entire room wails harder, which was of course a misstep by me. "I'm so sorry," I tell them hastily. "I only meant—"

What could I possibly have meant? They stare up at me, bewildered.

"You know what, why don't you all get something to eat, hm?" I suggest as a last-ditch effort. "I'll sit with him and tell him where you are if he wakes." They hesitate, and I manifest a look of pitiful fidelity. "I would just appreciate a moment," I half-whisper, and perhaps I should consider a career in daytime television, because they murmur their assent and file out, leaving me alone with Will's body and its inhabitants.

The moment they're gone, Will's eyes snap open. "Well, I'm afraid he's overindulged," pronounces not-Will grimly. "It's actually kind of embarrassing. It involved a dare between himself and one of his cohorts? I can't say I quite grasp the stakes, but that's what I gather."

"Well, boys will be boys," I remark, unsurprised. "So is he gone, then?"

"Indeed. There's nothing else in here but me."

"Dark," I register with a shiver.

"Mm, not especially," not-Will gently demurs. "It's really more of an echo situation than any visual impairment."

"I meant the mortality of it."

"Oh yes, right," the demon says. "Apologies, I'd forgotten."

"It's okay." I chew my lip. "So... do you take over his body, then?"

"I would, but unfortunately I'm not the right executive function. To maintain the same internal commands of this body would require the correct programming, whereas I am slightly different code."

"So what happens to you?"

"Well, I find another body," not-Will says plainly. "Normally not a problem, although in this case I might request your help, perhaps? Since I do hope to continue our symbiosis." He frowns. "Is that the word?"

"Relationship," I correct him.

"Yes, that." He sighs. "Apologies again. Without my host I struggle to recall the usual mortal lexicon."

"You mean even an omnipotent demon can't manage a simple translation without help?" I tease.

"Don't you require a calculator to determine gratuity?"

"Harsh but fair." It's funny how I can already see that he looks different. The usual sharpness to his features has become slightly amorphous. He—if those are even the demon's pronouns—will probably render Will unrecognizable within hours.

"I told you," not-Will reminds me earnestly, "I do have a tendency to overstress my hosts."

"Well, finding a new host is doable," I say, "but I guess I'm trying to figure out who I could get on such short notice. You prefer dummies, don't you?"

"Oh no, only for convenience. Intellect is vastly better and more interesting if I can manage it," not-Will says. "The only issue is how quickly the smart ones discover my presence. It's always a bit messy in the end. But ideally it'd be someone more complex."

"There's always Andrew," I realize like a pinprick to my thoughts. "Though he's not to your usual physical specifications."

"If he pleases you, he pleases me," says not-Will. "I find your presence stimulating enough. Perhaps we might even have a lovely pair of decades together if we were both careful? Or if this Andrew of yours could be persuaded to coexist peaceably."

I frown. "What does that mean?"

"Well, if we both agreed to share the body, then the disrepair over time would be considerably diminished," not-Will explains. "An amenable host would make for an entirely different set of rules."

"Oh." I wonder if Andrew could be persuaded. He *is* academically curious by nature, and he knows as much about the history and mythology of daemons as I do. He would know that not-Will wasn't necessarily malevolent. Perhaps he could even benefit from the obvious—the money, the refinement? Andrew is not very well-liked and he has always wanted to be.

I try to imagine spending my life with Andrew as I spent it with Will. Admittedly it's a bit tiresome to consider, though at least Meredith might let me rest. She's the one who's always wanted me to have the same perfect window-box of a life she hoped for herself, probably because she thinks of me as the person who's better suited for it.

What an idiot she is, I think with a helpless adoration. What a maniacal queen.

It occurs to me again that I've never particularly seen a future for myself without her in it. What did I really foresee after my doctoral program? The academic job market is abysmal, so not any professional success. No financial success either; what books would I possibly write? Satirical graphic translations of *Problemata*, probably, which at best would land me no farther than the sale section of Urban Outfitters.

I never see any deeper into the future than whenever I'll next drink cheap wine on my broken sofa with Meredith's glorious hair strewn lazily across my lap. And I suppose I've never actually looked for connections, have I? It's the same as Meredith settling for subpar men. What man has ever meant more to either of us than either of us?

Woeful sexuality aside, the only man I've ever really wanted to share my thoughts and feelings with was never a man at all.

"I suppose I have a somewhat eccentric offer," I say.

"Well, I certainly hope so," says not-Will approvingly. "It's why I liked you so much in the first place."

†

In the end Meredith and I make up rather quickly. I tell her that Will's out of the picture and that also, she's welcome to date Andrew if she likes, but she admits that after some consideration she actually has no interest in being some sad man's rebound. Besides, he's allergic to Hollandaise.

We help Lea move into Simon and Simone's gorgeous townhouse, which is just absurd. It's a strange version of a happily ever after, but an architecturally favorable one. I catch Meredith's eye while she stares longingly at the original wood floors and the fastidiously preserved white moldings, and she grimaces, but I shrug. *Someday none of this will be ours,*

I mouth to her, and she laughs. Together we steal a middling bottle of wine from Simon's cellar and also the faucet handles from one of the guest bathrooms. We figure it's what we deserve for handling all of this with something resembling grace.

Rae somehow digs up an industrial studio in Harlem that's... very her, which I'll leave up to interpretation as to whether it's a compliment. She is something of a pseudo-celebrity now, which she bears with an almost bewildering indifference, almost as if she hasn't noticed. During an art exhibit Lea drags us to, we discover that Rae has become the muse of a very famous Brooklyn artist. We agree amongst ourselves that this is only right.

I remove all of The Apps™ from my phone, finding them useless. I do, after all, own a technological marvel of a vibrator, and with an inheritance from an unknown "sponsor" that allows Meredith and me to make up Rae and Lea's share of the rent, all's fair in apps and war.

In case you're still wondering, yes, I took on the role of housing the demon, which has actually worked out wonderfully for us both. Thanks to his assistance I've quit the bartending job at the Olympia Club and my dissertation is nearly finished, plus we keep each other company whenever either of our thoughts wander. (We do have hours of energy conservation, for the record. As with all relationships, mutual coexistence is key.) I do know his name now, although I can't mention it here. No telling what sort of dissolution might follow.

As for Meredith and me, after a lot of soul searching and hard seltzers, we determine that there's simply no point waiting around for an idiot man to come along and give her the proper future she's always dreamed of. Ultimately it seems very silly and fruitless.

"I'm glad it never worked out with you and Will," she adds. "You really deserve so much better, you know."

I'm not entirely sure that's true. My motives when it came to Will were always slightly suspect.

Personally I think the wrongdoing was minimal, not-Will who is now not-me says in my ear.

Comforting, I reply.

I thought so.

"Well, *you* certainly deserve better," I point out to Meredith, gesturing to the magnificent polenta she's made for the two of us with the assistance of my newly transferred culinary expertise, "and anyway, who says a family needs a husband? Sometimes a family is just two wine aunts on a broken Ikea sofa." And an incorporeal demon, but I'll wait to tell her that some other drunken night.

"Or," Meredith says optimistically, "possibly a family is two wine aunts and a... sperm bank?"

That's a thought, comments the demon in my head.

Why, I ask, *do you plan to possess an infant?*

No, he tells me. *I just love babies.*

"Which isn't to say love is entirely off the table," Meredith adds, which is fair. Old habits do die hard. "I'm just beginning to think it can coexist alongside other things without having to be the necessary instigator," she says with a pointed little smirk.

"I don't see why not," I tell Meredith, who gives me the satisfied smile of a woman whose pieces have fallen into place. "I do appear to have countless marketable skills now that you've coaxed me into adulthood."

"Is that what this is?" she asks, amused.

Oddly enough, I think it must be.

GROW YOUR OWN OPTIMIST! (AUGUST - OCTOBER 2020)

WHEN DOWN ON HIS LUCK JAMIE PEREZ FINDS HIMSELF ACCIDENTALLY LOOPED INTO AN INSPIRATIONAL CHAIN EMAIL, he makes the unlikely choice to continue the chain and respond. Little does he know that the mysterious recipient of his impulsive catharsis knows how to help everyone but herself.

PART I: LIFE IS STUPID

From: Angelica Martin (amartin234@gmail.com)
To: Jamie Perez (jamieb.perez@gmail.com)

Subject: Writing Exchange!

Dearest friends,

We've started an email collective for encouraging our sisters during this difficult time of isolation! Please send a poem/quote/thought to the person whose name is below (Yes, yes, we're all strangers... it's fine! A stranger is just a future friend! ☺). Feel free to choose a favorite text/mantra/meditation that has affected you and send it to the person below:

Blake Barton (blbarton12@gmail.com)

After you've sent the short poem/verse/quote/etc to your person, copy this letter into a new email and send it to someone else! Keep the cycle of love going, sisters!!

Yours in solidarity,
Angelica

†

From: Jamie Perez (jamieb.perez@gmail.com)
To: Angelica Martin (amartin234@gmail.com)

Re: Subject: Writing Exchange!

Hi Angelica,

I think maybe there was a bit of a mix-up here? I'm actually a man (regrettably, ha) so I'm just wondering if maybe you want to send this to someone else. I'm sure someone just got their wires a bit crossed. —J.

†

Re: Subject: Writing Exchange!

Omg Jamie, I'm so sorry!!! But honestly I don't know how this whole thing was arranged or who it was that sent me your email, so… maybe if you could just send it on anyway?? I mean who cares, right? It's 2020, men can be feminists too :)

xx Angelica

p.s. nice to "meet" you!!!

†

SEB
(10:13 p.m.)

> so i somehow ended up in
> some kind of chain email
> inspirational quotes for women

lol so what lil nugget of wisdom
are u going to send the feminists

> idk man i'm kinda drunk

figures
just ignore it
nobody likes those emails
who tf even emails anymore

true

†

From: Jamie Perez (jamieb.perez@gmail.com)
To: Blake Barton (blbarton12@gmail.com)

Subject: Fwd: Writing Exchange!

Okay so I got an email about sending some kind of inspirational quote and I guess I'm supposed to tell you to live laugh love or something. Tbh I think it would be very derivative of me. I'm not actually a woman or a sister or whatever though I do get it, that whole thing. We should all be feminists and all that. I'm on board, believe me. I just didn't realize people still sent these sorts of emails, you know what I mean? I've apparently been mistaken in thinking society's moved on from dragging other members into the herd. The privilege of technology and social media was supposed to be the freedom to disengage if one so chose, but now here we both are, facing down an email from a stranger.

I wonder when you'll read this. Over breakfast maybe? I'm on my third glass of cheap whiskey, or maybe my fourth. I wasn't actually doing anything—just doom-scrolling to see what I'm supposed to care about these days—so what am I supposed to do now, ignore it? Sure, I could have replied "unsubscribe" and gotten back to my night, but I feel like what's missing in the world is the truth. The real truth, you know what I mean? Something actually honest. So here's my truth, which I've been mulling for the last six glasses or so.

Here's my essential thesis: Life is stupid. It's just a series of pointless things happening until we die. That's it. It's not even one pointless thing at a time, it's multiple pointless things at once. And we all tell ourselves that we're here for a reason, but really we don't have any better reason for existing than, idk, a mosquito. Like, what is the point of us?? Why are we here?? Soulmates are fake as shit and so is karma. Our imaginations are actually so tiny if you think about it. The universe is fucking huge, and the chances we meet our soulmate (if we even have one—which, if you're following, we don't) is like, a zillion to one. And if people actually get what they deserve, then how do you explain any of this? Nobody's turning fascists into pillars of salt and our plagues still only kill the people white taxpayers forgot. Also, there are murder hornets now?? Are you kidding me?? It's pointless. It's stupid. Nobody's contesting that.

But we keep doing it. Why? I don't know. Because life is just as random as it is stupid, I guess. And there's some beauty in the randomness. Like who knows, maybe one day you'll be drinking alone in your apartment and accidentally get an email from the feminist agenda that causes you to think that maybe being a part of something—anything—is still better than the alternative, which is the aforementioned drinking alone in your apartment. It's not beautiful in the conventional way. It's not pretty. But maybe it's just ironic enough to please the drunken eye.

Alright well in case you didn't pick up on it, I'm not a woman, and anyway below is the forwarded message.

Stay lit fam
—J.

ps how ironic is it that I have a girl's name and you have a boy's name? Unless you're actually a dude in which case. Lol. fucking life am I right

†

Angelica
(10:45 pm)

> ange, did you happen to
> include me in some kind
> of chain email

(10:56 pm)

> ange
> this guy's like, deranged

(11:13 pm)

...

> you're probably asleep huh

ugh you marrieds are so
boring

†

From: Blake Barton (blbarton12@gmail.com)
To: Jamie Perez (jamieb.perez@gmail.com)

Subject: Re: Fwd: Writing Exchange!

Okay, I'll bite. What, pray tell, the fuck

†

Jamie Perez to **Blake Barton:** Excuse me

Blake Barton: "Life is pointless"? Seriously?

Jamie Perez: Do you have any evidence suggesting otherwise?

Blake Barton: No

Jamie Perez: Well then there you go

†

Angelica
(6:45 a.m.)

lol how did you know it was me
actually don't answer that
did you keep the chain going at
least???

(7:15 am)

of course not

oh COME ON blake

I'm just really not in the mood
to be empowered

ugh, whatever
wanna skype in a bit??
I have to go for a run this morning
but it's been AGES since we actually
talked

> a run? you exhaust me
> but sure

✝

Blake Barton to **Jamie Perez:** Where are you located? I just want to know in case there's certain parts of the world that are more pointless than others.

Jamie Perez: SF, sort of.
Did not think I'd hear from you again, btw

Blake Barton: "Sort of"? That's the equivalent of leaving your jacket at my house so you'll have to come back for it.

✝

From: Jamie Perez (jamieb.perez@gmail.com)
To: Blake Barton (blbarton12@gmail.com)

Subject: left my jacket at your house

I'm in Richmond, but most people ask me if I mean the one in Virginia when I say that, so it's just easier to say Frisco. And don't think you're getting out of answering just because you decided to be clever

✝

Blake Barton to **Jamie Perez:** Okay first of all, nobody who's actually from the Bay calls it "Frisco," so jot that down. Secondly, I didn't decide to be clever, it just comes naturally. Thirdly I'm in LA. (Sort of.)

Jamie Perez: You think you're real cute huh? I see you. I'm not actually from here, which apparently you already know. I work in medical sales and I'm based out here right now.

Actually, that's a lie. I could probably just delete it or continue lying but whatever, it's not like any of this matters. I'm here because my girlfriend convinced me to move out here with her, but now she's having second thoughts. And by second thoughts I obviously mean she dumped me. It was gentle, actually. Very tender. I'm hardly even bruised. But I'm not supposed to go back to Austin until everything settles down, so... here we are.

Blake Barton: I thought you were drinking alone in your apartment?

Jamie Perez: I was drinking alone, I just never specified that the apartment was empty.

And that's seriously all you took from that?

Blake Barton: You're extremely forthcoming with personal information. Has anyone ever brought that to your attention?

Jamie Perez: All the time. Do you ever answer personal questions?

Blake Barton: You haven't technically asked me any.

†

Angelica

(8:45 am)

I'm back from my run!!
ready when you are

(9:03 am)

> hi sorry do you mind
> if we push to noon?
> I just have some client
> stuff to finish

totally, of course!

†

Hubs 🖤 🖤 🖤
(9:04 am)

pretty sure blake's about to
bail on me again :(

:(sorry babe

†

From: Blake Barton (blakeb@witchylady.net)
To: Rhiannon Rose (rhia.rose@gmail.com)

Subject: Re: New Client Consultation

Dear Rhiannon,

Thank you for choosing me to be your guide on this wonderful journey!
Selecting a path to self-improvement is one of the most rewarding things
we can do for ourselves. I'm so excited for you to take the first step toward
embracing the magic within!

As a reminder, the Witchy Woman holistic program has three different
pathways to personal wellness:

Green Witch (Basic Package)
- Daily recorded guided meditations
- Partial astrological profile
- Tarot consultation
- Subscription to our Well Witch series
- Access to our Kitchen Witch nutrition forums
- Monthly coaching sessions with a Witchy Woman mentor

Gold Witch (Advanced Package)
- Personalized guided meditations
- Full astrological profile

- Monthly tarot consultation
- Verified account in our Well Witch series
- Personalized Kitchen Witch recommendations
- Invitation to our Annual Wellness Retreat
- Weekly coaching sessions with a Witchy Woman mentor

Platinum Witch (Luxury Package)
- Personalized daily guided meditations
- Full astrological profile
- Weekly tarot consultation
- Verified account in our Well Witch series
- Personalized invitation to our Well Witch networking events
- Platinum Discount on all Witchy Woman products
- Personalized Kitchen Witch meal plans
- VIP access during our Annual Wellness Retreat
- Daily coaching sessions with a Witchy Woman mentor

The purpose of having a Witchy Woman mentor is to allow a professional life coach to open your mind and broaden your acceptance of the magic around you. As a practicing witch myself, my gift is my ability to connect to others using deep, meditative paths to empathy. I can already tell from your emails that you have such wonderful energy around you, so all that's left to do is help you find that positivity in yourself!

Once you've selected a preferred package, someone from the Witchy Woman administrative offices will get in touch before we begin your journey. From there, the magic is in your hands!

Cheers,
Blake

Blake Barton, Certified Life Coach
Witchy Woman Holistic Healing
San Luis Obispo / Santa Barbara / Santa Monica
blake@witchylady.net

✝

From: Jamie Perez (jamieb.perez@gmail.com)
To: Blake Barton (blbarton12@gmail.com)

Subject: Personal questions

Where do you live? What do you do for a living? Do you think aliens exist? Please advise.

✝

Angelica
(12:45 pm)

> sorry, does this afternoon work? I really underestimated how long this new client would take

omg girl don't even worry about it!!!! just let me know when you're free

✝

Blake Barton to **Jamie Perez:** Of course aliens exist. You should know that, right? Seeing how you think there's no difference between us and mosquitos. Anyway, even if aliens are only single-celled organisms (which I doubt they are) they have to exist. I mean, what are the chances that this is as advanced as it gets, right? We somehow managed as a society to talk ourselves back into measles. We're ripe for conquest.

Jamie Perez: I didn't say there was no difference between us and mosquitos. There's definitely a difference, but we're much worse off for knowing that.

✝

SEB
(12:45 pm)

                    linds is on a tinder date
                    right now in the other room
                    like a zoom date or something

dude
I can't believe I have to say this
but stop listening to ur ex have
phone sex

                    she's not and anyway it would
                    be zoom sex

even better
digital digital get down

                    can you, and I can't stress this
                    enough, not?
                    oh god his name is chad
                    his name is fucking c h a d
                    CHAD

ok??? so??? my name is
Sebastian
that's either a fuckboi or a porn
character, no in between

                    you're both and also i think
                    i'm going to be sick

u rly gotta move out bro

                    oh DO I seb
                    THANK YOU
                    for this incredibly novel
                    feedback

hey
don't take ur dumb decisions out
on me

†

Jamie Perez to **Blake Barton**: Full disclosure, I just googled you. Are you 25yo grad student Blake Barton, Blake Barton the teenage NBA hopeful, Blake Barton the holistic life coach (struck that one out right away tbh, no offense) or Blake Barton the 87yo art collector from New Hampshire?

Blake Barton: If you're asking whether I'm hopeful about my NBA prospects, the answer is duh, always. Also, it's kind of weird to email someone about how you googled them. Aren't you supposed to keep that sort of thing to yourself...? Wait, nvm, forgot I was talking to "life is pointless" guy. Is that in your LinkedIn profile, by the way?

Jamie Perez: So you're just not gonna tell me anything, huh?

✝

From: Blake Barton (blakeb@witchylady.net)
To: Rhiannon Rose (rhia.rose@gmail.com)

Subject: Re: New Client Consultation

Hi Rhia Rose, (Sorry for my initial confusion about what you prefer to be called!)

Thank you so much for such an enthusiastic response! I'm very excited to begin your Platinum Witch journey with us. When would you like to schedule your first daily meditation call?

✝

Blake Barton to **Jamie Perez**: Fine, you want to know about me? I commute from a dingy studio in the Valley to my clients who live in beach houses and ask me if I prefer sparkling or still as if I don't normally drink straight from the tap. They mostly keep East Coast hours and I'm three hours behind, so I basically never sleep. My friends have all collectively fallen out of touch with me except for one whose wedding anniversary is the same day mine was supposed to be. I haven't had "anything new to report" since my breakup, but she keeps asking as if one day I'll magically change my mind. I have a green thumb because patience is not a virtue, it's a skill, and I actively pretend not to hate yoga.

Your turn. What kind of person stays in their ex's apartment after they've broken up?

Jamie Perez: Uh, did you miss the whole thing about a global pandemic?

Blake Barton: Pandemic already implies global, there's no need to be redundant. And if you haven't realized by now how weak of an excuse that is, I don't know what to tell you.

Jamie Perez: You're a real ray of sunshine. Has anyone ever told you that?

Blake Barton: Yeah, whatever. Bye.

✝

From: Blake Barton (blakeb@witchylady.net)
To: Rhiannon Rose (rhia.rose@gmail.com)

Subject: Re: New Client Consultation

Hi Rhia Rose,

Thank you so much for clarifying your time zone. Traveling can be so good for the soul, and it's so wonderful that you're such an early riser! 7 a.m. EST it is. Looking forward!

✝

Angelica
(9:38 pm)

it was really fun catching up
with you tonight! really glad
we were able to chat,
even for a bit :)

yeah sorry I couldn't talk

for longer but I have
to be up at 4 for a client call

omg wow that's dedication

yep
thanks again for checking in,
good to hear from you ange x

†

From: Blake Barton (blbarton12@gmail.com)
To: Jamie Perez (jamieb.perez@gmail.com)

Subject: Sorry

Had kind of a bad day and took it out on you. No need to respond, just wanted to say I was shitty and you probably didn't deserve that (or maybe you did, I don't know your life).

You really do need to move out of your ex's apartment, though. The gyms are open now, man. Move on. Only saying that because you need to hear it from someone.

Good luck,
Blake

†

SEB
(10:23 pm)

is it weird if I'm emailing
about my personal life with
a total stranger

(10:28 pm)

actually nvm

†

Jamie Perez to **Blake Barton:** If I'm being honest, things were bad even before I moved in with her. I just figured it would be easier if I were there, or... I don't know. I thought I should prove myself to her or something, since everyone before her was such a catastrophic failure that it had to be a lack of effort on my end. I have a tendency to believe I can fix things, but it turns out I very much can't.

Blake Barton: Because life is pointless?

Jamie Perez: Whoa. Thought you'd be asleep by now.

Blake Barton: Yeah, me too. But I find that going to bed often leads to waking up in the morning, which is always less fun than it sounds.

†

From: Jamie Perez (jamieb.perez@gmail.com)
To: Blake Barton (blbarton12@gmail.com)

Subject: The hazardous state of consciousness

So you mentioned you were engaged before?

†

Blake Barton to **Jamie Perez:** What's with you and subject titles? And yes. Two years ago, for about a year.

Jamie Perez: I like things to have their place. Also, I wish I was engaged.

Blake Barton: Weird thing to say while living with an ex.

Jamie Perez: I think that's why I can't bring myself to move out, actually. I just really feel like I'm this piece that doesn't fit correctly. Like, I should be engaged at this age, shouldn't I? Or close? I should be thinking about a mortgage and a 401k, not barely paying my rent. I went to school, I did all the stuff I was supposed to. I eat right and I work out and all evidence seems to suggest I'll keep my hair, so what gives, right? I just assumed that everything would work out if I did all the steps correctly—so now I think part of me is convinced that I can't move on until I fix whatever the problem is. I'm supposed to have a life by now.

Blake Barton: Life... you mean that pointless thing we're all doing for no reason?

Jamie Perez: Touché.

†

From: Blake Barton (blakeb@witchylady.net)
To: Rhiannon Rose (rhia.rose@gmail.com)

Subject: (DRAFT) August Well Witch Goals

Dear Rhia Rose,

August is a time of impending harvest, and the ideal time of year for remembering that we reap the things we sow. For that reason, it's important to show gratitude for the offerings that come your way, and to recognize that what we put into the world is often what we get out of it. It is the perfect time for protective magic, creation, and offering! In order to better connect to the earth and the community around you, now is the time to consider a new ritual that will

†

Blake Barton to **Jamie Perez**: Do you have any rituals?

Jamie Perez: What, like going to the gym before work or something?

Blake Barton: Not habits, rituals. Things you actually think about while you're doing them, not things you do without thinking about them.

Jamie Perez: I'm assuming you mean something other than getting drunk "alone" in "my" apartment, which I'd have to think about. Do you have any?

Blake Barton: Officially? Yes. Off the record, I find that if I think about something for too long I immediately want to stop thinking about anything.

Jamie Perez: Hey don't take this the wrong way but... are you okay?

Blake Barton: Well, last night a stranger emailed me about how life is pointless, so...

Jamie Perez: You know, you keep misquoting me. I said life is STUPID. Which it is. But tons of stupid stuff is great. I mean, look at pugs.

Blake Barton: I'm not sure that's accomplishing what you want it to? Pugs are basically not even supposed to be alive. They can't hunt or sniff things out or live on their own in the wild, plus we bred them so they can't even properly breathe.
You know, I think life might actually, truly be pointless. We're all just running around trying to make enough money to stay alive until we die. And if money doesn't even make us happy, then what exactly are we doing any of it for?

✝

SEB
(1:31 am)

yo I think this girl
might be even more fucked
than I am

l'chaim
and go to bed

✝

305

From: Jamie Perez (jamieb.perez@gmail.com)
To: Blake Barton (blbarton12@gmail.com)

Subject: pugs are cute you heartless pedant

What if I moved out tonight?

†

Blake Barton: Oh for fuck's sake. Did you think I was hitting on you???

Jamie Perez: No--jesus, no, I'm saying what if I moved out tonight, would that prove you wrong? Because then I'd be a person whose life you changed, so that can't possibly be pointless.

Blake Barton: Okay, hold up. What makes you think I don't ALREADY change people's lives? I fucking change lives every day, okay Mr. Medical Sales. Because I worked instead of going to college, both my sisters could afford to go to school and now one's a lawyer and the other one's a doctor. Because of me, my ex didn't have to drop out of his PhD program and that's how he met the woman he left me for. So I don't really need you to tell me that my life has meaning, okay? It does have meaning. For everyone but me.

Jamie Perez: How did it feel to say something honest for the first time all night?

Blake Barton: screw you

†

BLAKE BARTON · @bbartonwitch · 2h
Now is the time to focus on your intentions! For a gratitude exercise, I like to use clear quartz and obsidian while centering my thoughts on a mantra about newness. Remember to give thanks for your blessings as the spiritual harvest grows near!

✝

Angelica
(2:41 am)
> do you think I'm a hypocrite
> nvm don't answer that

✝

From: Jamie Perez (jamieb.perez@gmail.com)
To: Blake Barton (blbarton12@gmail.com)

Subject: is it too late now to say sorry

Sorry for the Bieber lyrics. But look, I know I was a dick. I didn't mean to be, it's just that you don't seem like someone who appreciates it very much when people are nice to you.

I get that I haven't given up as much as you have, but it seems like maybe we have the same problem. We keep doing things because we expect a certain result. I expected to get love if I made the decisions based on love, but it doesn't work like that. You clearly sacrificed and you expected your sacrifice to return something to you, but that's not how it goes.

BECAUSE LIFE. IS. STUPID.

And part of life being stupid is staying up all night talking to a stranger and making more progress in one day than in three months of talking to a friend. It's that pugs are cute but also can't breathe. It's making decisions to help someone else but them not making the decision to help you back because you can't control people—you can only choose them. And it's also figuring out that the most cynical person you've ever spoken to in your entire life is some kind of witchy influencer on Instagram.

I'm sorry that I didn't inspire you properly, because yeah, I mostly peddle drugs that have worse side effects than the problems they're supposed to fix. But what I meant to say is that life is stupid and pointless and funny and surprising, and maybe soulmates and karma aren't real, but friendship is, and randomly meeting someone on the internet who gets the bottle out of your hand for the night is close enough to both.

Anyway, hope you have a good day, or a good life or whatever. No need to respond. I'm going on a little road trip, I think, so I might be incommunicado anyway.

It was really fucking weird to meet you, Blake Barton. And I mean that as a compliment.

–J.

†

Angelica
(6:11 am)

why would I think you're a
hypocrite??
oh and how was your client call?

†

From: Rhiannon Rose (rhia.rose@gmail.com)
To: Blake Barton (blakeb@witchylady.net)

Subject: Re: August Well Witch Goals

Blake,

cannot Thank You enough for this morning's call am Feeling Invigorated and Full Of The Universe's Spirit Etc Etc. Jw if it's Possible to also do a Call this afternoon as my Anxiety spikes after midday (mentioned I was doing a Cleanse I Hope???) Assistant will Ping with details–

BLESSINGS!!!
Rhia Rose

✝

Angelica
(6:34 am)

she's a total lunatic

self-destructive in
relationships, confuses
anxiety with blood sugar, has
more money than she needs
and is completely unaware that
she's swapped out her
problematic religious
upbringing with a slavish
devotion to astrology and the
occult

oh nooooo sounds awful!!

tbh I think it might be kinda
fun

✝

From: Blake Barton (blbarton12@gmail.com)
To: Jamie Perez (jamieb.perez@gmail.com)

Subject: get out of your ex's apartment and then open this message

✝

SEB
(8:34 am)

is it weird that I'm sitting
in a parking lot off the pch
looking at an unopened email

yes

would it be weirder if I

                                          went down to the beach and
just like, got myself off very
discreetly
while looking at the ocean

yes

                                          might do it anyway

I figured

                                          cool

there are probably worse rituals
to have

                                          rituals are things you think
about while you're doing them,
not things you do without
thinking about them

best way to think imo

                                          well
I guess you have a point

†

Subject: get out of your ex's apartment and then open this message

(XXX) XXX-XXXX

†

Maybe: Jamie Perez
(12:34 pm)

hey it's jamie

                                          hey jamie
has anyone ever told you that
you have a girl's name?

PART II: JOY IS FLEETING

From: Mark Carney (mcarney@ostettlerpharma.com)
CC: Frank Ostettler (fostettler@ostettlerpharma.com)
To: Jamie Perez (jperez@ostettlerpharma.com)

Subject: Re: NW Quarterly Sales Report, Block 4A

Dear Jamie,

Hope this email finds you well! Just wanted to touch base about your comments from yesterday's Zoom call. Given the times, I'm sure you're aware that we're learning not only as an industry but as a global economy just how much can be done remotely. Every day at Ostettler Pharmaceuticals we're pushing the envelope and working to advance the state of telemedicine in America—none more so than here in the Northwest Regional Sales division!

As our most recent transfer to the Northwest region of sales, I'm concerned you may not have been sufficiently briefed on our preferred terminology. For example, in yesterday's call you suggested that our recently designated Five Step Clarity Procedure felt "pushy," as in Step Four, Focused Deliberation (i.e., "You're saying your office would like to decrease this month's order of Revelin, the world's foremost preventative anti-depressant, despite no change in patient requests?") As I'm sure you recall from last month's orientation, we do not use the word "push," opting instead for more appropriate terminology such as "actionable information" or "progressive collaboration guidance." We also do not refer to Ostettler products as "drugs," as such terms can be extraordinarily misleading. Our business is the wellness of our human family, which we provide by virtue of compassionate dedication to modern patient care.

While we're very grateful to have someone of your caliber in our department, it appears that the Southwest Regional Sales division may have overlooked some of the training hours that we in the Northwest Regional Sales division believe to be essential. We ask that you please complete the following sixty hours of our Employee Reinvigoration Series, which we in the Northwest have worked tirelessly over the past four months to make available online! While all currently contracted clients will not be affected, please note that no new client paperwork will be approved until the Employee Reinvigoration Series and subsequent re-entry exam have been completed.

Hope you and your family are staying well!

All best,
Mark

Mark Franklin Carney, Division Team Lead
Block 4A, Northwest Regional Sales
Ostettler Pharmaceuticals, Inc.
San Francisco, CA

†

From: Jamie Perez (jamieb.perez@gmail.com)
To: Blake Barton (blbarton12@gmail.com)

Subject: compassionate dedication to modern patient care

Well, I just got pretty much exactly what I was expecting from my supervisor, who really needs to get a sports team or something because he sounds like he sleeps in a homemade Northwest Regional Sales jersey. Also, can we just go ahead and do away with "hope this email finds you well"? Like, the fact that the email is finding me at all is a pretty good indicator that I'm distinctly unwell, but good try.

Anyway, they're not calling it a suspension but it might as well be. There's been a stay at home order for as long as I've been part of this division, so my business is entirely new clients. Plus I think they're looking for any reason to be rid of me. I heard there's a class action suit going or something. Something about an opioid epidemic, I imagine.

I still haven't decided how I feel about my job since you asked. Like, is it immoral? I'm not dealing crack but aren't I, in a way? But then again I don't know, people do need it, and is it my fault that medicine has such terrible side effects...? If we could just ask the stars then I assume there'd be nothing to medicate, so personally this feels like a flaw in the design.

I get how people get addicted, for the record. People can get addicted to absolutely anything in my experience, not just pills. You can get addicted to lattes or to hearing people laugh. That's the whole thing with comedians, right? That they're basically all narcissists who get addicted to the high of making people laugh and then they can't quit. I always thought Linds (my ex) was like that with flirting—not in a bad way, she just got a high from meeting new people. Well, new men, specifically. She was addicted to the knowledge that someone was looking at her and I think I got addicted to being the someone who got to look at her. Not to like, objectify her or anything, because if I were as good at dating as she is then yeah, I'd probably want to do more of it too. God, I sound like that guy in *500 Days of Summer*, pretend I never brought it up. The point is I don't know who to blame for how dependent we are on that feeling of happiness, or I guess it's more like relief. Even if it's temporary—which it literally always is—none of us seem capable of resisting.

So anyway, 60 hours of workplace training here I come. Remind me not to attend Zoom conference calls after two car mimosas again.

†

Blake Barton to **Jamie Perez**: Hey, here's some focused deliberation for your 5 step clarity procedure: when I called you a drug pusher, I super did not intend for you to turn around and say that to your actual boss. And why are you emailing me? You have my cell.

Jamie Perez: I dunno, I thought you'd be asleep. I was going to text you earlier but I wasn't getting service at the beach, and anyway now I'm at a uniquely terrible AirBnB. I'm stealing wifi from the liquor store next door but there's no working showerhead. And once again, I can't believe you're responding to my heartfelt email with "why are you emailing me," but I'm guessing I'll get used to it. I've always been a little weak for women who are a little mean.

Blake Barton: You really, really need a life coach. And to find a nice girl, apparently, though I don't know, those might be a myth. I don't think anyone's actually nice. I think they just want other things badly enough that they're willing to say or do whatever it takes to get it.

†

SEB

(1:21 am)

yo. what's your take on nice people

suspicion

what?

I find them suspicious.
why are you so nice.
what's wrong with you.
that sort of thing

same, kinda. but surely that's a flaw, right?
or like a coping mechanism
or something

more like an insurance policy?
nobody is nice without an agenda

so then do you think it's better

314

if people are blatantly mean??

I didn't say that.
I just don't trust niceness.
anyone who's too nice to anyone
is getting paid

okay, so then explain your
mom

just because I don't understand
her specific form of currency
doesn't mean she isn't collecting
exorbitant amounts of interest

and anyway leave my mom out
of it, man. gross

✝

From: Blake Barton (blakeb@witchylady.net)
To: Rhiannon Rose (rhia.rose@gmail.com)

Subject: Re: URGENT!!!!!!!

Hi Rhia Rose,

Just wanted to follow up after tonight's call before we speak again for our morning meditation. As I mentioned over the phone, I encourage you to consider trying one of our Witchy Woman ritual baths. "Serenity," which includes some wonderfully aromatic lemongrass oil, is one of my personal favorites, as is "Calm," which creates a similar sense of inner peace while invoking the vibrancy of sea salt, allowing your mind sufficient room to wander.

Consider as you bathe the circumstances of your anxiety, and in particular your sense of injustice. Now is the time to discover your many parts! I encourage you to inhale a benediction and exhale a release; for example, inhale gratitude for your independence and exhale resentment for your ex-husband. There is a difference between the valuing of your past and the servicing of your anger. Would you be who you are if not for him? This is what I mean when I say to consider your many parts. Find the edges of yourself and ask: Am I a garden just beginning to bear fruit, or is there some underlying virus rotting my leaves? This is also what I mean by finding your tenderness. In addressing your needs, is it crucial to be gentle or forceful? After all, emotional pesticides can only go so far.

Please find the invoice for this evening's phone call attached. For any further inquiries, please contact our billing department.

Yours in prosperity,
Blake

\-

Blake Barton, Certified Life Coach
Witchy Woman Holistic Healing
San Luis Obispo / Santa Barbara / Santa Monica
blakeb@witchylady.net

†

Jamie Perez to **Blake Barton:** How's it going with that new client you have? I've been thinking about her ever since you told me that story.

Blake Barton: The one about how she's compulsively recreating her ex-husband in a series of lawn gnomes, you mean? Or the dreams where she gives birth to her own father?

Jamie Perez: I actually looked at those lawn gnomes and they're weirdly good.

Blake Barton: I know. They're exactly the right amount of disturbing.

Jamie Perez: But actually, I meant the story about her mother leaving their family for their minister. I mean you said she replaced her religious upbringing with astrology and stuff, right? So I keep thinking about it. Like, who is her god now? Gemini?

Blake Barton: Is that... I don't know what to do with that. Gemini is not a person?

Jamie Perez: Okay whatever, but I'm just saying. If everyone believes in something, then what does she believe in? Or I guess what I'm actually asking is what do I believe in.

Blake Barton: Okay, so what do you believe in?

Jamie Perez: On a good day? Human decency.

Blake Barton: ... and when was your last good day?

Jamie Perez: Point taken. What about you?

Blake Barton: On a good day? Karma. Not the thing we turned karma into, like our own personal vengeance translator or something, but the general sense of balance. That the universe is a self-regenerating organ. Self-healing. That sort of thing.

Jamie Perez: I like that, it's soothing. So is this a good day, then?

Blake Barton: Oh sure, absolutely. I just spent two hours on the phone explaining to my client that her ex-husband is not actually capable of haunting her from mirrors, given that he is not dead and is instead merely somewhere in Florida. This is what I live for.

Jamie Perez: Well, misery loves company. On a related note, seeing as I'm sure you were dying to know what I'm up to, it turns out I'm going to have to actually watch the entire 60 hours of this training. I thought maybe I could just run it while I was doing other things but there are interactive portions at irregular intervals, which is obviously very disappointing news.

Blake Barton: You realize this is extremely uninteresting to me, yes?

Jamie Perez: Yes.

Blake Barton: Okay. Just checking.

Jamie Perez: I guess doing these training videos is just as good as anything else I'd be doing from my shitty motel room.

Blake Barton: Don't you have like... nowhere to be and nothing to do? You could spend all your time with this weird work video or you could find something else to do during the day and just watch it at night. All you do after 10 pm is get existential anyway.

Jamie Perez: You make a depressingly accurate point. So what would you do if you could spend your day doing anything?

Blake Barton: I don't know. Drive along the coast. Get lost somewhere with no cell service. Find a remote cliff and scream.

Jamie Perez: There's a real feral quality to your darkness, Barton.

Blake Barton: I'm insulted it took you this long to notice.

✝

From: Rhiannon Rose (rhia.rose@gmail.com)
To: Blake Barton (blakeb@witchylady.net)

Subject: Re: September Well Witch Goals

Blake,

Have been Thinking about your garden Philosophy & find myself concerned it is Triggering unpleasant memories of my adolescence & intrusive thoughts (gardens are a Very christian mythos) so I will need to speak with you immediately in order to Harness these feelings & prevent my retreat into Personal Darkness. am VERY CONCERNED this will undo all our beautiful Progress

please contact my assistant to arrange our next call!!!!
Rhia Rose

✝

Angelica
(10:32 am)

This client is... very intense

Oh boy, what now??

eh, the usual. it's just that
we're not allowed to say things
like "you need to take this
down at least ten notches," so
like...
very challenging

Ughhh people are so weird.
Do you think she's listening to
you?

Oh, absolutely not. I mean
she's listening, but also
hyperfocusing on the things
she wants to hear. Which so
far seems to be anything that
reinforces her suspicion that
other people are conspiring
against her

Oof. So what are you going to
tell her?

To do some inner child work,
probably

Will that help?

A normal person? Yes. but
personally I think her god will
always be vengeful, she likes it
that way

????

Her god. as in the thing she
believes in

I know who god is blake...

†

From: Blake Barton (blbarton12@gmail.com)
To: Jamie Perez (jamieb.perez@gmail.com)

Subject: Re: compassionate dedication to modern patient care

Yummy noises. That's my god

†

Jamie Perez to **Blake Barton**: What?

Blake Barton: I used to live for the sounds people would make when they ate my food. Like, specifically my ex. Not that I'm an incredible chef or anything, because I'm not. But he would take a bite of something and make this extremely over the top sound that I would pretend to hate, but secretly I loved it. I'd cook new things all the time just to see if I could get him to do it.

Jamie Perez: You know you could have texted me this, right?

Blake Barton: I was continuing an old conversation, not starting a new one. Besides, you said you weren't getting very good phone service.

Jamie Perez: Alright, fair enough. You haven't mentioned your ex before

Blake Barton: He wasn't relevant before

Jamie Perez: I'd ask you what happened, but I know you won't tell me

Blake Barton: there's nothing to tell

✝

From: Jamie Perez (jamieb.perez@gmail.com)
To: Blake Barton (blbarton12@gmail.com)

Subject: starting a new conversation

I did take your advice, for what that's worth

✝

Blake Barton to **Jamie Perez**: You've decided to stop pushing drugs?

Jamie Perez: I do not "push" "drugs," I provide actionable items to wellness professionals. And what I meant was that I took your advice to do something with my time—spent today driving to Tahoe. Found a cabin in the woods and am currently sitting out on the porch watching this video training and emailing a reclusive stranger I barely know

Blake Barton: I'm not reclusive

Jamie Perez: Okay cool, good talk

✝

SEB
(4:32 pm)

so how are the woods???
are there bears

> I'm not sure this counts as
> those kinds of woods?
> it's like, basically a ski resort

well I'm still unsure why
you decided to do this.
certainly not if there are no bears

> I don't know, I was just
> scrolling instagram while

zoning out of this training
video and then I realized I
could just leave and wake up
somewhere more interesting

I've been telling you this
for months

yeah but it never sounds
exciting when you say it

does it sound exciting when
someone else says it???

I mean. kinda, yeah

†

Blake Barton to **Jamie Perez**: for the record, I'm glad you took my advice. My venmo is @bbartonwitch, feel free to shoot over my usual coaching fee at your earliest convenience

Jamie Perez: I can't believe you get away with this kind of robbery. Are people really just paying you money for you to be their friend??

Blake Barton: They're paying me money to listen to them, yes. but I'm not their friend

Jamie Perez: Next you're going to tell me you don't have any friends, right?

Blake Barton: I have one friend and she's already more friends than I need

Jamie Perez: You're about as nurturing as a cactus, you know that? Not that I'm complaining. The cacti is a strong and noble breed

Blake Barton: I get that a lot. "You'll get through this, you're so strong" and "you'll be happier without me, you're tough enough on your own." I love it. Classic

Jamie Perez: I'm assuming this is about your ex. You know that what he's really saying is that he wants someone to need him, right?

Blake Barton: Oh, so it's my fault now?

Jamie Perez: No, god, I'm just saying—you take care of people, you don't need them, so some people probably resent that. I'm guessing he left you for someone younger right? And like, dumber probably

Blake Barton: I'm not going to blame her for his decision.

Jamie Perez: Yeah, exactly, that's what I'm saying. Because you're smart, and he needed to be the smart one. Classic

†

Angelica
(9:31 pm)

Can you do me a weird favor?

Ummmm always

Can you look at Charlie's instagram?

Omg YES absolutely.
What am I looking for?

I don't know. Anything I guess

Okay hang on

(9:35 pm)

Omg so he broke up with that girl, there's a long post about them parting ways with a spirit of mutual compassion.
Who is he, gwyneth paltrow???
And now some other girl is always commenting on his posts, hang on

(9:38 pm)

Oh my GOD her account is
private but it says UofM 2021.
She's an undergrad!!!! Charlie!!!!
What the fuck!!!!!!

(9:41 pm)

Okay wow this was a deep dive
but I found her blog
and she definitely keeps hinting
at a secret boyfriend so, yikes.
Wowwwwwwwwwowwwowowwww

I can't believe I almost
married him.

You dodged a bullet FOR SURE

†

BLAKE BARTON · **@bbartonwitch** · **1h**
As summer comes to an end, this is the season of letting go: old grudges
don't have to stifle new growth. Find your light and let it guide you as we
return our spirits to the earth!

†

From: Blake Barton (blbarton12@gmail.com)
To: Jamie Perez (jamieb.perez@gmail.com)

Subject: (No subject)

How's the video training going?

†

Jamie Perez to **Blake Barton**: No subject title, really?

Blake Barton: Are you going to heckle me every time we do this?

Jamie Perez: Depends. Are we going to keep doing this?

Blake Barton: We're barely doing it now.

Jamie Perez: Okay, true. And to answer your question I just hit play ten minutes ago, so it's going as well as it can be. Not sure I'll be able to keep myself awake for very long, though.

Blake Barton: Too invigorated from your day of actionable items?

Jamie Perez: Yes, actually. Sort of. I went for a really long hike today.

Blake Barton: Sightseeing or soul searching?

Jamie Perez: Umm more sightseeing? That was the idea, anyway. I had some existential moments but they were coincidental, I think.

Blake Barton: Any new gems to add to the "life is stupid" and "joy is fleeting" collection?

Jamie Perez: It was a little more personalized this time. Well, no—actually, I was thinking about you. I mean I was thinking about me, but also you.

Blake Barton: Is this going to get gross?

Jamie Perez: What? Jesus, no. I was just thinking about how you always helped people in your life and were disappointed by them, but I don't help anyone and I'm still disappointed. So like, is there a way not to be disappointed, or... nah?

Blake Barton: Hang on, let me write this down: "People are disappointing," got it. Go on.

Jamie Perez: I'm serious though. Like, the only reason to exist is other people, right? Anything else is just capitalism or trying not to get eaten by bears. But it's a gamble, because for every person who brings something to your life there's probably someone else who takes something from it. And like, how do you make sure it's not a shitty gamble. That's the whole thing.

Blake Barton: That's the whole thing?

Jamie Perez: Pretty much, yeah.

✝

From: Blake Barton (blakeb@witchylady.net)
To: Rhiannon Rose (rhia.rose@gmail.com)

Subject: Re: INTRUSIVE THOUGHTS?

Hi Rhia Rose,

I apologize for the delay, but I was doing a monthly phone consultation with another client when you emailed this morning. As Kelly from our Administrative Offices already explained to you over the phone, as a Platinum member I am always eager to ensure your psyche is well-supported. However, I do have other clients, so if you still feel my services as a Witchy Woman mentor are not meeting your standards, I accept your wish to terminate the remaining services included in your Platinum membership and wish you the best of luck.

Whatever your decision, I do want to assure you that the feelings of discomfort you seem to be having as a result of your ritual meditations are not only quite common, but necessary. While you may personally feel that your memories surrounding the dissolution of your marriage are intrusive or toxic thoughts, I encourage you to consider the alternative: that learning a lesson about ourselves and others can be taxing, but still indicative of growth.

What I think is important is not to punish yourself for mistakes you've made in the past, but rather, to feel encouraged by the gamble you've taken. No risk, no reward. So you can either own the flaws in your experience and keep going, or you can stop now and never live at all. The choice, as always, is yours.

Yours in tranquility,
Blake

†

SEB
(8:32 am)

ok fuck you, that picture you posted is incredible and you know I only doom-scroll. did you do that hike at dawn?

kinda?
couldn't sleep so I drove to yosemite and then I was like well, might as well not waste any time

bro you are turning into a mutant

actually I think I'm just starting to realize something about life

....which is????

no idea.
I'm just saying that whatever it is, I'm just now starting to figure it out

†

Jamie Perez paid Blake Barton • 1h

coaching fees, plus interest

†

Blake
(9:32 am)

$5? Seriously?

                        I factored in a friends and
                        family discount if that's cool

The hubris here is staggering

                        you're the one texting me

I didn't want to think of an email
title

                        hey, I'm not mad. gives me
                        something to do besides watch
                        this training video

What are you supposed to be
learning now?
How to infiltrate the facebook
algorithms for people over sixty?

                        I honestly don't know,
                        I keep nodding off

Don't you have actionable items
for that?

                        hilarious.

                        how's your crazy client?

She tried to fire me, actually.
But then she unfired me

                        whoa, what'd you do?
                        Pull off an exorcism?

Just finally gave her some advice
she liked, I guess.
Actually she's trying to poach me
now

                        what??

Yeah she wants me to be her
full-time life guru

                        damn.
                        Though I'm guessing you

could charge her whatever you
wanted

I probably could, yeah

but you're... not going to?

I mean... if all there is to living
is the gamble we take on other
people, I'm not really sure this is
the one

(9:45 am)

Did you fall asleep?

nearly. Can I call you?

Why?

I don't know really. Just want
to

oh
yeah, okay

†

Outgoing: Blake Barton

"Hello?"

"Whoa. That is... not what I thought your voice would sound like."

"Oh good, bye then—"

"Oh come on—"

"I'm joking. What did you expect me to sound like?"

"Like... an old, old Russian woman?"

"What, like the Baba Yaga?"

"Yes, exactly."

"Interesting. I thought you'd sound like Darth Vader."

"And do I?"

"Yes actually, it's uncanny."

"Okay, I know you're mocking me, but I'm choosing to pretend it's a compliment."

"Fair enough."

"So what did you tell your client? That life is stupid?"

"Pretty much."

"And she was like oh cool, come live with me?"

"Basically."

"I can't figure out if that's the best job offer in the world or the worst."

"A little of both, probably. Though she's really not so bad. Just... lonely, I think, and with enough money to make it seem especially unfair."

"That feels generous—"

"I'm a generous person."

"—apparently so. I was going to say it felt generous but also, you do seem like you enjoy a certain amount of irony. Like maybe it soothes you."

"What, that a rich person isn't happy? Or that a drug pusher thinks life is pointless."

"Again, it's stupid, not pointless—"

"Sorry, sorry—"

"And yeah, kind of, because it proves my theory, doesn't it?"

"Which one? You have a lot of theories for a drug pusher."

"I'm not touching that again. And I meant the theory that, you know...
Well, okay—life is stupid, sure, but more specifically, you can really only
be so happy. Nobody has more than anybody else. Like okay, they do,
because privilege and racism and stuff—"

"Right, that stuff."

"—but say you get like, ten marbles. And everyone has ten marbles. And
some people like your client have ten marbles of money and zero
happiness marbles. And some people have three marbles."

"And some people have chain email penpals?"

"Right. Which is one potential marble."

"So do the marbles change form?"

"What?"

"Well, because joy is fleeting. According to you."

"Oh, well, no. I mean first of all I'm pretty sure you're misquoting me
again. But also, I think if you have a happiness marble then you probably
always have a happiness marble."

"So joy isn't fleeting...?"

"No, it is, definitely, but like, it comes back. It flits in, too, not just out."

"So one good turn deserves another?"

"More like... if it wasn't this, it'd be something else."

"Ah."

"Yeah."

(Silence.)

"I told her what you told me, actually."

"What?"

"My client. I told her what you told me."

"Which part?"

"All of it."

"All of it?"

"Well, I paraphrased."

"And that did the trick?"

"That did the trick."

"Huh. Interesting. I feel like you're trying to tell me something."

"Yes. I'm trying to tell you that I will not be reimbursing your coaching fee."

"Fair enough, but I still think you're trying to say something... else. Maybe even... something nice?"

(Silence.)

"No."

"Ah, okay. Well for the record, I Venmoed you because you changed my life, so we're even."

(Silence.)

"Also, I'm going to re-start the video now. Want to stay on the phone with me?"

(Silence.)

"Yeah, okay."

"Good. I was hoping you'd say that."

PART III: PEOPLE ARE DISAPPOINTING

From: Rhiannon Rose (rhia.rose@gmail.com)
To: Blake Barton (blakeb@witchylady.net)

Subject: Re: October Well Witch Goals

Blake,

Once again I find Myself wondering about the connection I have with others in my Life or perhaps in my Past Lives. As you say this is the season of the Witch and with the end of summer comes the season of Ancestral spirits. you have Said that this is meant to be about gratitude but I find myself overburdened with Resentment. how can I be Sure that my ancestors are listening or that their Intentions are as pure as mine? as you Know I have been forced to carry many Emotional Hardships in my Life and while it is not my fault (you have made this very clear to me which is one of many reasons I value your ability to Focus my Thoughts) I still feel there is some doubt clouding my Mind and I am Concerned this will inevitably lead me to a destructive spiral. As you are probably aware by now my Empathy is my Curse. hope to speak about this soon, can be free in fifteen minutes but no later than an Hour

Blessings!!!!!
Rhia Rose

†

From: Blake Barton (blbarton12@gmail.com)
To: Jamie Perez (jamieb.perez@gmail.com)

Subject: Re: Re: Re: no subject, stop it with the subjects Jamie seriously not every email needs a subject

What are your thoughts on cottagecore

†

Jamie Perez to **Blake Barton**: Would it really be so hard to just send me an email titled "apropos of nothing, I know I've worked hard on my Cool Girl persona but it turns out I'm listening to Taylor Swift again"? It's honestly a matter of expediency at this point. Did you know the modern attention span is only like, seven seconds? And now all I can think about is the fact that this email has a completely irrelevant title to the subject at hand

Blake Barton: Don't let this go to your head but you're the worst person I've ever met

Jamie Perez: Thank you

Blake Barton: Answer the question

Jamie Perez: I've literally never thought about "cottagecore" in my life. I had to google it. It looks like... I don't know, pumpkin spice lattes but in architecture form?

Blake Barton: First of all the PSL is essentially THE symbol of western capitalism, so it's the complete opposite of cottagecore. Second of all how dare you. I'm leaving

Jamie Perez: Have you been watching that Anne of Green Gables show on Netflix? (I definitely haven't, he says, innocently.) (In my defense she's a chatty delight and also, GENERATIONS of readers will readily confirm that.) Or wait, hang on—have you finally realized your destiny to become the village witch? Personally I think you'd be very good at it, if that has not occurred to you already

Blake Barton: My only ambition at this point is to become unreachable to society. I'm tired of emails and phone calls. I'm tired of exchanging currency for goods and services. What is this? It's meaningless. I'm ready to tend some sheep and grow some herbs and rely on the earth before dying unexpectedly of typhoid

Jamie Perez: Okay, so this is definitely the Anne of Green Gables effect. Or maybe Little Women???

Blake Barton: Your attempts at becoming a feminist ally may have gone a step too far

Jamie Perez: Hey, leave your toxic masculinity out of this. Unless you've got a potion for that, in which case we're back to the village witch thing

Blake Barton: I hate to give you credit but it's a really good idea. Live in the woods? Make herbal remedies? Curse some dicks? Ideal

Jamie Perez: Told you. And for the record, I could probably dig up some stuff for typhoid. It is one of the things I offer as a capitalist purveyor of actionable items

Blake Barton: Why are you in my cottage fantasy to begin with? I didn't invite you in

Jamie Perez: Oh sorry I just assumed I was there. Like, possibly as one of the dicks you were cursing

Blake Barton: Nah. I imagine your virility has enough trouble without my help

Jamie Perez: While that shot to the groin is, as ever, impeccably mean, the rock climber whose guest house I'm staying in might happen to disagree with you. Not to be excessively gratuitous, but rock climbers really don't get enough credit for their grip strength

†

Angelica
(11:34 am)

Why are people so
consistently disappointing?
They're never what you want
them to be

Aww what now? That client again?

It's all stupid. also, you gotta
stop sending me these
cottages. And this "affordable
old houses" feed. And
whatever this french manor
house restoration thing is

you don't like them???

No, I fucking love them,
that's the problem. I
don't have time to daydream
about absconding from society.
The dream shatters every time
I open my email or happen to
stumble on my sister's
instagram

Omg her new house is so good

No, her new house is
expensive, there's a
difference. She and Justin
hired a decorator and there's
basically no trace of her
anywhere in the whole thing

You mean Grayson??
You gave the toast at their
wedding

I know this phrase gets
morbidly overused
but I truly could not care less

You can't hate him forever, B.

If Ryan wants to quit her job and
be a mom that's her choice, just
like you dropping out to pay for
her tuition was your choice. You
don't get to decide what her life
looks like

Excuse me, I'm the one with
the life coach certification.
what exactly are your
credentials?

I teach kindergarten.
Irrational tantrums are kind
of my bread and butter

I'm not a child ange

She says, childishly.
And wait, is this "people are
disappointing" thing about
Ryan? Or your client?

It's not about anything. It's just
a fact.

†

From: Jamie Perez (jamieb.perez@gmail.com)
To: Blake Barton (blbarton12@gmail.com)

Subject: You might be onto something with this cottage stuff

Then again, it does seem like maybe the fact that we can't actually interact
with anyone is making me want to do that from an ivy covered cabin. Or,
as you say, the woods

Haven't heard from you in a bit. Everything okay? Missing my nightly
dose of the Rhia Rose show. plus I'm sure you're dying to hear about the
Northwest Regional Team's new diversity initiative

†

From: Blake Barton (blakeb@witchylady.net)
To: Rhiannon Rose (rhia.rose@gmail.com)

Subject: Re: WELLNESS RETREAT

Hi Rhia Rose,

As I'm sure you know, with things as they are in the world we felt it would be more appropriate to cancel our in-person Wellness Retreat this fall. But don't worry! The online shop will be open with discounts on all our Witchy Woman products, and I will be providing several remote workshops on meditation and spiritual wellness. While I appreciate your very generous offer to sponsor the event, we at Witchy Woman are primarily concerned with preserving the health and safety of our community.

If you have further questions, please direct them to our administrative offices. Looking forward to our morning meditation!

Yours in peace,
Blake

Blake Barton, Certified Life Coach
Witchy Woman Holistic Healing
San Luis Obispo / Santa Barbara / Santa Monica
blakeb@witchylady.net

†

From: Jamie Perez (jamieb.perez@gmail.com)
To: Blake Barton (blbarton12@gmail.com)

Subject: I'm way too invested in this betty love triangle

Are you going to take responsibility for my obsession with this album?
Please advise.

✝

BLAKE BARTON · @bbartonwitch · 3h

The need for escape is common as the season of the witch approaches!
During your Autumn meditations, be sure to inhale your blessings
(friendship, laughter, life) and exhale your grievances (betrayal, anger,
envy). Remember that every step forward gets dragged two steps back by
bad feelings, personal resentment, and toxic relationships. Open yourself
to the ancestral spirits who may help you find health and success!

✝

From: Jamie Perez (jamieb.perez@gmail.com)
To: Blake Barton (blbarton12@gmail.com)

Subject: Seriously?

Okay, usually I have some idea why you're mad at me (as in, usually you
tell me in a very upsetting way) so I have to say it's not very chill of you to
leave me hanging

Don't tell me this is about the rock climber.

✝

SEB
(10:03 pm)

straw poll:
do we think misanthropic life
coach is pissed at me because
I talked about doing stuff
with another girl, or...?

341

do u really need to ask whether
someone you refer to as
"misanthropic life coach"
is behaving misanthropically?
if so she may be misnamed

                                    I really regret bringing it up to
                                    her

ok why'd you do it then

                                    I don't know

                                    I mean I guess maybe on some
                                    level I wanted to push her into
                                    like, admitting something. or I
                                    don't know

                                    she's more sensitive than she
                                    pretends she is.
                                    maybe she thought...

                                    I don't know what she thought

no offense but it sounds like
maybe u do

                              ✝

From: Blake Barton (blbarton12@gmail.com)
To: Jamie Perez (jamieb.perez@gmail.com)

Subject: Re: Seriously?

This is not about the rock climber.

                                ✝

Jamie Perez to **Blake Barton:** You're just... not going to explain yourself?

Blake Barton: I've got a remote wellness retreat to plan and a madwoman to pacify. I'm busy

Jamie Perez: Like hell you are. Just tell me the truth—are you upset that I was with someone else?

Blake Barton: Are you actively insane? I don't care what you do. I have enough to deal with in my life. We don't even know each other.

Jamie Perez: Oh, come on. Bullshit. You know that's not true.

✝

From: Mark Carney (mcarney@ostettlerpharma.com)
CC: Frank Ostettler (fostettler@ostettlerpharma.com)
To: Jamie Perez (jperez@ostettlerpharma.com)

Subject: Re: New Client Request Form

Dear Jamie,

While your recent completion of the remote Employee Reinvigoration Series was a significant step toward enhancing your contribution to the Northwest Division of Regional Sales, we are concerned that the diminutive number of your prospective clients that are signing on with our Diversity in Healthcare Initiative may show a critical lack of motivation on your part. As you know, during these times, we must rise to the occasion and be the leaders in our healthcare communities. It is our primary goal this fall to increase our proactiveness in attending to the needs of our diverse Northwest region.

While we in the Northwest are pleased to see your entrepreneurial spirit in signing new clients to Ostettler contracts, we are concerned you may not be discussing our diversity awareness program effectively. Please schedule a time to chat sometime today so we can discuss how you might improve your DHI client pitch.

Looking forward!

All best,
Mark

Mark Franklin Carney, Division Team Lead
Block 4A, Northwest Regional Sales
Ostettler Pharmaceuticals, Inc.
San Francisco, CA

✝

RECENTS

Outgoing: Blake Barton Today
Outgoing: Mark Carney Today
Outgoing: Blake Barton Yesterday
Outgoing: Blake Barton Sunday
Outgoing: Blake Barton Saturday
Outgoing: Blake Barton Friday
Incoming: Potential Spam 10/8/20
Outgoing: Blake Barton 10/8/20
Incoming: Blake Barton 10/7/20
Outgoing: Blake Barton 10/6/20
Incoming: Blake Barton 10/6/20
Outgoing: Blake Barton 10/5/20
Incoming: Blake Barton 10/4/20

✝

SEB
(11:01 pm)
YOU WOULD THINK.
THAT BEING THE ONLY

NON-WHITE MALE IN
THE OFFICE. WOULD
MEAN THAT I AM
ALREADY
CONTRIBUTING TO THE
"DIVERSITY INITIATIVE."
AND. YET.

and yet I would be wrong?

AND YET YOU WOULD
BE WRONG

bro, you hate this job.
just say fuck the lemons and bail

oh cool just bail, sure,
in this economy why not

you've got savings, don't you?
there's this account on instagram
with all these listings for super
cheap houses all over the
country. just buy one of those
and raise goats

jesus, have you been listening
to the new taylor swift album
too?

uhhhhhhhhhhh no.
I just always see cool shit in my
feed and you're the only person
I know who probably has a spare
90k lying around

I thought you only doom
scroll? And I wouldn't call my
dad's life insurance check
something I keep "lying
around"

potato potato, man.
raise goats, be free

✝

RYAN BARTON KAZNECKI · **@rybartonkaz** · 2h

It's a boy!!!!!! 🐻 [VIDEO]

↳ reply from **@bbartonwitch:** congratulations ry 🖤

†

Angelica
(7:34 pm)

Ryan just called me

I saw your comment on her post!
Is she excited?

Yeah. And apparently
Dylan is engaged too

Oh, that's great!

Yeah

Are you... upset?

She's engaged, not dropping
out of her residency program
or anything. I'm happy for her

. . .

What?

Nothing,
I'm just waiting for the other
shoe to drop

There's no other shoe.
I can't be happy for my
sisters?

I mean... historically?
Not exactly

Do you really think I run
around hating everyone in my
life just because they don't do
exactly what I want them to do
at all times?

I wouldn't put it that way

So that's a yes??

Sry babe, buuuuut it's not a no

✝

From: Kelly Chan (kellyc@witchylady.net)
To: Blake Barton (blakeb@witchylady.net)

Subject: Fwd: RETREAT?????

Blake, this client is a FUCKING NIGHTMARE, I do not understand
how you are dealing with her literally at all. You must be the saint of your
family or something, holy balls.

Listen, I know everybody's pissed about this, but I don't think the Zoom
retreat idea is really going to work. We've worked out all the social
distancing stuff and corporate is giving us the go-ahead—by which I mean
they've said "go ahead" and I've got no choice but to listen. I know you
spent a lot of time on the meditation sessions and the distance yoga but it's
all getting scrapped, I'm so sorry.

\-
Kelly Chan, Client Coordinator
Witchy Woman Holistic Healing
San Luis Obispo / Santa Barbara / Santa Monica
kellyc@witchylady.net

✝

From: Jamie Perez (jamieb.perez@gmail.com)
To: Blake Barton (blbarton12@gmail.com)

Subject: People are disappointing (including me)

If you're mad about what I said, I'm sorry. I shouldn't have made jokes or
been disrespectful. She was nice and funny and I liked her a lot. I didn't

mean to make it sound like it meant nothing to me. So if the problem is just me being a misogynistic pig, hopefully that helps, and then maybe you can just skip the rest of this email and call me back.

If you're mad about what I did... to be honest, I would have chosen to talk to you instead of her, but I've been trying to give you space lately. I have no idea what you want from me or even what you think of me. I've been wanting to tell you that for a long time, but... I don't know. You don't exactly give me lots of opportunities to be real with you, but I could have tried. I'm sorry I didn't.

If there's something here, you should tell me. I know you don't want to hear that and maybe you're going to tell me it's gross for me to feel something about the person I spend all my time talking to these days, but one of us has to be honest, right? Whenever anything happens, you're the first person I want to tell. You're the person I fall asleep to and wake up with, even if it's only on my phone. If that's just friendship for you, that's fine. I know you're not exactly on good terms with all your friends these days, and I get it if that's what I am for you. But if there's more than that, I'd like to know.

People are disappointing. They do the wrong things. I did the wrong thing and now you're doing the wrong thing, and I think you know that. I know I said soulmates were fake the first time I ever spoke to you but maybe we do get something good, something close. Even if that something is just someone who makes you feel less lonely despite all evidence that you're both alone. So even if it means arguing all night—even if it means admitting to something we'd both rather not admit to—I'm hoping we can find a way to move on.

I know you hate this. I know it makes you feel icky and seen or whatever, but maybe you need that? It seems like you could probably benefit from having someone who sticks around to fight with you instead of just letting you disappear. And I get that maybe you don't want that person to be a guy with no future who just quit his job—and/or a guy who was living with his ex-girlfriend until he sent you a drunk email that you didn't even want to answer. But in my defense, you did! And that means something to me.

And everything that happened after that has meant something to me, too. And I get that I probably seem like an idiot to you, and in a lot of ways you're right that we don't actually know each other. I don't know what your eyes look like when you laugh or whether you scowl when we fight. I don't know if all those times you heckle me, you're actually smiling. But even if you're actually that mean, I like you and I want to know the answer. I know enough about you to know that much for sure, so either you're in or you're not, but don't run. Whatever your answer, I'll understand.

Either way, I need you to find a way to tell me.

✝

From: Blake Barton (blbarton12@gmail.com)
To: Jamie Perez (jamieb.perez@gmail.com)

Subject: (DRAFT) Re: People are disappointing (including me)

I don't want to run from you. I just don't know how to stay.

✝

SEB
(2:31 pm)

anything?

no

:(sorry man

it's fine. it was a longshot anyway

maybe she just needs time?

it's been a week, seb.
I'm thinking the problem is me, not time

well it's her loss

✝

Angelica
(3:43 pm)

You're not actually going to that
retreat, are you???

> No choice

You're going to do hot yoga
in a room packed full of
people??? Surely this is not a
good idea

> Probably not.
> But they have health
> insurance.
> And probably access to some
> secret government vaccine

I'm sure they do. but you don't

✝

From: Blake Barton (blbarton12@gmail.com)
To: Jamie Perez (jamieb.perez@gmail.com)

Subject: (DRAFT) insert betty lyrics here

So, I don't think I told you about this—or maybe I did, who can
remember—but that client is now making us hold the wellness retreat in
person, so that's like, months of work down the drain and also, now I have
to attend. In person. Which is fine. It's not like I'm at risk or anything. I
mean statistically speaking yes of course I'm at risk, but who cares, right?
I'm not engaged, I'm not married, I have no kids, so there's nobody for
me to infect. Even if I did get sick, it probably wouldn't matter.

I guess I just thought for a second that maybe it would matter to you, but
then I threw that away once I realized I wanted it to be true, which makes
a lot of sense if you're me and probably no sense at all if you're you. If I
were my own client I would tell myself okay, I get it, you've been burned

before, but like... suck it up, right? Why do you insist on being some kind of self-fulfilling prophecy where you push people away just so they prove you right? So someone left you once. Big deal. People leave people every day. People are disappointing. Everyone knows this. What matters is how you deal with it.

And with you I just thought maybe

†

Angelica
(2:31 am)

> You know what I like about
> my clients? I don't have to get
> attached to them. They don't
> disappoint me because
> disappointment is just par for
> the course
>
> But even the people I love
> I end up hating a little bit.
> I know it's not fair, but I
> kind of hate you even though
> I love you. You got married
> and I didn't and you're happy
> and I'm not and I hate that.
> I love Ryan and I hate her too
> because she's giving up the
> shot I could have had. I love
> Dylan and I hate her because
> she gets to dream about
> wedding dresses and I'm not
> allowed to say anything about
> the fact that mine's still in my
> closet slowly turning brown. I
> hate the only guy in my life

because I don't hate him yet,
not at all, but I know that
someday I will. Either that or
he'll hate me, which would be
way worse.

So, do I want to risk my life
going to this retreat because
my clients are rich enough to
make me? No, I don't, but I
probably will, because I don't
have to hate them, because
they don't mean anything to
me. I take their calls instead of
his because I know they need
me and I'll never need them.
But with him, with you, with
my sisters, it can only ever be
the opposite. And that terrifies
me.

†

Angelica
(6:42 am)

I don't think terror is quite as
bad for you as you think it is

And for the record, I don't have
to need you to love you. I can
just love you, and I do.

†

From: Jeff Indra (jeff.indra@bofa.com)
To: Jamie Perez (jamieb.perez@gmail.com)

Subject: Re: Loan Pre-Approval

Dear Jamie,

Below is your loan scenario for the property you intend to purchase. As you can see, the cost of the property itself and the broker's fee is mostly covered by your down payment, and the remainder of the loan offering will be directed toward the cost of renovating the property. So long as you have a reasonable renovation schedule and the appropriate paperwork filled out along the way, it shouldn't be a problem.

Again, congratulations! It's a great investment. That property will be gorgeous with a little love.

Jeff

Jeff Indra
Sr. Wealth Management Loan Officer
Financial Consumer Lending
Houston, TX

✝

Angelica
(7:13 am)

Thanks ange

You don't have to thank me
for being your friend, B.
But DO respond to my
instagram messages.
Like, now please

Ugh I'm supposed to be
packing for my retreat.
And if it's just more cottages
I swear to god

It is, but I think you want to see
this one

I mean obviously I do but still

Wait

Wait wtf

Right???
Am I crazy or is that the same
jamie from the group emails????

Whatttttttt the fuckkkkkk

☦

RECENTS

Outgoing: Jamie Perez   12:34 PM
Outgoing: Jamie Perez   10:06 AM
Outgoing: Jamie Perez   9:14 AM
Outgoing: Jamie Perez   8:01 AM

☦

SEB
(12:35 pm)

So now she wants to talk

you're a homeowner, buddy.
in this economy you're midas.
sure that home happens to be in
the middle of bumfuck nowhere,
but still

You're the one who talked me
into it

was I????
I mentioned it once and
the next thing I knew you were
like,
I quit my job and bought a house
in the fucking acadian woods

                                        It's a good house
it's basically a witch's cottage

                                        Yeah exactly. Cottagecore
is that like straightedge?

                                        What? No.
                                        unless you count the latent
                                        anarchy

this means nothing to me but
whatever, at least it's closer to
me than Frisco

                                        Don't call it Frisco,
                                        nobody calls it Frisco

again, whatever.
so are you going to talk to her?

                                        Idk
????

                                        I feel my answer should be no

mmmhmmmm whereas
I feel that is an answer in itself

                                        But if I cave now then I lose,
                                        right? You're the one who
                                        plays these games
bro, played.
I PLAYED those games.
now i'm married and I live
in the fucking suburbs

                                        so?
so do you want to win a game?

or do you want to have a life?

†

JAMIE PEREZ · @jamieb.perez · 7h

I did a thing

↳ reply from **@bbartonwitch**: hope that village has a witch
  ↳ reply from **@jamieb.perez**: it could. put your money where your mouth is

†

From: Blake Barton (blbarton12@gmail.com)
To: Jamie Perez (jamieb.perez@gmail.com)

Subject: I get it, you're the king of cottagecore

But don't say things you don't mean.

†

From: Jamie Perez (jamieb.perez@gmail.com)
To: Blake Barton (blbarton12@gmail.com)

Subject: Who says I don't mean it?

Come with me. I'm going to need help anyway. Surprisingly enough this is my first cottage in the woods and a witch would be spectacularly useful

†

From: Blake Barton (blbarton12@gmail.com)
To: Jamie Perez (jamieb.perez@gmail.com)

Subject: That's insane

You don't even know me

†

From: Jamie Perez (jamieb.perez@gmail.com)
To: Blake Barton (blbarton12@gmail.com)

Subject: I know you

And anyway, if it doesn't work, then whatever. At least I'll have someone to keep me company on the drive

†

From: Blake Barton (blbarton12@gmail.com)
To: Jamie Perez (jamieb.perez@gmail.com)

Subject: Re: That's insane

Sorry, but this title bore repeating.

You might wind up hating me.

†

From: Jamie Perez (jamieb.perez@gmail.com)
To: Blake Barton (blbarton12@gmail.com)

Subject: Re: I know you

Sorry, but same.

And yeah, I might. And you might hate me, too. But I think we deserve a chance to find out, don't you?

†

Blake Barton to **Jamie Perez**: That's it? No "where's my apology" or "I'm waiting on the reason for all the phone calls you've dodged"? Just... come with me, no explanation necessary?

Jamie Perez: You can tell me later. I gotta get back on the road for now— I'll be in L.A. in about two hours. When I get there, I'm going to text you, and either you're going to get in the car and come with me or you're not.

Blake Barton: Why did you drive to L.A.??? I don't know if you've noticed but Maine is in completely the other direction

Jamie Perez: You know why. See you soon.

†

Angelica
(6:42 pm)

What are your thoughts on me doing something objectively stupid

It's been a long time
since I've seen you do something
that wasn't objectively smart.
Or worse, wildly selfless

Is that a yes or a no

Well I guess... will it give
you something you actually
want?
Because going on a "wellness"
retreat with the client who's
driving you crazy seems like
maybe not it

These are my only options?

†

From: Rhiannon Rose (rhia.rose@gmail.com)
To: Blake Barton (blakeb@witchylady.net)

Subject: EMERGENCY

I HAVE ONCE AGAIN BEEN VISITED IN A DREAM BY MY EX-HUSBAND. CANNOT WAIT UNTIL TOMORROWS RETREAT. PLEASE CALL IMMEDIATELY...

☦

Angelica
(6:45 pm)

At some point you gotta stop
looking for signs, B.

☦

Jamie
(7:21 pm)

I'm here. You ready?

> There's a lot of range to Los
> Angeles... you're probably not
> even close

Well, I've come this far.
I can go another ten minutes or so

You started sharing location with Jamie Perez.

Today 7:23 pm

> Probably more like forty

Lol, fuck LA.
So is that a yes, then?

> Depends.

You do understand that this is stupid, don't you?

Sure, but life is stupid.
And joy is fleeting and
people are disappointing and
all the other greatest hits of
human survival.
So if there's no point, why not?

What exactly are you planning
to do when you get there?
Just fix up a cottage and start a
podcast?

Why not? Better than my other
plans

This is all so painfully
Millennial

Well, in this economy...

You're serious about this?

I'm serious about this.

You're sure?

I'm sure.

(. . .)

†

BLAKE BARTON • **@bbartonwitch** • **1h**

If you've been waiting for a sign, this is it! Do the scary thing. Take the impossible chance. If this is your opportunity to finally say yes instead of no, then take it! The world is waiting, and it is wide and lovely for you.

GEOFF AND THE MAIDEN

Anisha Song was forty-two years old when she awoke to find her first husband Tomaz dead of a stroke beside her in bed. Tomaz was a bit older than she, but even so it was unnatural. He was a young man still, by all accounts, with plenty of life left to live. He ate well, hydrated beautifully, exercised like a madman (in Anisha's opinion). Tomaz was so handsome his students routinely tried their hand at flirting with him. He was gentle with his refusals. She'd seen him do it many times. He understood the haze of adoration, the edge of desire, the coupling of both in the nymphets who filled his lecture halls. They made Anisha feel old. Tomaz agreed.

His hair was only softly gray. Anisha stroked his temple and said with a sudden vigor, "Tomaz, I'm so sorry."

"I told you it would keep happening," said her second husband, who was, had been, and would always be Death—well, not really. That would be a simplification of everything He was to Anisha, and she to Him. That day, she would think of Him as being prodigiously Geoff, but He was still technically Death to anyone who wasn't Anisha, who had been dragging her feet for some time as to the subject of their engagement.

Geoff was not as handsome as Tomaz, but infinitely more beautiful. And more patient, too.

Anisha let out a sigh. "But you said I could have a normal life."

"And so you have," Geoff mildly agreed. "Don't you think? Nobody normal gets forever."

Anisha stroked Tomaz's brow with a sigh, thinking again of when they

361

met. He'd thrown up on her shoes and she'd thought to hell with him, I hope he dies.

She smiled fondly down at him before looking up again at Geoff. "You're sure that if I...?" The word *agree* came to mind, but Anisha could only feel the weight of the word *quit.* "If I stop..." Trying. Living. Choosing. "Being stubborn. Then...?"

"Things need not change," Geoff confirmed with a nod. "There is no requirement for monogamy in the classic sense. Only a more spiritual fidelity. Vows and such."

"Does that make sense?" Anisha had spent her life being shockingly monogamous. Not that she'd ever thought that would be the case. She had no interest in the care and keeping of men; Tomaz was an exception. Geoff was more of an unavoidable vocational circumstance, and also, not technically a man. "I mean," she amended, because expecting things to be presented rationally was a very high ask indeed, "are you sure there's no other way?"

Geoff gave a grave, sympathetic nod, which Anisha took to mean she'd had forty-two years to learn exactly what would happen next and did not need vocal prompting.

"Fine." Anisha was very disappointed. This would be to lose three decades of a fight. Four if you counted the years during which she'd been trapped but unaware of it. "I'll do it."

To His credit, Geoff didn't tolerate excessive sentiment. Within moments, Tomaz took a breath.

"Anisha," said Tomaz, frowning up at her from where he remained unnaturally still on the bed. Life appeared to return only gradually to his extremities, one finger-wiggle at a time. "I'm beginning to think you're right about the dangers of sleep apnea. I also regret to inform you that we may be out of eggs."

"I'm afraid we're also out of time," Anisha remarked with a drastic tone of levity, considering whether she might cry and then realizing no, better not to startle him. Rein it in. "Tomaz, I want a divorce."

Only then did Tomaz become aware of Geoff's presence in the room. At the moment, Geoff was flipping through one of the novels on Tomaz's side of the bed. It was excellent. Tomaz had exceptional taste in books. And films. And food. Tomaz always knew exactly what to cook or what restaurant to go to. He knew where to find the best view of every city. He knew the nature of time, and that Anisha had been slowly choking the life out of him since she turned twenty-one and kissed him so inexpertly that she bit her tongue, and then saw stars.

"Oh, Anisha," said Tomaz, raising one finger gently to the edge of her cheek. "Okay. Okay."

✝

It had set in quite early, or so Geoff would tell Anisha on a day where He was really more of a Megan. There was no real way to explain that. On a day that Geoff was being particularly Nurmagomed He told Anisha that she, too, appeared as other things to Him, sometimes more frequently than day to day. Sometimes hour to hour, occasionally moment to moment. She was of marvelous complexity and had a tendency to flex. But on the day that He was Megan, She told Anisha that the effects of Anisha's condition (or rather, the effects of the pre-negotiated contract about which Anisha had yet to be informed) came on early, perhaps as a result of Anisha's own early puberty. She got her first period in the sixth grade, during gym class. Which was just as well, since most of the class grew distracted by the hail of dead doves falling from the sky.

"I had a feeling this might happen," said Anisha's mother Reena when she arrived to pick up Anisha that day from school. There was a health crisis or something, avian flu she supposed.

Reena took Anisha for frozen yogurt. "There's a slim but unignorable possibility that you may be courted by a spirit representing Death," Reena explained. "Your father wasn't concerned and neither was your grandmother, but I felt quite sure there might be a risk with you. I can't explain it," Reena added. "I just saw it on your face when you were born. You'd been here before and you were very displeased to be back. I could just tell."

"What?" said Anisha.

"Before your dad died he told me a story," Reena said. "About how some generations back one of his ancestors had bargained with Death, promising an heir for a bride. I wish he were here now. I'm not very good at storytelling. I'm more of a 'name all the elements on the periodic table' kind of person. Stories elude me." Reena was a doctor. She had been Anisha's father's doctor when he came to the emergency room with a bullet in his hand. That was sometime in his twenties, ten or so years before the bullet in his chest. (He didn't have a dangerous job—he was a teacher, like Tomaz. But lightning occasionally strikes twice.)

"Well, try," suggested Anisha, because it seemed an important story if it made doves rain from the sky dead.

"Fine. The point is someone in your bloodline is owed to the spirit of Death, whoever they are, in matrimony. There are supposed to be five signs, I think," said Reena. "God, I wish I had a cigarette. Smoking kills but it also relaxes."

"Noted," said Anisha. "The signs?"

"I don't remember all of them," Reena said. "Your father was always a bit hazy on the details. Dead animals were one, I know that. Gifts of blood. I remember asking him what the fuck he meant—sorry, that's not a nice word, don't say that at school—I asked him what he meant by 'gifts of blood' and he said he had no idea and then we got... distracted." Reena's cheeks colored slightly. "So I never really pressed him. And then when you were born I thought oh shit, I should really have written them down."

"You could call Grandma," said Anisha, and Reena blanched.

Ten terse minutes later Reena hung up the phone with Anisha's grandmother. "So, actually, dead animals is the second sign," said Reena. "The first is gifts. Very possible this all got mixed up over time, though. Anyway, it's gifts, dead animals, words of affirmation, physical touch, quality time."

"That doesn't sound right," said Anisha. And it wasn't. When Geoff was exceedingly Megan He pointed out to Anisha that those are love languages. Which wasn't technically incorrect. But in this case, Megan (who would do so under the guises of Hilditrut, Chōko, Marquis, Yulia, and Earl, respectively) specified that actually, the signs were *all* gifts, and the first gift was dreams. By then, Anisha had been having dreams about Geoff for a very long time. At first it was just a voice in her ear indistinguishable from her conscience. Eventually, though, she recognized it was coming from something alien to her, or possibly fractional, like a habit sloughed off over time. But not, as it were, intrinsic.

When Anisha was nineteen years old her first husband Tomaz threw up on her shoes. Then he looked up at her, dazed, and said, "You look like a feeling I had once."

And eventually, Anisha would come to realize that feeling had a name.

†

365

Anisha, once an aspiring ballerina, had gone to a prestigious dance camp when she was sixteen years old. It was a time of sexual awakening, disordered eating, the expression of timeless ennui in artistic form. The camp was bucolic New England at its summeriest and Anisha was bunked in a small cabin, one of six, with three other dancers, two that would go on to either feature prominently in the New York City Ballet or die tragically young (not Anisha's doing, but not necessarily not her fault). The fourth dancer in their little quartet was actually Geoff, but Anisha didn't know that at the time. She hadn't yet met Geoff and therefore wasn't yet aware that Geoff could also at times be Jacklyn.

Anisha would meet her future second husband within minutes of arriving at the camp. Her mother Reena had rented a car and driven her up, having traded a weekend of on-call duty with another doctor who needed someone to cover for his extramarital affair. (Reena was a generally utilitarian person and did not need to approve of someone's actions in order to take advantage of the cards such actions conveniently dealt.) Upon arrival, Anisha would become fast friends with Jacklyn, who was parentless for reasons Anisha did not initially ascribe to the circumstance of Her (Geoff's) existence, and realize that Reena's plans of staying through the weekend to spend time with Anisha before she settled in for an entire summer away were actually—come to think of it—deeply embarrassing. Anisha quickly told Reena she'd be busy and wouldn't have time for the serene picnic by the lake or tranquil stroll through the picturesque town for which Reena had so valuably and unconscionably bartered.

Reena's smile flickered only for a moment. Because again, Reena was very utilitarian, and had been something of a wayward youth herself. She figured it was only deserved. Reena's own mother had felt Reena too thoroughly Westernized, her culture too readily discarded. Reena had not gone to summer camps, though she had always wanted to attend one. She went to a drab, institutional state school because it was the practical thing to do, and because paying for her mother's chemo and her own school tuition was virtually impossible otherwise. Reena was happy she could give Anisha the things she herself didn't get to have. It was also Anisha's right to squander Reena's feelings as she wished. Such was the nature, and the privilege, of daughterhood.

Reena returned to the city. The girls found a dead possum underneath Anisha's bed. They played spin the bottle and kissed the boys they snuck into their room. They found a dead cat in one of the shower stalls. Anisha had dream after dream about autumn. They danced and stayed up too late and woke up again groggy and danced. They broke and reset as people, as future deaths. Anisha found her name spelled out in blood across the cabin's only window but quickly scrubbed it out before the others awoke. They kissed more boys. They kissed each other, giggled, and did not discuss it when it happened occasionally, again. Anisha had a dream about her father, who said my my, how you've grown. They found a dead mouse on Anisha's pillow, curled sweetly like it had been waiting for her to come home. They danced until their hearts beat percussively to La Bayadère and Coppélia. They got drunk in their ice baths at night. Anisha temporarily fell in love with Jacklyn but didn't know what to call it, how to name that kind of uncertainty. Desire sweetened terror, friction temporarily anesthetized fear. Jacklyn held Anisha's hair while she vomited up her girlhood. Anisha missed eleven of Reena's calls.

At the end of the summer, Anisha performed in their company showcase as Giselle. By the end of Giselle's seven minute descent into madness, Anisha saw that her mother was weeping silent but steady tears, like she wasn't aware she was crying. Anisha thought, fleetingly, Mommy.

As Anisha took her final bow she felt something give out in her knee. It was sudden and sharp and though at the time she had no reason to think so, irreversible. Jacklyn had to help her off the stage. Anisha realized then, like a lightning strike, that she already knew Jacklyn and had dreamed of Her before. A dead cockroach lay belly up beside the stage.

The doctor told Anisha there was something wrong with her tendon. Part of it had deteriorated so much it was essentially dead, and needed a graft. They resurrected her patella to the extent that they could but it wouldn't hold her weight anymore, not like it used to. Anisha no longer had the lightness she hadn't known was so essentially her gift, so she never saw her mother cry again.

✝

Anisha met her first husband Tomaz at a party off campus when they were both students at Columbia—Tomaz a graduate student, Anisha an undergrad who had been invited to the apartment by someone she knew from the restaurant where she waitressed part time. Reena had been dead for six weeks on the day Tomaz threw up on Anisha's shoes and she wished malevolently upon his spirit. The next day, she discovered Tomaz was her teaching assistant.

Geoff was intensely Mihkkal around that time. By then Anisha was starting to accept that she was being courted in a way that was very unsanitary but also easily blamed on the state of the Columbia dorms. Mihkkal was nearly seven feet tall and identified as non-binary but accepted the use of either They or He. In any case They told Anisha that the thing with Reena had been hereditary and not technically related to Their presence but also, They were obviously drawn to Anisha, and thus that sort of thing would likely keep happening. More of a side effect than a goal.

Anisha didn't clock it at first when they began speaking to each other. She knew in an abstract way—the same way she had known it with Jacklyn—that Mihkkal was Geoff and that she owed Him something. Which was not technically unlike her relationships with other men. Anisha was seventeen when she first spoke politely to a man at the restaurant where she waitressed, who would later briefly stalk her. It was very alarming for Anisha, obviously, and Reena had gotten so upset she fainted. It had taken several hours for her to wake. Later, Anisha would find the man's obituary with a note. *You are promised to me and I will care for you always. Yours eternally, Mihkkal.*

Anisha discovered that Tomaz was her TA but thought nothing of it. He seemed embarrassed about the shoe vomit incident but didn't dwell on it, which she liked. Tomaz was a first year doctoral student in the English department, Anisha pre-med, so for her the class was merely an elective. A comparative literature course on world myths. She got particularly invested in her midterm paper, a study on the various identities of Death (she thought it best to know thine enemy/contracted future spouse) and spent nearly four hours talking to Tomaz about possible sources until he got a sudden look of horror in his eyes.

"What is it?" asked Anisha, about to mention that if it was just Mihkkal—who showed up from time to time—he needn't worry, everything was fine. Then she saw the dead branch hanging off the tree behind her. "Oh, it gets much worse than that."

"What? No, nothing," stammered Tomaz—who, it must be said, had never been a stammerer. Nor would he ever be again.

The next day a new TA showed up in Tomaz's place. He'd quit as a result of a scheduling conflict, the professor said. Anisha got an A on her midterm paper in large part because of her conversation with Tomaz, who had shifted the direction of her research and also the nature of her thoughts.

Mihkkal became briefly Yasmeen. Anisha did not go home for winter break because she had nowhere to go home to. When classes resumed in January she signed up for two pre-med requirements, Spanish, and a class on evolution. She worked through the summer, finished her sophomore year, then her junior year. Three months after that she bumped into Tomaz at a Starbucks, his arm around a woman.

"Hi," she said to Tomaz, who blinked when he saw her.

"Hello." He excused himself to speak privately with Anisha, parting ways with the woman he'd had his arm around, who had papers to grade.

Tomaz stood wordlessly beside Anisha as she waited for her latte. (Mihkkal was the barista, but Tomaz would not notice Them until many years later, when Mihkkal was already Augusto.)

"You threw up on my shoes at a party once," remarked Anisha.

"I know." Tomaz shuffled his feet. "I'm not—" He paused. "I don't normally drink so much."

"Did something happen?"

"Yes. Well, no. Not that day. But also, in a way, every day."

Anisha looked at him and Tomaz said with a shrug, "My brother."

"Oh. Yes, my mother."

"How long ago?"

"Almost three years now. You?"

"Five."

"I'm sorry," Anisha said politely.

"It's not your fault," said Tomaz.

"Sometimes it is," she murmured, before adding, "You said I reminded you of a feeling."

"Did I?" He looked at her quizzically.

"Maybe you didn't mean it. I mean—maybe it didn't mean anything."

They were silent for a moment.

"You know, I always sort of thought you might have left that literature class because you fell in love with me," Anisha commented.

"I did," said Tomaz.

"I never heard from you after."

"It didn't seem appropriate."

"What if I fell in love with you, too?"

"Did you?"

Just then Mihkkal announced to Anisha that her latte was ready. Helpless, she launched herself on tiptoe and kissed Tomaz, who would later prove to be very, very talented at such things despite an atrocious initial performance. In fairness he had been taken by surprise, and Anisha had thought she was being practical. Killing a cat, or some other act of violence upon her curiosity.

Two years into medical school, Anisha would discover that her intentions to become a doctor were greatly impractical. Life was too fragile for her to be around. Side effects or something. She understood two things by then: that she was cursed and her clock was ticking. She got the feeling it would all be much easier if she just gave in.

Geoff was Onyekachukwu then, Onyeka for short. He was looking at Anisha with something very close to sympathy. "Are you ready?" He said in His gentlest voice.

She thought about it. About the way it felt to achieve such beauty that her brilliant, stoic mother wept. About the dream of her father, a gift from Onyeka when He had been Yulia. About everything that had been taken from her.

"No," she said. Instead she typed Tomaz's name into Google and messaged four different accounts before she found him.

I just wanted you to know that I destroy everything I touch, she offered in fair warning.

Don't let this go to your head but I think I'm going to let you, replied Tomaz, which was when it really began to end.

†

After they filed the divorce papers, Tomaz took Anisha home and poured her a cup of tea. She had a sip and then pushed it aside, instead climbing into his lap and grinding on him with mounting desperation. He carried her into the bedroom and they had slow, companionable sex for probably the two hundred thousandth time. She came twice. Then she rearranged their bookshelves and made lentil soup and scrubbed the toilet bowl with a toothbrush and then it was dark and Geoff was Mladenka in a crown of braids.

"I can be Geoff if you prefer it," She said.

"Let's just get it over with," said Anisha.

Her wedding to Tomaz had been an elopement. Anisha had no family and wasn't really the wedding type. Tomaz might have done it, the whole party thing, because Tomaz was really very sparkling in social situations. The shoe vomit had been an isolated incident.

Anisha had already been putting off marriage so long that people began to think there was something seriously wrong with her. After all, who wouldn't want to marry Tomaz? Only an idiot or someone precontracted to marry Geoff, the latter of which took too long to explain at parties.

"You won't be happy with me," Anisha told Tomaz after the seventh time he asked her to marry him. "You want a family. I'm not going to have children."

"For very understandable reasons," Tomaz agreed, because he had already grown accustomed to his occasional glimpses of Geoff. (It wasn't total constancy for Tomaz, but it was certainly often enough. Somewhere, inevitably, Anisha would bump into Geoff at least once throughout the day, and statistically speaking Tomaz was bound to be with her on those occasions about fifty-percent of the time.)

"I'm not even sure what the point would be," Anisha said.

"Well, I just think it'd be fun to look you in the eyes and promise my life to you," said Tomaz. "Everything that came after that would just be an exercise in gratuity."

Anisha felt again the singular sensation that she'd found someone much too good for her and that she would ruin him irreparably despite that being the one thing she did not want to do. Well, losing him was the one thing she did not want to do. But ruining him was a close second.

But her wedding night with Tomaz was another event. Now she was with her second husband, who was Mladenka. Anisha thought about her first kiss with Geoff, who had been Jacklyn at the time, and shivered. "Giving in to your cursed ancestral demands doesn't change anything," she said. "I still love Tomaz. I'm still choosing to be faithful to him. Sexually if not institutionally."

Mladenka looked as if She would be sick. "I do not want to participate in your corporeal customs."

"Okay, then what do you want to do?"

Mladenka gave a small flourish of Her hands before presenting Anisha with a small braided crown of flowers. "Adore you," She said.

"That's it?" Anisha wasn't sure if it was over or if it was starting or if any of it was even real. She felt incredibly grumpy and middle-aged, though Tomaz told her she couldn't allow her to call herself that for at least another three years. Forty-two was young, young, young. Tomaz was imperfect, obviously. He bit his nails and fundamentally could not multitask. He was an academic who was not always sympathetic to her vocational bouts of melancholy; he had moments of extreme, crushing selfishness that left Anisha with feelings of profound, echoing loneliness. His body had grown soft in places whereas Geoff was often chiseled, voluptuous, and/or young. But love was space and love was softness and love was freedom and love was peace and love was compassion and love was comfort and love was terror and love was fearless and love was prophetic and love was uncertain and love was promising a future before you knew what it would hold and love was a laugh and love was a fixture and love was new and love was old and love was middle-aged and love was looking each other in the eyes just to say the word forever and love was earnest and love was urgent and love was forgiving and love was frozen yogurt and love was regret and love was the baby she wouldn't get to have and wouldn't have to mourn and love was not needing forever and love was a side effect of grief and love was weeping in a dark auditorium to the stylings of Coralli and Perrot and love was the picnic she should have taken and love was the father she'd never get to meet and love was kindly overlooking the small altar of dead rabbits in the honeymoon suite that was really just the slovenly apartment they could barely afford and love was I can let you go so that you can be free and love was this city and love was this moment and love was everyday and love was Tomaz. Mladenka who was Geoff who had been. Jacklyn who had also, in Anisha's mind, been her father, who had been such a constancy in her life that they knew each other's every thought, smiled at her and said, "Let me show you the garden."

Then She opened a door that hadn't been there before and Anisha stepped through it into the starry skies of night.

ABOUT *the* AUTHOR

OLIVIE BLAKE is the *New York Times* bestselling author of *The Atlas Six* and several other books, including the *Witch Way* anthology *The Answer You are Looking For is Yes* and the novella *La Petite Mort.* She lives in Los Angeles with her husband, goblin prince/toddler, and rescue pit bull.